People of a quest

QUINTUS — Young adventure-seeking soldier in a strange land

REGAN—Strange, adopted daughter of the queen

BOADICEA—A warrior queen and instigator of the British tribal revolt against the Romans

CONN LEAR—Leader of all the Druids at Stonehenge

CATUS—Brutal procurator of Nero

VALERIANUS—Crazed Roman leader of the West

BRAN—Quintus' strange quiet guide on his mission to the Druids

The Mistletoe and the Sword

Anya Seton

AVON
PUBLISHERS OF BARD, CAMELOT, DISCUS, EQUINOX AND FLARE BOOKS

AVON BOOKS
A division of
The Hearst Corporation
959 Eighth Avenue
New York, New York 10019

ISBN: 0-380-00583-2

First Avon Printing, February, 1974.
Fourth Printing

AVON TRADEMARK REG. U.S. PAT. OFF. AND
FOREIGN COUNTRIES, REGISTERED TRADEMARK—
MARCA REGISTRADA, HECHO EN CHICAGO, U.S.A.

Printed in the U.S.A.

The Mistletoe and the Sword

FOREWORD

This story happened in England in A.D. 60–61. It is entirely based on history and follows in every particular the only contemporary sources that we have, *The Annals of Tacitus* and the *Roman History* of Dio Cassius. Dozens of authors have since speculated on the facts offered by these two sources; I have consulted most of these and found that *Boadicea: Warrior Queen of the Britons* by Lewis Spence (London, 1937) is the most detailed and convincing.

Boadicea, her daughters, the evil procurator, the governor, Suetonius Paulinus, Seneca, and General Petillius Cerealis are all historical characters, so was Postumus Poenius, prefect of the Second Legion, who actually behaved in the mysterious way I have shown, though I have used my own interpretation of why he did so.

It may be interesting to know that General Petillius Cerealis of the Ninth Legion himself became governor of Britain ten years after this story ends. A very good governor.

There is much uncertainty as to the extent of Druidism during this period, but most authorities agree that Stonehenge was used, though not built, by the Druids.

For the sake of simplicity and ease in locating I have used the modern names for Roman places in Britain, but the endpaper maps show the Roman ones. And for the same reasons I have followed one consistent system in the naming of characters because Roman nomenclature is confusing. Also "Boadicea" is the fairly modern name for what was originally "Boudicca."

A complete list of my source books on Roman Britain and the Celts would be tedious, but the works of R. G. Collingwood, and Jacquetta Hawkes were perhaps the most useful.

A.S.

CHAPTER I

QUINTUS, standing in the prow of the Roman war galley, was eagerly peering through swirling fog ahead, toward a glimpse of high white cliffs.

That was Britain at last! The savage misty island that he had dreamed about all his nineteen years, or at least it seemed that long. For Quintus could not remember the time when he had not known the strange story of his great-grandfather Gaius Tullius' weird and horrible death.

I'll find it, he thought with growing excitement. I'll find that place of the golden tree and the stone circle if I have to search through every inch of this barbarian land!

He lurched on the heaving deck as a great wave hit the galley. He grabbed at the painted eagle on the prow and lost his footing. Green water sloshed over him, and he collapsed with a clatter of shield, sword, and armor on the wet deck. The galley slaves, though straining at their oars to keep the boat headed for shore in this rising wind, nevertheless snickered.

Quintus heard them, flushed, and ignored them, while he pulled himself up. It was beneath the dignity of a Roman soldier to act as though galley slaves existed. But he glanced nervously toward the stern where his officer and ten other cavalrymen were huddled. Fortunately his officer, the centurion Flaccus, was seasick, and the others, having, unlike Quintus, no private reason for desiring duty in the wild half-conquered island, were grumpily huddled in their cloaks.

The wind blew harder, the waves mounted, and Quintus began to wonder if they were to be blown back across the channel to Gaul. Though it was autumn and not sultry, lightning suddenly zigzagged across the sky, and the galley slaves set up a wail. "Neptune! Neptune! Deliver us!"

Quintus muttered a few prayers himself, but chiefly to Mars, the god of war, for whom he felt affection. He promised Mars a sacrifice if they landed safely, but it was not for his own safety he was so much concerned as for that of the transport which immediately followed them. That vessel contained the horses, including Quintus' horse, Ferox, of whom he was much fonder than anything in the world except his mother, and his little blind sister back in Rome.

Ferox was a huge, intelligent, black stallion and as fond of fighting as his name implied, or indeed as Quintus was himself, though Quintus had had little opportunity to fight yet. He had entered the Roman army only last year when he was eighteen, and there hadn't been anything but dull guard duty in Rome. It was a distant cousin on his mother's side who had finally wangled Quintus' transfer to these troops that were being sent to Britain. The cousin had influence. He had even sent a petition to the Emperor Nero about it.

Thunder crashed over their heads, torrents of rain drenched them. Quintus set his jaw and let the icy trickles stream off his bronze helmet and down his back beneath the leather cuirass. The galley slaves might groan and curse at discomforts, but a Roman soldier must take what came, stoically.

Fortunately the rain flattened the waves, and in a little while the galley's keel grated on a pebbly beach, not at all where they had meant to land, but it *was* land. And the horse transport soon loomed out of the murk and beached near them.

Quintus ran down the shingle to help the horses. Ferox whinnied and snorted when he saw his master and floundered obediently through the shallows where Quintus received the black stallion with a relieved pat and low word of greeting, "So there, old boy—thanks be to the horse goddess that you're safe!"

Two of the other horses were not. They had broken their legs by falling on the heaving deck, and Quintus turned away his head, ashamed of the rush of moisture to his eyes, as a soldier cut the injured beasts' throats. There was certainly no time for sentiment. Flaccus, the centurion, was ramping up and down the beach, barking orders to his men, and cursing the climate and everything about this miserable island, where he had already served several years, before a trip back to Italy for recruits. It was penetratingly cold and dripping wet, quite unlike anything these southern-born troops had ever felt, but they saddled their horses, mounted, and fell into ranks, with the ease of long discipline. They climbed a steep cliff and made their way inland to a camping place.

Nobody bothered them. The silent forest seemed as uninhabited as the heaving ocean beneath the white cliffs. There was no sound but the rain, and as they made camp, Quintus was disappointed. He mentioned this to his friend, Lucius Claudius Drusus, who was Roman-born and young like himself but far more aristocratic since he was distantly connected with the late Emperor Claudius.

"I thought we might see some action when we landed," said Quintus morosely, settling himself on the ground beneath the partial shelter of his shield, and stretching his steaming leather sandals toward the little campfire. "I thought the natives were hostile—that's why they sent for us to build up the Ninth Legion."

Lucius shrugged, thrust his sword into the simmering pot, and speared himself a hunk of mutton. "I wish I was back in Rome," he said shivering. "The sun'd be shining, there'd be the smell of flowers, we'd be all going to the games in the Circus Maximus, there'd be beautiful girls with gilt curls and sweet smiles. Jupiter! Even Nero's fat head up in the royal box'd look good to me right now. The gods, of course, preserve our august Emperor-god," he added hastily.

Flaccus thrust his long, glum face over the fire and said, "You two elegant young Romans make me sick. This tribe here in Kent is friendly but if you *got* this action you've been wanting, Quintus Tullius Pertinax, I bet you wouldn't like it so much neither. One of these blue-painted savages come screaming at you in a war chariot, and you'd be bawling for your mama and your cosy little white marble villa, and your rose water baths, *that* you'd be!"

Quintus' temper flared; he thought of a dozen scathing remarks to hurl back at his officer but managed to swallow them. He contented himself with muttering to Lucius, "That dog of a Spaniard, nothing but a colonial himself!" For the Roman army consisted of men drawn from all the

13

conquered countries in the vast empire, and this Ninth or "Hispana" Legion, which they were on their way to join, contained many Spaniards, to whom the young Romans from Rome felt quite superior.

As Flaccus disappeared to administer some reproof at the other side of the camp, Lucius said to Quintus, "Why you ever moved heaven and earth to get sent out here to Britain, I'll never understand! Now *me*, I couldn't help it. My father thought it'd be good experience and discipline for me. By Mars, I'll count the days till I get home again!"

Quintus was silent. He had told nobody, not even Lucius, of the story that had so fired all his childhood, of the queer feeling that in Britain his fate awaited him, or of the impetuous vow he had made long ago. Not a practical vow, his mother had said, too dangerous, and virtually impossible to fulfill. And she had added gentle words of warning designed to curb her son's impulsive tendencies. So he had stopped talking about the quest for the golden tree and the stone circle, but he had not been able to stop thinking about it at times.

Quintus munched on some mutton and shivered a little in the cold rain as he stared out into the silent pressing forest. Suddenly a thrill went through him. It must have been quite near here, he thought—that long ago battle when Gaius Tullius was captured.

"What's the matter with you, Quintus?" asked Lucius, yawning and putting down the jug of wine he had been drinking from. "All you do is gawk at those trees!"

Quintus started. "I was wondering where that first battle of Julius Caesar's happened. I had a great-grandfather there too, and——"

"Oh Jupiter," interrupted Lucius, yawning again. "Can't you find something better to wonder about? What's it matter *what* happened in this wretched place over a hundred years ago! I wish Caesar'd stayed in Italy where he belonged, then *I* might be there too."

Quintus laughed. "Hardly a patriotic sentiment. Rome wouldn't be mistress of the earth today if Julius Caesar'd stayed home."

"Maybe she wouldn't," agreed Lucius without interest. "Here, move over, you're hogging most of the fire."

This was not true, but Quintus was used to Lucius' grumbles and was fond of him, partly because they were the only two in this company who had actually come from the city of Rome itself.

Quintus obligingly moved over and soon both young men were asleep.

When Quintus awoke the next morning the rain had stopped, and by the time he was astride Ferox and riding next to Lucius on the road through the forest he felt eager for excitement. This was a good road they were marching on, twenty feet wide, and made of paving blocks topped with gravel. Straight as a spear it led toward London through the land of the Cantii, a peaceful Kentish tribe. The Roman legions had built this road and many others like it since the second and successful invasion of Britain seventeen years ago when the Emperor Claudius had actually come here himself and made a triumphal march to Colchester.

"Imagine!" said Quintus to his friend, "Claudius' elephants plodding along here—didn't he have camels too?—miserable natives like those over there must've been terrified." He jerked his chin toward a village he had just discovered to the right of them. There were several round mud houses huddled inside a circular palisade made of sticks. A woman was squatting by the opening in the palisade pounding something in a stone bowl. She wore a shapeless garment that had once been striped and squared with color, but it was very dirty. A naked little boy stood beside her. He was very dirty too, and as the legionaries passed on the road, both the woman and the boy raised their heads and stared narrowly, unsmiling.

"What a funny color their hair is," said Quintus, gazing back at his first native Britons. "Red like brick dust, and shouldn't they salute us or something? After all they're our subjects." He spoke with the instinctive arrogance of Rome, and the woman's cool level stare annoyed him.

Lucius shrugged. "Too stupid," he said languidly. "I've always heard that these redheaded Celtic savages are very stupid. O Roma Dea—how I wish I was back in civilization! It isn't even as though we'd have anything to do here except police some dismal outpost in one of these everlasting forests. The Britons are perfectly quiet now and glad enough to enjoy Roman comforts, and good government, and the security we bring them. The interesting

15

times of Julius Caesar and Emperor Claudius are all over."

Quintus nodded and sighed, "Yes, I guess so, though Flaccus says there might be trouble up north."

"Oh, Flaccus," said Lucius with contempt, glancing ahead at their officer. "He's jumpy as a chicken; all those Spaniards are."

The two young Romans rode on in silence behind Flaccus, but ahead of the rest of their company of eighty-two men, called a "century," because, in the old days, it had always consisted of one hundred men. Lucius and Quintus both held minor office and had a limited amount of authority. Lucius was an Optio; Quintus a standard-bearer, carrying a tall staff topped with the Ninth Legion's number and emblems. It rested in a socket fastened to his saddle. Sunlight twinkled on their embossed bronze armor, on their helmets with arching crests of clipped red horse-hair, on their oblong shields, and the scabbards of their short deadly swords. Quintus and Lucius rode without stirrups, like all the cavalry, and were both excellent horse-men. When a white figure suddenly appeared from behind a large tree and waved its arms in front of them, the horses shied without disturbing the young men's balance in the saddles, though Flaccus nearly fell off his horse.

"By Hades, what's the meaning of this!" cried the centurion furiously, recovering himself and glaring at the apparition in the road. "Hey, you old man, get out of the way!"

The old man shook his head and said something in a heavy guttural language, while he stood squarely in the middle of the road, his skinny arms outstretched. He wore a long grayish white robe, and he had a gray beard through which gleamed a golden necklace with a dangling mottled stone shaped like an egg. There was a crown of oak leaves around his partly bald head, and Quintus started to laugh. "Here's the funniest sight I've seen since our Saturnalian games," he chuckled to Lucius.

"Keep quiet!" shouted Flaccus angrily over his shoulder to Quintus. Then he beckoned for the interpreter, who came up and saluted.

"Find out what the old goat wants," said Flaccus, "and be quick about it or I'll ride him down."

The interpreter saluted again and addressed the white-robed man. This interpreter was a British hostage, who had been captured in the Claudian campaign seventeen

16

years before and taken to Rome where he had spent the intervening years and learned excellent Latin. He was tall, rawboned, and sandy-haired; a middle-aged man. His name was something unpronounceable like Neamhuainn, so the Romans called him Navin.

"This old man," said Navin, at last turning back to Flaccus, "is our Arch——" he checked himself, went on quickly, "that is, I mean he's one of the British priests, sir. A Druid. His name is Conn Lear, he is a very important man." Navin paused, and Quintus, watching, had a sudden impression that the old man somehow understood the Latin the interpreter was using, and was listening intently. Navin went on after a moment. "Conn Lear wishes to warn you not to go further up country with your troops, sir. He says you must return at once to Gaul while there is still time. That his people want no more Romans in this land."

"What!" shouted Flaccus between fury and astonishment. "You dare to tell me this impudent drivel! Navin, you're crazy, and most certainly this old man is."

"Possibly, sir," said Navin tonelessly. His light blue eyes gazed up into the officer's dark ones. "But that is what he said."

The priest suddenly put his hand on the interpreter's arm and murmured something else rapidly and earnestly. Navin listened, then turned to Flaccus. "He says that *he* means no harm to the Romans, but that all the omens and auguries point to fearful trouble. The sacred hare has run its course through Stonehenge, the great stone circle in the west. The mistletoe has been found on three oaks near the Holy Well of Mabon, and the sea has turned red as blood near Colchester. The British gods have spoken. *Turn back!"*

"Phuaw," Flaccus spat onto the road at the priest's feet. "Seize him!" he cried to Quintus. "Bind him and haul him along with us. We'll get to the bottom of this nonsense when we get to headquarters."

Quintus jumped off his horse, eager to obey. So *this* was a Druid! he thought with angry excitement. It was white-robed priests like this one that had killed his great-grandfather. All that stuff about stone circles and mistletoe made it certain. "Here, graybeard," he cried, striding up to the quiet Druid and holding out a leather thong to bind the man's wrists, "come along now."

"NEGO!" said the old man sternly in Latin, and added Celtic words which Navin, who stood by impassively, interpreted. "He says you have no right to bind or coerce him. He came only to warn."

Quintus hesitated in spite of himself. There was power in the old man's steady glittering eyes.

"Hurry *up*, Quintus Tullius!" shouted Flaccus, snapping the bridle. "Haul him off to the rear, you're delaying our march."

Quintus thrust out his hands with the thong, and at once something happened. It was as though his hands hit an invisible wall. Quintus' vision blurred for a moment too; all he could see was the Druid's fierce eyes. Then there was a whirl of white, and he heard Flaccus' furious voice. "By all the gods, you fool—you've let him go! Run after him!"

" 'Twould be no use, sir," said Navin calmly. "These Druids have magic tricks and many hiding places in the forest."

Quintus blinked and reddened. "I'm s-sorry, sir. I don't know what happened—it was his eyes——"

Flaccus, most surprisingly, did not burst into the torrent of abuse with which he usually disciplined his subordinates, instead he bit his lips and cast an uneasy glance toward the thick grove where the Druid had vanished. "This infernal country," he said beneath his breath, "there's many strange things . . . well, no matter. The old man was crazy." He kicked his horse while raising his sword high as marching signal to the ranks behind.

All that day and part of the next, until they reached London, Quintus continued to feel perplexed and embarrassed at the way the old Druid had somehow made a fool of him. He tried to talk about it to Lucius, but that young man soon grew bored and took to humming Roman love songs to himself, especially one that the Emperor Nero had written which celebrated the charms of a lady called Acte. Lucius substituted the name of a pretty Greek dancer he had yearned for back home and managed to forget the rain, which had started up again.

But Quintus still thought about the meeting with the Druid which had made the old story come even more vivid than it ever had in Rome, and as they plodded on, he went over again all that he had heard from his father and tried to remember new details.

The tragedy to Quintus' great-grandfather, Gaius Tullius, had happened a hundred and fourteen years ago when Julius Caesar had tried to conquer Britain.

Gaius was an officer in the Roman army of those days, a centurion, or captain, of the Seventh Legion. And in 54 B.C. his legion was ordered to Gaul where Caesar was making preparations for invading Britain.

Caesar had made a quick reconnoitering trip into Britain the year before, but the great general had had bad luck, or even, it was whispered in Rome, had shown poor strategy. The Romans had never seen tides like those of the northern seas, nor such quick violent storms, and several disasters overtook their fleet. Moreover the Britons turned out to be fierce strange fighters, who hotly resisted the Roman invasion. Caesar tamely returned to Gaul and decided to try again the following year. This time Caesar took with him eight hundred vessels of all classes and five legions and cavalry, some thirty-two thousand men in all, so that the British lookouts who guarded the great white cliffs by Dover were dismayed at sight of the huge force and withdrew into their secret forests while they decided on the best resistance.

Gaius Tullius was a tough, brave soldier, and his Seventh Legion was a crack one. He was delighted when Caesar ordered it forward to take a stockaded hill fort that the barbarians had built a few miles inland. The Seventh Legion took the fort easily, but no sooner did they plant their flaunting eagle standards along the stockade than a panting runner brought word of new disaster back on the landing beach.

Again, like the year before, Caesar had underestimated the force of wind and water. The tides had risen, a fearful storm had blown up, and the entire fleet had been smashed to bits.

Gaius had been standing near the general when this news came. He had seen the bald head redden, the flash of the eyes, and the sharp thinning of the lips, as Caesar grimly gave the order to retreat—back to the beachhead. It was very humiliating, especially as there were jeers and taunts from the British captives they had taken—big, fair-haired men with blue tattooings on their faces, who wore helmets horned like bulls and long gaudy plaid trousers that the Romans thought ridiculous. But there was nothing ridiculous about British fighting. This Gaius discovered for himself ten days later when new boats had been built and Caesar marched forward again into the interior. The British had profited by the interval. They had summoned a great force from all their nearby tribes, not only the Cantii of Kent, in whose territory Caesar now was, but the Atrebates from further west, the Trinovantes from Essex, even the Iceni who lived way up in Norfolk. And the British had chosen a general of their own, Cassivellaunus, King of the Catuvellauni tribe, who had a capital north of the little village of London, at a place called St. Albans.

This British army encountered Caesar's in Kent about twenty miles from the coast, and the Romans did very badly and lost many men. A temporary setback which Caesar barely mentioned in the account he later wrote of this campaign. The heavily armed Romans were confused by the darting agility of the Britons and particularly by their extraordinary methods of fighting in low war chariots, which were furnished with whirling scythes on the wheel hubs, and which could be maneuvered as deftly as the shaggy little ponies that pulled them.

Caesar soon worked out a better defense and tactics. He crossed the Thames River and eventually made his way to King Cassivellaunus' capital, which he subdued, but for Gaius the war was finished in that first defeat.

He and a friend of his called Titus, another centurion of the legion, somehow got cut off from the main body of their cohort, and were captured by some little dark warriors from the mountains in the west of Britain. These little men, delighted to exhibit as prizes two Roman officers, thereupon carried the bound Gaius and Titus in a wagon back toward the west.

Titus survived to tell the grim story and its sequel to Gaius' son in Rome—the same story that Quintus had heard so many times from his father as it was handed down the years. Now, remembering it in the very land where it had happened, Quintus felt the shiver that had always chilled his back as his father had gone on with the tale.

As Titus told it, he and Gaius had suffered much from shame at their capture and from hidden fear of what would be done to them. The wagon bumped day after day through the wild black forests. Their captors did not harm them, in fact they fed and treated them too well, and Titus, who understood some Celtic, told his friend that amongst the fierce, little blue-faced men there was constant talk about "the place of the great stones, the place of sacrifice," and that they talked of the sun-god, of sacred oaks and mistletoe, of Druid priests. And when they mentioned these, the British warriors cast uneasy glances about them and seemed afraid.

At last one day their captors came to a giant oak on the edge of a great open plain. On this plain there were circles of strangely formed stones, standing as tall as houses. The Britons stopped near the giant oak and threw their captives on the ground so roughly that one of Gaius' rawhide bonds loosened, but this he did not notice at first because of his amazement.

The oak tree sparkled with gold. Its branches were hung with golden bracelets thick as a finger, and a sharp golden sickle rested in a low crotch of a branch beneath a great ball of mistletoe.

The British tribesmen threw themselves on hands and knees and seemed to be worshiping the oak tree. Then they pointed to the distant circle of great stones standing on the plain, and they ran off toward it, leaving only one man on guard. This guard took several long pulls of the honeyed mead he carried in a drinking horn and squatted down quite near Gaius and drowsed.

"May the gods of our fathers be merciful," Titus had whispered to Gaius. "I heard what they said—they mean to sacrifice us over there in that circle of stones, to cut us into bits for an offering to their god. They've gone to fetch their priests."

"No," Gaius whispered, while he worked one hand loose from the bond. "We'll not be minced up yet." Suddenly with his freed hand he hit the unsuspecting guard so mighty a blow on the head that the man crumpled silently on the ground.

Gaius seized the Briton's knife, cut his own bonds, and Titus', but there was no time to escape, for the tribesmen came running back, and with them a dozen white-robed, long-bearded Druids, shouting and waving golden spears.

Titus did not remember exactly what happened then, except that as they were surrounded, Gaius reached back up into the tree for a better weapon than the knife and pulled down the golden sickle, which caught on a trailing frond of the mistletoe ball, dislodging the plant which fell to the ground.

At this the Druids and tribesmen let out a wail of horror. They stared at Gaius with glittering snake eyes and began to move forward slowly in an ever narrowing circle around their sacred tree and the Roman who stood backed against it.

"Run, Titus," said Gaius in swift Latin, "they've forgotten *you!*" He brandished the golden sickle. Again the gasp came from the advancing Britons, and then, at a sharp command, the Druid priests drew their arms back as one man and hurled their golden spears. Gaius fell, quivered once and was still, while the Britons crowded around murmuring, staring with shuddering awe at the trampled mistletoe and the sickle in the Roman's hand. Titus did escape then, running back into the forest. Nobody noticed him, but as he went he heard a Druid cry in a great voice, "Do not touch the dead Roman. He must never be touched. He has profaned our gods. He shall lie here as he is, forevermore, in sacrifice!"

This was the end of the story Titus told when, after incredible luck and difficulties, he got back to Rome. But little Quintus had always asked one earnest fearing question. Would, then, his great-grandfather's bones still be lying there in the heart of Britain under an oak tree? And Quintus' father had solemnly answered that perhaps it was so. Here Julia, his mother, would weep and say that it was because of this that bad luck had come to the Tullius family, that it offended all the spirits of their ancestors to have one of them lie unavenged, and that this had brought a curse on them all.

In truth, matters had gone badly with the family since Gaius' death. It had lost favor with the emperors and become impoverished. There was much ill health and many early deaths. Quintus' father died young of fever, the four brothers before Quintus died one by one, his little sister, Livia, was born blind.

"Someday when I am big I shall go to the dark island of mists," Quintus, as a child, had boasted to his mother, "and find the golden tree and poor Gaius Tullius beneath it. *I* will see that he has the proper burial rites at last, and I'll take some of that gold and bring it back to you."

Julia always smiled sadly, reminding him of how much time had passed since those days, that the tree might be no longer standing, and that it was cruel to trouble her heavy heart with foolish talk about the impossible.

22

And yet, mused Quintus, riding along the Roman road toward London, I always had a feeling that I'd get here someday, and I still have a feeling that the quest will succeed, but how? and where? and when?

This he could not guess, but his curiosity about this strange new land was keen and some miles before they reached London, he summoned Navin, the British interpreter, to come and ride beside him.

"It must feel queer to be coming home after all these years in Italy," said Quintus thoughtfully. "Where did you live here?"

A faint grim twinkle appeared in Navin's blue gaze. This was the first Roman soldier who had spoken to him as a human being, instead of as a barbarian captive or a useful piece of machinery. "I was once a chief—the nephew of King Cymbeline," he said quietly. "I am a Trinovante, from the country north of the Thames, where Colchester, your capital, is." He paused a moment, then added, "It *is* strange to be coming home. To be here"—he glanced at the dull dripping skies, at some rough mud huts glimpsed through a grove of birches—"after Rome."

Lucius suddenly stopped humming and leaned over. "By Venus, I should think so indeed! I vow you'll be in as great a hurry to get back as the rest of us. When I think of the glorious warm sunlight, and the delicious joys of the baths, and our food, our wine and music—yes, even our orators! The beautiful bustle of the Forum, the splashing of our fountains—O Roma Dea, Roma Dea," groaned Lucius invoking the spirit of his beloved city.

"Rome for me was not quite like that," said Navin, while a shut look came over his big-boned face. "This," he added with a peculiar emphasis, "is *MY* country."

Lucius shrugged and went on humming to himself, but Quintus noted the Briton's intonation, and for the first time a prick of doubt pierced his Roman superiority. Good old Navin had been traveling with this company ever since he was assigned to it in Rome. A quiet, courteous man, thoroughly Romanized in clothes and speech, and grateful, one naturally assumed, for the fine treatment he had received. Indeed all the British captives had been positively pampered; everyone knew that. And look at the royal reception the captured British King Caractacus had got from the Emperor in Rome too. It was no wonder the

23

British had settled down so peacefully under the enlightened Roman rule.

As for that Druid's—Conn Lear's—warning yesterday —well that was surely superstitious nonsense. But I wish I'd understood exactly what he was saying, Quintus thought.

He turned around and called back Navin, who had dropped behind. The interpreter brought his horse up level with Ferox again.

"I'd like to learn some British words," said Quintus. "Teach me."

Navin looked startled, again the twinkle appeared, and he gave the attractive eagle-nosed young face a quizzical glance. "It is seldom indeed that a Roman concerns himself with the language of his subjects, O Quintus Tullius."

"Well, I think it might be useful. I like to know what's going on. For instance, what's 'horse'?" He patted Ferox's sleek neck.

"We have several dialects," said Navin, "but I will give you words that can be understood by most Britons."

By the time they had crossed the long wooden bridge over the Thames and entered the straggling little town of London, Quintus had memorized about twenty common Celtic words and was quite ready for some other distraction. But he did not find it in London, which was a dull place, except for the water traffic. The river was full of round woven fishing coracles and some trading vessels from Gaul, and there was a hubbub of sailors on the waterfront. The town itself was mean and ugly. The houses were one-storied and mostly made of wattle and daub thatched with reeds; even the military and government buildings were of unadorned wood. Here and there on the outskirts one of the retired Roman soldiers had built himself a villa, but though many thousands of people lived and did business here it seemed to be only an overgrown village.

"No decent forum," moaned Lucius, as they passed the open market place of trampled earth, "no public baths, no circus—not even a temple."

They drew up before the military headquarters and Flaccus went inside to report the arrival of his company. He came out again almost at once.

"We're to proceed immediately to Colchester," he said. "Seems the governor's there."

"I thought, sir," said Quintus, "we were to stop in London, then go north to Lincoln to reinforce the Ninth?"

"Since when do you question orders!" snapped Flaccus. "They've changed. That's all. Some one of these native kings has died, and there's a commotion about it."

He turned his back, flicked his horse, and gave the signal to march.

"So much for London," said Lucius, shrugging and easing himself in the saddle. "Not that I'm tempted to linger. . . . Ah, more forest ahead, I see," he added, as they headed east. "The charming variety of the scenery here intoxicates me, and the climate——" for it began to rain harder.

"Oh, quit grumbling," said Quintus good-humoredly. "After all they're sending us to the capital, and they say it's really quite a place. Maybe there'll be lovely British maidens, and even some fun."

"Ha!" said Lucius morosely, expressing profound disbelief.

But actually Colchester was a fair provincial city. It had been the capital of that part of Britain under King Cymbeline, and the Emperor Claudius, on his visit, had given orders to turn it into a Roman capital.

The young men's spirits rose as they saw paved streets, stone villas, corner wineshops like those at home. The government buildings and basilica and palace stood on the edges of the forum, which was properly furnished with a rostrum for orators to stand on, a mammoth statue of a winged Victory, and little altars to Jupiter, Mars, Minerva, and other gods. But one scarcely noticed those because the center of the forum was occupied by an enormous building, big enough to shelter a thousand people, and obviously a temple with its dozens of white and gold columns, its elaborate carved cornices.

"Now WHAT is that?" cried Quintus, amazed at this unexpected magnificence, and Navin who had remained near him and taught him more Celtic words during the boring three days' march from London, answered dryly, "That is the Temple of Claudius, dedicated to our divine and late lamented Emperor who is now, of course, a god."

"Not bad," said Lucius grudgingly, preening himself a little, for he was proud of his relationship to Claudius and hoped that it could be used toward future promotion, and eventually toward speedy return home.

Quintus had a less personal reaction to the gorgeous temple. "And do the British really worship here the spirit of their conqueror?" he asked slowly of Navin.

A muscle flickered in the corner of the Briton's mouth. "Undoubtedly," he said, in an odd tone, "but you forget, sir, that I have not been home in a long time."

This man knows something we don't know, Quintus thought, or am I imagining it?

As they continued to march along the edge of the forum toward headquarters, Quintus cast curious looks at the townfolks. There were Roman citizens in thick white wool togas, slaves in short tunics, well-to-do Britons in gaudy tartan trousers and capes held with bronze brooches, and poor Britons huddled in mangy goatskins. But all of them, even the Romans, shrank to the wall as the legionaries marched by and gave the proper arm's length salute crying, "Welcome, Eagles of Rome, welcome!" Evidently the populace was well trained.

Flaccus went off to report, while his two subordinates accompanied their men to the barracks. Quintus saw at once to the stabling and grooming of Ferox and, when he rejoined Lucius, he learned that they were summoned to appear before the governor at once.

The "imperial" palace was warm and comfortable, the chilled young Romans discovered gratefully. The shivery dankness outside had increased with the incredibly early nightfall of this northern climate. The palace was solidly built of marble and snug brick. The atrium—the great central hall—was roofed over as it would never have been at home, and the mosaic floors were well heated by hot-air flues from below.

A slave ushered Quintus and Lucius into the frescoed hall, which was lit by six torches and a bevy of little oil lamps. They clearly illumined a portentous group gathered around a parchment littered table.

"The High Command!" whispered Quintus, staring up the hall at two throne-like chairs. One was occupied by a bull-necked, red-faced man in elaborate gilt armor who could only be Governor Suetonius Paulinus, the military ruler of Britain. The other throne contained a small, fat man with hunched shoulders and the dome head and hooded eyes of a frog. His white toga was embroidered in gold and so banded with purple that it was not hard to identify him either—he was Decianus Catus, the Emperor Nero's procurator for Britain, in charge of all its civil affairs, and only slightly less powerful than the governor. Or perhaps he did not consider himself less important at all, for he talked continuously in a shrill, insistent voice, which quite drowned out Suetonius' occasional gruff interjections.

"I wonder what they wanted *us* for," murmured Lucius after twenty minutes of unrecognized waiting by the entrance. Flaccus was there too, halfway down the room, and several other centurions, as well as senior officers—tribunes and prefects.

Four legionary generals, or legates, were milling around the governor and the procurator, and some other patricians in togas, but it was difficult to hear what was going on, until Catus suddenly stood up, banging his puffy white hand on the table, and shouting, "I tell you, this is the chance I've been waiting for! We'll show these chuckleheaded savages we mean business. We'll call in the loans and help ourselves to all that ripe juicy treasure the Icenians have been traitorously hoarding. The huge tribute we'll send back to Nero—the gods keep His Imperial Majesty in health and grace—*that'll* startle him!" Catus' pursed pink lips drew back in a smile. "The Emperor will be pleased with all of us," he added quite softly, staring—as though he dared him to deny it—at the governor who rose also, while his gold-hilted sword clattered against the table.

"If—Decianus Catus—you will stop talking long enough to listen to me," cried Suetonius, his heavy jowls quivering, "you might learn that I am in complete agreement with you, and have no intention of interfering with your little plans for the Icenian nation. My interests are elsewhere—in the west. I am going to stamp out this disgusting Druidism once and for all, if I have to chase each one of the scurvy priesthood into the Irish Sea."

Ah, thought Quintus, that's interesting. So we're to fight the Druids, are we? He had edged unobtrusively along the wall to a nearer viewpoint where he could hear and see much better.

And the talk went on. There was a tall old man in a toga who was called Seneca and made occasional comments which the others listened to respectfully. This

Seneca was a philosopher and author—Quintus had read some of his books at school—and it also appeared from the conversation that he was rather surprisingly a money-lender as well. Then there were the generals who commanded the four legions in Britain—the Second, the Ninth, the Fourteenth, the Twentieth. Quintus recognized the legion each general was in command of by the badges, but he looked hardest at the legate of the Ninth, the "Hispana" Legion from Lincoln. For this was the post to which his company was assigned, and this man, Petillius Cerealis, would be his own commanding officer. He looks all right, Quintus thought, with relief. The general seemed very young for so much rank. He had keen hazel eyes and was slightly built but he gave a pleasant impression of competence and strength.

After a while Quintus began to understand what it was all about. There was a large country north of here in East Anglia that belonged to a wealthy tribe called the Iceni. They had had a King, Prasutagus, who had died a week before, leaving no heirs but his Queen, Boadicea, and two young daughters. To be sure the Icenians had a peace treaty with Nero and had been co-operative in the matter of paying tribute and giving up all their weapons in observance of a Roman decree. Also the King had named Nero coheir with his wife and children, as a gesture of confidence. But Catus, the frog-like procurator, saw no reason for these facts to bother anyone now the King was dead. Prasutagus had reigned over a prosperous kingdom and was reputed to have amassed a huge fortune in gold. It was idiocy to let a weak woman and a couple of girls stand in the way of acquiring all of it.

"Well, that's settled," said Governor Suetonius at length to Catus. "Your own guard here should be ample to handle the business. But I'll give you a special detachment—a vexillation of picked men, besides. After all, the Icenians have no weapons and won't dispute you anyway. As for me I'm off tomorrow into Wales with the main army."

General Petillius of the Ninth suddenly put out his hand. "Your Excellency," he said to the governor, "I fear that the Icenians may resent this plan more than you think. I've heard that the Queen Boadicea is a proud and passionate woman. Besides, this course seems to me hardly— hardly just."

The governor, who had been gathering up some parchments, turned and stared. His red face grew more purple, but he had reason to trust Petillius, and he spoke with restraint. "Do you suggest that my administration of Britain is lacking in justice?"

The young general smiled apologetically. "I suggest that these measures against the Icenians may damage Roman prestige."

"What utter bosh!" interrupted Catus in his shrill high voice. "The whole country wants a lesson taught it; there've been mutterings and disobedience lately. We must show who's master!"

Suetonius glanced at the fat procurator with some distaste, but he spoke with courteous finality to Petillius. "I understand your objections, my friend, but I agree with Catus. Besides, this Icenian matter is unimportant—it's these slippery Druids who're causing the trouble—— That reminds me——" He looked down the room toward Flaccus. "O Centurion of the Ninth, where is the young standard-bearer who had the encounter with the Druid priest?"

Flaccus saluted, turned around, and spying Quintus, said, "Go to the governor—and, Your Excellency, my Optio there—Lucius Claudius was also a witness." Lucius stepped forward eagerly.

Both young men walked down the room and stood by the table. After a few questions, Lucius, to his mortification, was dismissed before he even had a chance to insinuate his relationship to the Emperor Claudius, but Quintus was kept much longer.

"Do you think," asked Suetonius, frowning, "that the Druid cast an evil spell on you, so your hands were paralyzed?"

"Not exactly, Your Excellency, it was more the power in his eyes. I—I felt like a fool."

Suetonius nodded while inspecting the young standard-bearer. A fine specimen of Roman manhood, big, well spoken and well educated. The quality of recruit they're sending us is improving, he thought. "I don't know who this straggler was," he said, reverting to the Druid priest, "I thought we'd got them all combed out and bottled up on their 'sacred' island of Anglesey, off Wales, where I'll finish them off once and for all. But we'll take care of *him*. Tertius Julian!"

An officer of the governor's own guard stepped forward. "Yes, sir."

"Take a detail of men down into Kent, find this priest, and execute him, then rejoin me in Wales."

Again General Petillius intervened. "But, Your Excellency, from the accounts, the Druid said he was friendly to the Romans and came only to warn."

"Well, imprison him then," said the governor impatiently. "Put him in that dungeon below the guardhouse in London, but be careful he doesn't work any tricks on *you*," he said to his officer.

"Not on me, sir," said Tertius Julian, throwing Quintus a look of patronizing amusement.

The governor shrugged dismissal, Quintus stepped back, but the procurator suddenly spoke up in his wheezy whine and demanded the vexillation the governor had promised for disciplining the Icenians. "And I'll take that one to begin with," he said, pointing a stumpy finger at Quintus, as though he were a cut of beef to be purchased. "He looks like a good man."

Quintus' heart sank. He had not the slightest desire to find favor in the procurator's eyes, nor to take part in what sounded like a messy and inglorious bullying of women and children.

But there was no help for it. Quintus remained in Colchester as a temporary member of Catus' new guard, while the Ninth was on the march toward Lincoln next morning, including most of the newly landed cohort and Flaccus and Lucius—to the latter's unbounded annoyance. For he had been given no time to taste the pleasures of Colchester and was frankly jealous of what he considered Quintus' preferment.

"Well then," said Quintus, as the friends said good-by, "we're neither of us pleased. I'd *like* serving under General Petillius, and I don't like that Catus. I'll be glad when this business in Norfolk is over and I can get to my proper legion. By the Furies though—why didn't I get sent with the governor to fight the Druids, that's what I *really* wanted to do!"

"Because," said Lucius, irritably flicking a blob of mud off his elegant bronze breastplate, "the army never by any chance lets you do what you want to do. *Quod est demonstrandum.*"

Nor, thought Quintus glumly, do I have the slightest

30

chance of finding that huge stone circle in the land of the small dark men to the west, either. Already he had discovered that this country was much larger than he had realized, and he perforce put all thoughts of his quest out of his mind for the present.

Quintus lived at the Colchester barracks for some days and kept fit when off duty by throwing the discus with fellow soldiers, or galloping Ferox along the hard-frozen tracks outside of town. He flirted mildly with a Gallic wine merchant's daughter and drank a moderate amount of her father's wares. And he awaited without enthusiasm Catus' orders to accompany the procurator into the country of the Iceni.

These orders actually came on a cold winter's morning when a sifting of snow fell from the gray sky. And Quintus found himself starting north as one in a company of two hundred of the roughest, most brutalized men he had ever seen—the procurator's hand-picked mounted guard.

CHAPTER II

IT TOOK THEM THREE DAYS to cover the sixty miles between Colchester and Caistor-by-Norwich in Norfolk, the land of the Iceni, because though the guard were all mounted they must not go faster than Catus' slave-borne litter. The procurator lolled in a sort of cushioned bed on poles, gilded and ornamented with imperial eagles. It was warmed, too, by a charcoal brazier, while Catus reclined in a nest of foxskin robes from which he called constant orders to the harassed slaves who ran alongside, especially Hector, a beady-eyed Sicilian, who by cunning flattery had become Catus' steward and confidant.

The guard was commanded by a gigantic Belgian centurion called Otho, who had the look and temper of a wild boar. He mistreated his horse and bullied his men, but with Catus he had a smooth deferential manner, and the procurator showed him high favor. Though the guard were all technically Romans, most were auxiliaries of different nationalities who came from many parts of the far-flung empire, and were fierce fighting machines, as stupid, most of them, as the gladiators who pummeled each other in the Roman circuses. Quintus found them thoroughly uncongenial and, whenever they struck camp in the dark night forests, hunted out Navin who had come along as interpreter.

On the third afternoon they emerged from the forest and saw a haze of smoke from a thousand fires, and a huge circular mound of earthworks, high as a tree, that surrounded the city of the Iceni.

"Ha!" cried Catus, leaning from the litter, his eyes sparkling with greed. "They look prosperous. That's the finest native town *I've* seen!"

A good many of the buildings were of stone and in the middle of them rose a large two-story edifice. It had many windows curtained by deer hides and a large bright golden shield fastened to the stone wall above a great portal.

"Obviously the palace," said Catus. "And where did they get enough gold to make a thing like that!"

The cavalcade drew up at the gate in the earthworks, and Otho, the centurion, banged on it with his sword, shouting, "Decianus Catus, imperial procurator of Rome, desires to enter!"

At once the gate swung back and an old man came forward bowing and crying a Celtic greeting. Navin stepped up. "He says the Queen has been eagerly awaiting you, O Procurator. Welcome and enter!"

Catus smiled and winked slowly at Otho. The guard and Catus and his servants moved through the narrow crowded little streets. Shy faces peered at them from doorways, then disappeared. A giggling, nervous little girl ran out from a round stone house, thrust a pottery cup of amber liquid into the procurator's hand, then ran back again.

"They are honoring you, Excellency," explained the interpreter. "That is their precious heather ale."

"Pah," said Catus, sniffing it, and he dumped it on the ground.

There were several wooden steps leading up to the palace portal, and on these steps stood four women. The central figure was so astonishing that a gasp came from the advancing Roman guard, and Quintus stared astounded.

Queen Boadicea was a majestic, full-bosomed woman, as tall as Quintus. She was over forty, but her hair, which cascaded down to her knees, was still the color of ripe wheat, or of the golden gorget that hung like a half moon on her breast. She wore a plaid robe of red and violet, belted by a golden circlet. Her face was broad, with high cheekbones; above them her eyes glinted a proud ice-blue.

As the procurator's litter drew up before her, she inclined her stately head and said in accented but correct Latin, "You are welcome, Romans. I knew that you would come to comfort me for the loss of my beloved husband and help me govern my people in his stead."

She smiled and, descending the steps, held out to the procurator a branch of white-berried mistletoe.

"What's this?" mumbled Catus, staring at the mistletoe.

"It is our most sacred totem," said the Queen solemnly, "I give it to you in token of the friendship between Rome and the Iceni."

"You'll give a lot more than a hunk of vegetable before you're through," said Catus below his breath, as he hopped out of the litter and contemptuously waved to a slave to take the mistletoe branch.

The Queen's eyes narrowed at this rudeness, but she bowed slightly, and said, pointing to two of the girls on the steps, "These are my daughters."

The princesses were large, redheaded girls of about eighteen. They looked as forceful and regal as their mother, but they had not quite the beauty she must have had in her younger days. The buxom, fair-haired princesses produced a chorus of lip-smacking and whistles from the rest of the guard, and several coarse jokes, but Quintus' eye was caught by the third girl who had been hidden behind the princesses, for she was much shorter than they. Her hair was not flamboyant like the other women's; it was a soft bright chestnut with gleams of light in the curly tendrils that fell below her waist. She wore no jewelry except an enameled bronze brooch that fastened her plaid robe. She had a small delicate face and a pair of very large blue-gray eyes, which were surveying the Romans with curiosity and some distrust.

The Queen turned with her daughters and ushered Catus through the portal; the other girl turned too and her eyes met Quintus' frankly approving stare.

At the moment when their glances crossed, Quintus felt a shock of interest. More than interest, a peculiar sensation of sympathy, and a sudden desire to touch that soft curly hair. His expression must have changed for she gave him a faint startled smile and then turned and ran through the portal after the others.

Nothing unusual happened that night. Catus remained in the palace with Otho, his captain, and all his slaves, and Queen Boadicea entertained them most hospitably. Quintus and the rest of the guard encamped outside the town, to await orders, which Quintus felt would not come.

The Icenians had received them graciously and trustingly and surely even Catus would not make too outrageous demands. Romans did not war on women, or without provocation. Tomorrow no doubt they'd all march back to Colchester again with whatever booty the old skin-flint had prized out of the poor Queen and that would be that. Except for a slight regret that he would not see the unknown girl again, Quintus was relieved.

He was also quite wrong in all his expectations.

The next morning the Roman guard was summoned back to the palace and ordered to come on foot while leaving the horses outside the town. Otho met them in the courtyard. "Fun's going to begin pretty soon, boys!" he shouted. "Procurator says to have some swigs of the good Roman wine these buzzards had hidden. There it is!" He jerked his chin toward two huge amphorae that had been hauled out to the courtyard. Red wine trickled down their curved sides. It was obvious that Otho had had a head start on the wine, and his men, with roars of ap-preciation, began at once to catch up. Quintus did not join them. He was not thirsty, and he was disgusted. These wine-bibbing rowdies were totally unlike the disciplined Roman soldiery he had trained with. Of course, he thought with contempt, Catus was not a general, nothing but a civilian.

He glanced toward the portal of the palace as a ring-ing, angry woman's voice inside cried out in Latin, "Nev-er! Never shall these things be done. It is not *possible* that the Emperor Nero would so abuse his faithful allies!"

Quintus glanced at Otho and the guard who were milling around the wine jars, and he pushed open the heavy wooden door.

It was dark in the low long hall, and smoky from a great central fire, but in a moment he could see the tense group around Catus and Queen Boadicea. They were both standing near the fire; Boadicea towered over the procura-tor, who was surrounded by his crouching slaves. Behind the Queen stood a dozen of her Icenian nobles and kins-men. They were tall, gold-bearded men in horned helmets and they were unarmed, as Roman law had decreed. They looked uncertain, anxious, straining to follow the Latin language, which their Queen had learned so well.

There were women too, huddled in the corner by a great loom filled with half-woven cloth. Quintus saw amongst them the two princesses, and the small girl with chestnut hair.

"Am I to understand," said Catus softly, darting his bald head toward the Queen, "that you refuse our glorious Emperor's commands . . . ?"

Boadicea quivered, her face grew pale, her eyes flashed, and she cried with furious scorn, "Commands that I abdicate . . . ? That I turn my kingdom and people over to *you*, that I give you my children's *inheritance* . . . and bow down as abject slave to Rome . . . ? Yes, O Procurator. I *refuse!*"

"Ah . . ." said Catus, smiling on a long, satisfied note. He turned and barked a command to his chief slave, Hector, the Sicilian, who jumped up and darted for the door where he saw Quintus. "Back to your post," Hector hissed, "the time has come."

Quintus frowned but he went to the courtyard where the slave was relaying Catus' order to Otho. The Belgian centurion's little pig eyes gleamed, he shook his head to clear it of the wine fumes. "Form ranks," he shouted. "Into the palace! Let no Icenian escape, but do not kill unless you must!"

The two hundred men drew their swords and rushed forward, Quintus with them obeying automatically. They stormed into the hall and so quickly had it happened that the Icenians were motionless at first. Then they fought with fists and teeth and stools and flagons, whatever they could lay their hands on, but the Romans thwacked fierce blows with the flat of the sword. They jabbed and slashed too, while Catus' slaves joined in. The procurator himself, safe on a table out of the brawl, capered with glee.

The Icenians were soon tied up and stacked like wood in the corner of the hall, while Otho seized and bound the Queen herself and threw her to the ground.

"Stand her up," shrilled Catus, "Boadicea shall feel how Rome punishes those who defy her might!" He gestured to Hector who ran up with a huge black three-tailed whip. Otho jerked the Queen to her feet and held her at arm's length while the slave, giggling, plied the great whip. It hissed and snapped through the air, the long snake-like scourges wrapped again and again around Boadicea's body. Her plaid robe tore to ribbons, blood trickled down her shoulders and matted the golden hair. She uttered no sound, but stood stone quiet under the lash, her face gray as ashes, her eyes sunken and terrible as those of a corpse.

36

It was her daughters who screamed, and Quintus, angry and sickened at these sights, whirled to see that two of the burliest soldiers had grabbed up the red-haired princesses and were carrying them from the hall.

Catus turned too and laughed. "Let them go," he said. "My soldiers have led a dull life of late, they deserve a little fun. . . . Cease," he said impatiently to the slave, who dropped the whip. "No doubt the Queen has learned her lesson. Put her over there out of the way and ransack the palace—here, we'll start with that chest!"

While Catus spoke, Quintus had suddenly caught sight of the girl who interested him. She had tried to hide behind the loom and a squat Frankish soldier was lunging for her.

Quintus reached the Frank with one bound and knocked him spinning on the floor. "Here, quick!" he said to the girl, and as she only stared at him with dumb horror, he picked her up and rushed with her through the door which led onto a side court. As the chill air hit her, she gasped and began to struggle frantically, hitting him in the face, trying to scratch his eyes.

"No, no—don't!" cried Quintus. "I won't hurt you." He dared not put her down because the Frank was clattering through the door after him. "You little idiot," he said angrily, as he ran with her across the court, "I'm trying to help you!"

She understood little of his actual words, but the sense of them reached her. She quietened and suddenly whispered something and pointed to a round building raised on high piles. It was a granary and Quintus saw what she meant. He flung her up through the open door, climbed up himself, and pulled the six-foot ladder after him, as the Frank arrived shouting furiously.

"It's no use, my friend," said Quintus, peering sardonically down at him. "You can't get up here. Go find yourself another girl."

The Frank looked up at Quintus' drawn sword poised for action, at the young Roman's cold watchful eyes, then he shrugged and walked away.

Quintus sheathed his sword and turned into the granary. The girl lay crumpled, sobbing, on a heap of grain. He sat down beside her and awkwardly patted her shoulder. "I think you'd better stay here a while until I figure out some way to get you far off from—from what's going on in that palace."

She spoke some Latin and understood most of what he said this time. She shuddered, covering her face with her hands, and whispered something in her own language. Then she translated it slowly. "I *hate* you, Roman," she said through her teeth. "I will *hate* you till I die."

"I know," said Quintus. "I don't blame you. That was a rotten business in there. You mustn't believe all Romans are like that."

She raised her head and gazed at him with the huge gray eyes. "Romans are beasts—like wolves—they betray, devour—you too."

"I don't think so," said Quintus gently, "but never mind that. What's your name, by the way?"

She had ceased crying and looked at him steadily in the darkness of the granary. He saw that for all her fear and smallness, she had a thoroughbred control. After a moment she pronounced a Celtic name.

"Regan?" he tried to repeat the difficult sound. "Is that your name?"

"Near enough," she answered. "I am Queen Boadicea's foster child. My parents are dead. She has been a mother to me. Never shall I forget what has been done to her this day—and to my foster sisters, the princesses."

Quintus said nothing. On impulse he put out his hand and touched the soft disheveled hair that rippled down her back. She jumped as though he'd struck her, throwing her hands out to ward him off.

"Listen, Regan," said Quintus stiffly, folding his arms across his breastplate, "I like you, and mean you no harm. You mustn't be scared of me. Now where can I take you that you'll be safe? Think!"

She relaxed gradually, sitting up straight on the pile of grain and examining him through the thick lashes of her half-closed eyes. His helmet with its arching crest of red and its engraved eagle gleamed in the half darkness—the odious panoply of Rome. But above the leather chin strap, the lean weather-tanned face and the steady dark eyes were attractive.

Her look softened, she started to speak, when from somewhere outside there came a long sobbing wail, anguished cries to Celtic gods for help, and a shout of drunken laughter.

She whitened, fear came back into her face. She started

to tremble though she tried to control it. "I must go to Boadicea—I must help——"

"No, you don't," said Quintus. "If you go back in there, I certainly couldn't protect you against all Catus' rabble. But we can't stay here either. You must know some house in town where you can hide. A poor one," he added grimly, "that Catus won't bother with."

Her breathing slowed and she bowed her head, knowing that he was right. "Pendoc," she whispered after a moment. "The potter. He has always protected me. His hut is down there by the river."

Quintus nodded and, going to the granary door, peered out cautiously. Nobody was in sight except three of Catus' slaves squatting by a wall and squabbling over a pouch full of Icenian coins they had found. Quintus did not bother with the little ladder. He jumped down and held up his arms for Regan. "I'll carry you," he said, speaking very distinctly so she would understand. "You must lie across my shoulder and pretend you have fainted."

She nodded with a frightened little smile. While he pulled her down from the granary and adjusted her light body over his left shoulder, he thought with sudden warmth, she trusts me now, poor child. Though she was about sixteen and he not quite twenty, the protection he was giving her made him feel infinitely older. In some ways she reminded him of his little sister, Livia; in some ways only, for as he carried her according to her whispered directions, through a maze of littered alleys down a slope toward a thatched hut, he felt a new strange tenderness that even his sister had never aroused.

They were challenged once. Three of the Roman guard were busy ransacking a stone house that belonged to one of the wealthier Icenians. They were piling up shields, bracelets, household goods on the doorstep for the later inspection of Catus. "Halt, Quintus Tullius!" cried the soldier in charge. "Centurion's been looking for you. Get up to the palace!"

"That's where I'm going," called Quintus gaily, trusting that the maze of alleys had confused the man's direction.

"With *that?*" cried the soldier, pointing to Regan's limp body.

"I thought Otho might be interested," answered Quintus, and added a rough bit of army slang.

39

The man guffawed and started walking toward Quintus, who moved fast, turned a corner, and started to run.

"Here," whispered Regan. "Here!" She slid down from his shoulder and pulled him after her through a door that was curtained by a cowhide.

Inside the small round hut it smelled of wet clay and pigs, who were snuffling after garbage on the packed earthen floor. The potter was a big scarfaced man with long sandy-red hair. He jumped back from his wheel with an astonished grunt as Regan and the tall Roman legionary burst in.

The girl explained in a string of urgent Celtic. The potter answered, drawing himself up and staring at Quintus with narrowed hostile eyes.

"It's all right," said Regan, "Pendoc says he'll take care of me. But he knew nothing of what's been going on. He's—he's very angry."

Quintus sighed. The potter, indeed any Briton, had a right to be angry, but Pendoc's continuing harsh excited speech to Regan was destroying the girl's fleeting trust. Quintus could see it. She turned and would not look at Quintus. Her small pretty face hardened to a stony mask. Quintus caught the word "trap"—one that Navin had taught him—and understood. There was no use protesting that he had no sinister purpose in rescuing Regan, that he deplored this whole shocking treatment of the Iceni. It was obvious Pendoc would not believe him, and that Regan no longer did.

"Farewell," he said to the girl. "May Jupiter and Fortuna both have you in their keeping, Regan."

She looked at him then. "ROMAN gods——" she said with blistering contempt, and turned her back.

Regan's contempt bolstered Quintus during the following three days that he spent in the Icenian city. After all he was a legionary under oath to the Emperor to obey orders without question. And it was not fitting for a Roman to go sentimental and soft or fraternize with natives who were, on the whole, being civilized for their own good. He almost managed to forget Regan and the peculiar new feelings she had roused in him.

And after all, thought Quintus sardonically, as they started on the march back to Colchester, the Icenian incident was finished to the satisfaction of Catus, anyway.

The procurator was extremely pleased with himself,

Quintus, who rode near the slave-borne litter, could hear his jubilant comments. Accompanying their cavalcade were twelve carts full of booty—bronzes and beautiful British enamels, gold gorgets, torques and brooches, coffers full of Icenian coinage, and the huge golden shield that had hung over the palace door. There were six new slaves too, or hostages, as Catus with unusual delicacy preferred to call them. These were some of the Icenian noblemen who had been surprised in the palace. Around their necks they now wore heavy iron collars attached to chains which bound them to each other between two Roman soldiers who held the ends.

"It'll do the Trinovantes good to see these," said Catus repeatedly to Hector. "Object lesson. I've noticed them in Colchester lately—very lax in worshiping our divine Claudius in the temple."

"Shockingly lax, O Beloved Master," agreed Hector, bowing as he trotted along beside the litter. "Yes, it will do the Trinovantes good to hear how you have broken the spirit of the Iceni."

Catus tugged at his ear lobe. "That Boadicea—she never uttered a sound when we flogged her, or afterward when I so considerately allowed her to retire to her own apartments with those stupid screaming girls of hers. You'd think they'd all been *seriously* injured."

Quintus jerked Ferox's bridle and to his own amazement heard himself saying to the procurator, "Would *you* not consider it serious injury, Your Excellency, if your home were sacked and your kinsmen enslaved, if you were publicly whipped, and your daughters dishonored?"

Catus jerked around, staring up at the young man on the big black horse. "You speak like a fool! These barbarians don't have feelings like Romans do." His eyes narrowed and he said, "You've been a disappointment to me, Quintus Tullius Pertinax. I've been watching you. Half-hearted soldiering, lazy—now insolent. I had thought to get you promoted, maybe command my personal guard. As it is, I shall see that you return at once to your legion, where I trust your General Petillius Cerealis will beat you into shape."

"Yes, sir," said Quintus, respectfully, reining in Ferox and dropping back to the rear, where he had trouble hiding his satisfaction from the other soldiers, who were pleased by the Roman newcomer's fall from favor.

They camped that night at a ford on the river Stour which was the boundary between the Icenians and the Trinovantes. Here there was a rough Roman fort containing a cabin where Catus decided to spend the night rather than endure the few remaining miles to Colchester. His slaves at once set about the usual routine. They heated water and scented oils for the procurator's bath. They arranged his cushioned couch for him to recline on while he ate the delicacies he demanded even in the wilderness —jellied eels, larks stewed in honey, poppy-seed cakes, all washed down with a flagon of imported Gaulish wine.

Quintus observed the dishes being rushed into the procurator's cabin. May Hygeia send him indigestion, thought Quintus maliciously, invoking the goddess of health. The guard had to be satisfied with the usual marching ration of hard wheat cake and dried fish, supplemented tonight by boiled mutton from an Icenian sheep. Quintus made a tour of the fort and glanced at the six prisoners, who had collapsed in a heap on the ground, hollow-eyed, silent. Their big blond heads slumped forward on their chests. Blood trickled from sores in their necks made by the iron collars. "What've THEY had to eat?" asked Quintus of the captives' guard.

"Nothing," said the guard, gnawing on a chop. "Procurator gave no orders to feed 'em."

"Well, *I* do," said Quintus. "Give them some of our rations, and if I weren't still serving under Decianus Catus I'd say the man is an utter imbecile. If he wants his captives dead, he should kill them. If he wants them to be useful slaves, he's got to keep 'em alive."

"True enough," said the guard, shrugging. He gathered up a handful of wheat cakes and took them to the Icenians. Otho had been left behind in the Icenian city with a dozen men to maintain order and also to hunt around in case any valuable booty had been overlooked. In his absence another officer and Quintus had been given temporary command.

It had been one of those promising late-winter days, when the sun was warm and the air smelled of spring. There were patches of snow still, beneath the holly bushes and towering oaks in the forests, but through the brown earth pushed green spikes of cuckoopint. Thrushes and blackbirds sang at their nestings, while deep in the wilderness on each side of the Roman road the wild things were mating; the foxes, the red deer, and the wolves.

Quintus too felt the restlessness and yearning of spring. In the twilight he wandered outside the fort and quite a way along the riverbank, which was marged with reeds where moor hens and coots were paddling. He thought how different spring was here from the sudden lush flowering back home. He pictured his mother and Livia sitting in their frescoed atrium, listening to the splash of their fountain. The sun would be hot, his mother's Persian lilies would be in full scented bloom. He sent them both a homesick greeting, and then suddenly he thought of Regan.

On the eve of their departure from the Icenian city he had gone back to Pendoc the potter's little hut to say good-by to her, to try—though he did not quite admit it —to wipe that last contemptuous look she had given him from his memory. The hut was completely deserted. The potter's wheel and the pigs, too, were gone.

It was reasonable that Pendoc should take the girl away—doubtless to one of the many caves and hiding places in the forest where the other Icenians had fled. For the Roman destruction had continued. Wanton fires had been lit, many of the buildings destroyed. In a short time the Icenian capital had become a city of the dead, hushed, empty, except for the Queen and her daughters, who were barricaded in a wing of the ruined palace.

But I'd like to see Regan again, Quintus thought. To tell her—to make her understand—what? He was a Roman and she was a Briton. The Romans were conquering and subduing the Britons. What more was there to explain?

Impatient with himself, he shied a pebble amongst the waterfowl and idly watched them scolding and fluttering off.

A twig cracked behind him and he jumped around, his hand on his sword.

It was Navin who stood behind him in the shadows, watching with a sardonic lift to his bushy red eyebrows. "You're far from camp alone, Quintus Tullius," Navin said quietly. "There are wild boar and wolves in the forest. And there may be other enemies too—for a Roman."

Quintus smiled. He had developed considerable liking for the interpreter and he knew that it was returned, and yet he had not the faintest idea what Navin really thought or felt. Navin had kept to himself during the days of sacking the Icenian city, except when Catus called on him to interpret. He had made it clear that the fate of the Icenians was a matter of indifference to him. He was a Trinovante, and the two nations had not been friendly with each other.

"I was wandering along and doing some thinking," said Quintus laughing ruefully, "about a girl, as a matter of fact. A little Icenian named Regan that I—I, well, took care of, back in that disgraceful brawl Catus produced."

"Yes," said Navin. "I heard that you rescued the Queen's foster child. Regan is not an Icenian."

"She isn't?" said Quintus, startled.

"No. Regan comes from a different part of Britain, though she is distantly connected with Boadicea. When her parents died, her grandfather——" Navin paused and it seemed as though he changed his mind about something he was going to say. He went on quickly. "Regan's grandfather brought her here six years ago to be raised by the Queen."

"Oh?" said Quintus. "Then isn't that Pendoc an Icenian either?"

"No. Quintus, you ask a great many questions and think too much. Until you give it up you'll never make a good Roman soldier."

Quintus flushed. "I *am* a good soldier," he said hotly. "Just because I don't lick the sandals of that fat civilian fool of a procurator——"

"And you've not yet learned to hold your tongue and hide your thoughts," continued Navin imperturbably. "But you will have to."

Whatever Quintus was going to reply he forgot as something about the Briton startled him. He stared through the waning light. "Navin! You're in native dress!"

The belted tunic, the high military sandals, the brass badge of the hostage all were gone. Instead Navin wore tight plaid trousers. A tartan cape was thrown over his shoulders and fastened by a huge brooch of Celtic scrollwork. His chin and upper lip were covered with red-dish stubble where before they had been carefully shaven like the Romans. And on his forehead was a circular patch of blue, the woad sign of the warrior chief.

"Even so," said Navin, nodding and watching Quintus.

"But what does it *mean?*"

"That I have found things not to my liking in Colchester or in London, and throughout the country of the Trinovantes which once my father ruled. That in Rome I was lulled into believing that my people benefited by Roman progress, that they were contented. It is not true. I find them thrown out of their homes in favor of Roman veterans who bully and despise them. I find them crippled by debts. And now Seneca, that philosophical moneylender, has suddenly called in all the debts—without reason. My people can't pay."

"Well, that's bad," said Quintus unhappily. "The Icenian incident was shocking I know, but——"

Navin held up his hand. "The Icenians today. The Trinovantes tomorrow—and soon all the other tribes. That's enough, Quintus. I too have said more than I should."

There was silence. Quintus was dismayed, and yet he thought: they can't really do much. The tribes aren't even friendly with each other. This poor Navin will be caught and brought back. Then an unpleasant realization struck Quintus. It was his duty to seize now, this instant, what was, after all, an escaping and defiant hostage. His hand moved slowly to his sword hilt.

"No, my Quintus," said Navin quietly watching. "You are very far from camp—and listen. . . ."

All through this conversation Quintus had been half conscious of the yelping of foxes. As Navin motioned for silence, there was a short sharp bark nearby from a thicket. It was answered by others to the right, the left, and further off, and others fainter yet in the distance. They were surrounded by the harsh strange barks.

"Foxes——" said Quintus quickly. "They always make a noise like that when they're mating. . . ." But cold ran down his spine, for Navin's eyes had changed as much as his clothes had. They were now wary, sardonic.

"Those are not foxes," said Navin. "Quintus, this is the last time we meet as friends. Go back now to the fort. You won't be molested. The time isn't yet ripe. . . . Go——"

Quintus turned and obeyed. As he walked glumly along the riverbank he felt the impact of a hundred watching hidden eyes. There were rustlings and movements in the blackness of the forest just beyond eyesight. And Navin stood where Quintus had left him, stern, implacable. Quintus reached the fort and reluctantly went to report this threatening incident to the procurator.

Catus was lolling on his couch listening to Hector strum a little lyre. When Quintus approached saying, "O Procurator—I'm sorry but something's just happened I think you should know," Catus impatiently wiped some cake crumbs from his chin and, turning on his elbow, frowned.

"Well, well. What is it? You KNOW I'm not to be bothered at this hour. Jupiter! I *never* get any peace and quiet!"

Quintus briefly related the encounter with Navin, and the procurator, who was drowsy, full of wine, and completely unwilling to bother with anything, said pettishly, "And you consider this stupid story important enough to disturb me with! I never liked that Navin anyway. Let him dress in anything he wants to and flounder around in the wilderness. He'll come back when he gets hungry, all right."

"But, sir, you don't understand. Navin means trouble. There's resistance getting underway, and those fox barks——"

"Those *fox barks!*" cut in the procurator with scorn. "You're always imagining things, like that Druid in Kent. I suppose you think they were ghost foxes."

Quintus reddened, but he said as quietly as he could, "No, sir. I'm quite sure they were made by Trinovantes, by Navin's own clan which, I know, has the fox for its totem."

"Well, let 'em all bark in the woods then—sounds just like the Britons." Catus rolled over and poked in a red pottery dish for a candied fig. "Go away," he ordered, turning his back on Quintus, and said to his slave, "Go on playing." Hector picked up the lyre.

So what in Hades can *I* do, thought Quintus angrily, as he walked out.

The next noon they reached Colchester again, and Quintus thankfully received orders to depart next day for the north, for Lincoln, where General Petillius and the Ninth Legion were stationed. He was to travel with a squad of auxiliaries who were bound further north into Yorkshire where the Romans had a fort in the wild country of the Brigantes.

Quintus enjoyed himself that night in Colchester. He went first to the great public baths and had a thorough steaming and soaking and rubbing down. Then he went to see a gladiator fight a bear in the circus. The gladiator got badly mangled but in the end he killed the animal with his bare hands. It wasn't like the wonderful spectacles at home, but it was exciting. And there were dances afterward, performed by some Spanish slave girls who belonged to a wealthy Roman merchant of the town.

Nor did Quintus neglect his religious duties. He entered the magnificent Temple of Claudius and bowed down before the statue of that Emperor-god, as everyone was expected to. In the vast shadowy temple there were other little altars and he duly lit some incense on that of the soldier's god—Mars. He paused by the altar of Venus, the goddess of love, and thought suddenly of Regan which was of course utterly ridiculous. He was annoyed with himself, passed on quickly, and went out into the forum where the colossal winged statue of Victory shone white against the sky. In the forum there was the usual bustle of togaed Romans and town-dwelling Britons, and Quintus, back in a city atmosphere as normal as home, began to think that perhaps he *had* been foolish to give so much importance to Navin and his fox barks. Or indeed to that whole time he had spent with the Icenians. Well, anyway, he thought, he'd soon be seeing Lucius and other friends in his own cohort—even Flaccus seemed worthy after Catus' ruffians. He bought himself some wine at the corner shop, teased the admiring and very pretty winemonger's daughter, and altogether passed an agreeable evening.

During the night a peculiar thing happened. Quintus' barracks were close to the forum, and it seemed to him afterward that mixed up with his dreams, he had heard a loud noise at some point, a sort of shattering crash outside, but it had not really awakened him. He was, however, awakened at sunrise by the murmur of many voices and the shuffling of feet.

Quintus rubbed his eyes, yawned, and went out just as he was, in his undertunic, to see what was going on. It was a hushed crowd that thronged the edges of the forum, all staring down at something on the marble pavement below. As Quintus edged through to look, a woman's voice cried out on a long quavering wail, "It is an omen! A dreadful omen!"

What is? thought Quintus, and then he saw. The colossal statue of Victory had fallen off its pedestal. It lay broken into a dozen pieces on the pavement of the forum.

"An omen! An omen!" The frightened whisper ran like wind through all the crowd. "Victory has deserted the Romans."

What utter nonsense, Quintus said to himself, and at that moment the old philosopher, Seneca, suddenly appeared on a balcony and put Quintus' thoughts into sensible words. "Fellow citizens and Britons!" Seneca shouted waving his arms. "There is no omen of any kind connected with this unfortunate accident. There was wind in the night and the statue was top-heavy, no doubt. We will at once erect another one!"

The crowd listened respectfully to the grave and portly Roman, but Quintus heard some hissing words behind him. They were in Celtic, but he caught their meaning—venomous hatred of Seneca. He turned instinctively and caught two more words hissed in a sneering voice. Something about a rope, and the wind. He stared behind him. Yes, quite near there were Trinovantes, for all that they wore Roman clothes. Their type was unmistakable, the height, the light hair. But he could not tell who had spoken. There were a dozen of them, and their big, rawboned faces were all expressionless, turned up toward Seneca.

Quintus walked back to his barracks to prepare for the march north. "Rope . . . wind," he thought, puzzled, and in a moment the solution came. Without a doubt it was not the wind but a stout rawhide Trinovante rope that had pulled down the statue of Victory in the night, had shattered the hateful symbol of Roman dominance.

He wondered if Catus would believe this if Quintus told him, but he knew that it was hopeless. Well, it they stop at *symbols* it'll be all right, Quintus thought. But again later, when the sun was warm and he set out west with the auxiliaries on Stane Street, his apprehension seemed silly. It was market day, the entire town hummed cheerfully. British peasants from the country had set up little stalls and hawked their produce in deep Celtic voices. Some of them sold lengths of woven cloth or bronze trinkets ornamented with ruby enamel, some sold the red glossy Samian ware they had learned how to make from the Romans. Some sold beaver skins and capes of woven kingfisher feathers. A trading ship from Gaul had anchored in the river Colne, and its crew mingled cheerfully

48

with the crowd. There was music and laughter, even the Britons seemed to be enjoying themselves. While above the whole scene rose the majestic gold and white Temple of Claudius, as solid and permanent as Roman power, no matter how many statues tumbled down.

"I'm really sorry to leave Colchester, after all," Quintus observed to one of the auxiliaries as they rode out of town. "It's a nice little city." Nor did he have the faintest intuition that the next time he came here there would be no Colchester at all.

CHAPTER III

THOUGH THE FIRST PART of the journey to Lincoln ran through Trinovante country, nothing unusual happened; in fact until they turned north on the highway called Ermine Street, Quintus saw hardly anyone at all. There were no sounds except those made by themselves and the birds.

The third day, they passed along the edge of the fens. Quintus gazed out over the distant tangle of green marshes and wondered if there were fever mists in them like the Pontine marshes outside of Rome. At any rate, fever or no, these fens were a treacherous secret maze of islands and twisting waterways always avoided by the legions and indeed by the Coritani tribe, who dwelt on the western border of the marshes. There were quite a few villages now that they were out of dense forest land, and there was a peaceful feeling, because the sun stayed out for two whole days and shone on the backs of grazing sheep and shaggy little British cows. The Coritani tribesmen, who were very tall like the Iceni to whom they were related, seemed friendly. There were actually smiling faces as the auxiliaries marched by, and sometimes children ran out from the round wattle-and-daub huts to offer the soldiers bunches of anemones and buttercups.

The foreboding of trouble and disaster which Quintus had felt back in Icenian country now vanished completely. Though he was partly relieved, he was also faintly disappointed, as he resigned himself to the prospect of routine barracks life in Lincoln, and decided to concentrate on earning a promotion and finding some way to get

50

sent to the west where he might start on the quest for Gaius' remains.

After so many hours of marching through the flattest country Quintus could have imagined, it was a welcome change to see Lincoln's sudden high hill jutting up against the sky. At last the company trudged up the steep road to the top and entered the oblong fort at Lincoln, station of the Ninth Legion.

Quintus was received with enthusiasm. Not only had he been popular with the men, but he was a welcome distraction. The Spanish centurion, Flaccus, ordered that broiled fish from the River Witham be added to the evening rations and issued an extra amphora of red wine as well.

"Flaccus isn't such a bad fellow, after all," said Lucius languidly, as they all lounged in the barracks hall after dinner. "He's as bored as the rest of us, up here on this hill, so we all go hunting when we're off duty, and we've had horse races and discus throwing. The baths aren't badly fixed up either for a piddling little outpost like this. Good steam room, and a dice game always going on around the massage table."

Quintus laughed, looking at his friend with affectionate amusement. "Anybody ever do any work, up here?"

"Oh sure," answered Lucius, wrinkling his nose. "Roads. Miles of 'em. We're pushing north to the Humber. And patrols. Besides the usual drills and parade, *you* know."

"Patrols . . . ?" repeated Quintus thoughtfully. "Any trouble with the natives?"

"Oh Jove, no—our Parisii tribe here are gentle as rabbits. They love us, they palm off all sorts of worthless junk on us, and their girls . . ." Lucius' sleepy eyes brightened suddenly, "Big, strapping blondes, they——"

Quintus sat up straight and interrupted sharply, "You better not fool-around with their girls, Lucius. These Britons all have a strict code of honor——"

"Oh twaddle!" said Lucius rudely. "What in the world's come over you down there in the south? You come back clucking like an old hen. Bet you're out of condition too, all this pampering by the procurator." He suddenly delivered a fierce half-playful punch at Quintus' stomach. Quintus gasped, doubled his fists, and retaliated. They threw off their tunics.

Soon with the ease of long practice they were in the

51

thick of a fairly scientific wrestling match; rolling, scuffling, grunting, and thoroughly enjoying themselves.

The other men gathered around and laid bets. Flaccus watched with an indulgent and slightly envious eye. For all that these two were the patrician young Romans that he sneered at, they were tough and fit. Their strong-muscled bodies scarcely reddened beneath the pummeling they gave each other and they were well matched, though Lucius was slightly stockier and slower. Quintus had nearly knocked the wind out of Lucius, when the fight was abruptly ended by a messenger from the general who announced that Standard-bearer Quintus Tullius Pertinax was to report at once.

The young men disentangled themselves and got up. "Continued later," said Quintus, panting and grinning at Lucius. "I almost had you."

"Like Hades, you did!" wheezed Lucius. He growled some extremely vulgar taunts with what breath he had, and everyone laughed. Quintus did too. He was never angry with his friend, no matter how hard they scuffled, or who won, though Lucius was of more uncertain temper, and hated to be beaten.

Quintus washed his face, buckled his breastplate and shin greaves, put on his helmet, picked up his shield and the cohort's standard, then presented himself to the general.

Petillius Cerealis sat at a camp table in a bare white-washed room, frowning at a map. He raised his alert young-looking head as Quintus came in, and said, "Good evening, Standard-bearer." Quintus responded and waited. The general was in no hurry. His sharp eyes inspected Quintus from helmet crest to sandals. When he had finished, he said sternly, "Your sword hilt needs polishing, and your left sandal thong is frayed. Your whole appearance is slipshod. See that these matters are fixed by morning."

"Yes, sir," said Quintus.

"I know you've been on the road for days," continued the general, "but I have pride in my legion. We've a hard job to do here and an example to set. No detail is too small to count."

"Yes, sir," repeated Quintus, and despite the reproof, felt a liking for the man as he had in Colchester, especially when the hazel eyes suddenly twinkled as they did now.

"The report on you sent by the procurator, Decianus Catus, is not particularly flattering." Petillius shoved the map aside and fished a small piece of parchment out from a pile of dispatches. "Let's see now—uhmm—'slack, insolent, at one time actually insubordinate, given to association with the enemy. . . .' "

"The ENEMY!" cried Quintus, forgetting himself. "By the spirit of my father, sir, how anyone could call those wretched Icenians the ENEMY—and the way we treated them, the procurator . . . by Mars, I guess they're enemies *now*, all right—but——" He clamped his lips together as the general raised his eyebrows. "Sorry, sir."

"I gather," said Petillius, leaning back in his chair, "that the procurator's disappointment in you was also vice versa," and to Quintus' great relief, there issued from his general's throat an unmistakable chuckle. "Now what really happened in the country of the Icenians?"

The spring passed pleasantly enough in the fort, on top of Lincoln's high hill. Quintus' duties were not hard. Frequently, under one of the tribunes or senior officers, he supervised the road building, and though this bored Lucius, Quintus had an aptitude for engineering and took an interest in the continual problems to be met. He learned the routine of clearing the way, while leaving brush and trees ranged alongside as fences. He learned to choose and lay the paving stones, to see that the gravel was packed properly, to build bridges and fords, and drive the new highway straight as an arrow's flight through every obstacle, as they penetrated further and further into the northern wilderness.

The legionaries were well housed and fed; the baths—as Lucius had said—made a fine clubhouse and recreation center. They even had music, for two of the foot soldiers played the lyre and flute. It was not a bad life at all. Quintus was too busy to think much about Regan or the Icenians. And he had a gratifying prospect to hope for. Flaccus one day had said that the general was soon intending to send some dispatches to the Second Legion headquarters in the far west at Gloucester. Quintus was interested by any mention of the west, where Gaius Tullius' remains were, and he wondered if he might be chosen as one of the official messenger's escorts. "You apply for the job and I think you'll get it," said Flaccus one night

53

in the baths, as they came from the steam room. "It's a sure thing nobody else wants it. Too much devilish magic goes on in the wild country between here and Gloucester. People turned into stones and stood up in a circle to shriek every night; animals that talk and cast spells on you—little black gnomes that burn you up in wicker baskets!"

"Oh come, Flaccus," said Quintus grinning, "where'd you get all that stuff?"

The Spaniard shook his head darkly. "Oh, I've heard. . . . That's Druid country *that* is in the west. Our Governor Suetonius may think he's got 'em all chased to Anglesey, but I've heard there's plenty left."

"I wonder how our revered governor is getting on with his campaign," drawled Lucius. "We might as well be on the moon for all the news that ever comes up here. . . . Jupiter, that's *cold!*" he cried, as he suddenly plunged into the small swimming pool.

"You should've waited longer to cool off, idiot," said Quintus from the edge of the pool. "What's your big hurry tonight anyway?"

Lucius dove under the water and swam the length of the pool without answering.

So it was those blond girls in the British village at the foot of the hill, Quintus thought. He gave an uneasy sigh. If the general ever found out how Lucius sneaked out of the fort almost every night and what he was up to— but there was no holding Lucius when it came to girls, even though the whole garrison had been given strictest orders not to enter the village. But Quintus had no intention of being told again that he clucked warnings like an old hen. So when Lucius clambered out and made for the dressing room, giving Quintus a wink behind Flaccus' back, Quintus waved to him cheerfully, saying "See you later—I hope."

To his great surprise he saw Lucius in half an hour, the time it had taken him to run down to the village and climb up again.

Quintus was throwing dice with a couple of standard-bearers from other cohorts and his teasing greeting died on his lips when he saw Lucius' face. "What's happened ——" he began, and stopped as Lucius shook his head and jerked it sideways toward the corner of the hall. Quintus followed. "Trouble?" he asked briefly, restraining himself from an "I told you so."

"Not what you think," said Lucius. All his languid airs were gone, his face was pale and his round eyes worried. "Quintus, there's nobody down there in the village. It's deserted. Not a soul, even a dog."

"Well, that's not so strange. They've gone off hunting or on some religious expedition, they do that——"

"No, no," said Lucius impatiently. "You don't understand. Their furnishings are gone, everything, the ashes scraped out of the fire holes, their supplies. It looks as though they've gone for good, and yet they and their ancestors've lived there since long before Julius Caesar came to Britain. That isn't all"—he went on as Quintus was about to speak—"look at this!" He drew a large clay tablet from under his cloak and held it out gingerly. Quintus peered at it and made a horrified sound. Rows of little figures had been crudely carved on the tablet, figures with crested helmets and breastplates. One figure held a standard with an emblem that was unmistakable. The standard of the Ninth Legion. Something else was unmistakable, too; spears were shown piercing each of the little figures' breasts, and the whole clay tablet was sticky with fresh red blood.

The young men looked somberly at each other. "Where did you find this?" said Quintus at last.

"In the center of their village courtyard, on a stone they use for an altar to that victory goddess of theirs. They'd been burning the—the insides of some animal on it."

"Well . . ." said Quintus, on a long breath, putting down the bloody tablet, "the message seems clear enough. Charming little thing. We'll have to take it straight to the general."

Lucius bit his lips and stared down at the tile floor. "How are we going to say that we—uh—happened to find it?"

Quintus was silent a moment while he felt a distinct shock and almost contempt, quickly mastered. "You want me to say *I* found it, Luce?" he asked evenly.

His friend's eyes shifted and he spoke very fast. "Well, but you're a favorite of the general's. He wouldn't really punish *you*. The old boy can be mighty unpleasant when his orders are disobeyed. I—well, I didn't tell you, but I was in a lot of trouble with him before you came."

"All right," Quintus cut in. "I'll lie about finding the tablet, but I'm not so noble that I'm going to take blame for *all* the monkey business you've been up to. Come on!"

The young men walked silently to the general's quarters, while Quintus held the sinister tablet by one corner. When they were admitted, Quintus said, "General Petillius, here is something we feel you'd want to see at once. It comes from the altar in the British village, but the Parisii have cleared out. Entirely. No trace of them."

The general examined the sticky red tablet long and carefully, but his face showed nothing. His eyes were frigid when he looked up at Quintus. "How did you happen to visit the village? You know my orders."

Here goes, thought Quintus with distaste. "I was on the ramparts and heard some strange noises from below, sir. I decided to investigate."

"You must have exceptionally sharp ears, since the village is over a mile away and the wind in the wrong direction. Did it occur to you to report these remarkable noises to a superior officer before taking independent action?"

"No, sir," said Quintus, staring at the wall above Petillius' head.

The general's stern eyes moved from Quintus' face to the flushed and subtly defiant one of Lucius.

"Our Britons here have always been extremely friendly until recently," said the general, "but there has been a change, and this"—he indicated the tablet—"is a declaration of war. I should like to know the reason."

Both young men were silent.

"Can you think of any reason why the Parisii should become suddenly hostile to us, Quintus Tullius?" said the general, each word dropping like a stone.

"No, sir," said Quintus, his eyes on the wall.

"Can *you*, Lucius Claudius?" continued the implacable voice.

"Oh, no, sir," said Lucius quickly. "None at all."

There was another silence, and the general sighed. Then he stood up with decision and called a sentry. "You," he said to Quintus, "will accompany this sentry to the guardhouse to await my decision on your disobedience.

56

. . . You," he turned to Lucius, "report at once to your centurion. The whole legion will now be alerted. An attack on the fort seems likely."

Quintus followed the sentry with a sore and heavy heart. As he crossed the parade ground, Lucius ran up to him and whispered, "I'm sorry, Quintus, I—I'll get you out soon. You'll see."

Quintus did not answer.

The guardhouse was an underground prison below the west gate tower. It contained six cells, very small and pitch black, with ventilation holes, and stone floors, nothing else. Quintus was shoved into one of them and given a jug of water. His sword and armor were taken from him. The thick oaken door banged shut, the iron bolt clanged through the sockets. He was alone.

It was afternoon of the next day before there was a sound on the other side of the cell door. The bolt shot back and Quintus, blinking in the sudden light of a little lamp that someone carried, finally recognized Lucius.

"It's all fixed now, Quintus," cried Lucius in an excited voice. "You're to come out!—general's orders."

Quintus made a harsh sound. "So you finally told him the truth. . . ."

"Shut up!" whispered Lucius, quickly glancing at the guard who stood in the corridor. "No, it isn't that—I didn't have a chance yet—but something's happened. Come on—hurry up!"

Quintus' resentment toward Lucius and his relief at being released were both forgotten in amazement when he saw the parade ground. The entire legion of six thousand men was there in full battle dress, and forming into cohorts under the shouts of the centurions. The cavalry, already mounted, were quieting their prancing horses in a square near the stables.

"Jupiter Maximus! What's up?" Quintus cried. "Have we been attacked?"

"No," Lucius answered. "We're on the move. A messenger came. The Iceni have risen. We're going to the relief of Colchester. It's besieged."

During the desperate forced marches of the next three days, Quintus learned what had happened. An exhausted Roman messenger had tumbled into the Lincoln garrison at noon of the day Quintus spent in jail. He brought a frantic summons for help from the procurator, Catus, who was in London. The Iceni and the Trinovantes both had risen with Queen Boadicea as their leader. She had turned into an avenging fury. Her forces marching down from Norfolk had killed on the way not only every Roman but every Briton friendly to the Romans. And they had marched on to Colchester. There were thousands of them—nobody knew exactly how many, but there were women amongst them. Warrior women like the Queen. Something terrible was happening in Colchester. The procurator wasn't sure what yet—he had only been able to send a few of his guard to its relief. He had sent a messenger to the governor way off in Wales with most of the army, but the gods only knew when Suetonius could get back. Petillius and his Ninth Legion must come at once and put down the insurrection.

"By the divine spirit of our august Emperor, I implore you to hasten," the procurator had written. "I hear some of the other tribes have joined the rebellion, the Coritani, your own Parisii."

The general had read this message aloud to the assembled legion. It was obvious why Quintus had been released from jail, aside from the fact that he was needed to fight with his men. The general had realized that the Parisii flight and defiant tablet were part of the great concerted rebellion and doubtless had little to do with any action of Lincoln's garrison. Lucius had not had to confess. The minor incident had been forgotten in the crisis.

All the same, Quintus thought, as he rode down Ermine Street on Ferox, my name hasn't been cleared. And he could not help wondering if Lucius ever would have told the truth about the visit to the village. There was no outward difference in the relationship between the two young men. They shared their scanty marching rations together, snatched sleep side by side in each night's camp, but Quintus' trust was shaken. It was painful, but fortunately there was scant time to brood on personal matters. They were constantly on the watch for attack. But there was none. The Coritani villages beside the fens were deserted too. They could see marks of the broad British wagon wheels on the road ahead of them, so that some force must have passed that way, but until they reached Braughing where Ermine Street joined the Essex Stane

58

Street there was no sign of trouble. At Braughing there had been a small permanent stockade for the accommodation of passing troops; Quintus had stopped there on the way up. A time-expired Roman veteran had lived within the stockade with his wife and children, and acted as quartermaster.

Now there was nothing left of the stockade or its cluster of wooden buildings, nothing but a heap of ashes, while from the branches of a great oak tree, outside the ramparts, dangled four hacked corpses, the bodies of the Roman veteran and his family.

At this sight, the legionaries became silent, though before they had been lighthearted—pleased by the break in the monotony of garrison life, joking about how quickly they were going to subdue a yapping pack of natives led by a *woman*.

"Imagine fighting with women!" Lucius had laughed earlier on the way down. "We'll spank all the little dears and send them home to their pots and pans."

Lucius' jokes no longer amused Quintus and he merely said, "You didn't see Queen Boadicea. She's as strong and proud as any man. So for that matter," he added, "are many of our Roman matrons."

Braughing's fate was sobering but still did not prepare them for the sight of Colchester, which they reached next day. The smell of smoke had met them two hours before they got there, and as they came near, it became intolerable, suffocating. Quintus' whole concentration for some minutes had to be given to Ferox, who plunged and trembled and finally bolted sideways up a little hill.

Here Quintus managed to soothe the horse and incidentally to get a good look at Colchester. Except that it simply wasn't there. The forum, the government buildings, and basilica, the neat streets of villas and shops, the theater had all become heaps of smoking rubble. Quintus blinked and looked again. The enormous, magnificent white and gold Temple of Claudius wasn't there either. In its place was fire, a vast bonfire with flames leaping high enough to touch the clouds.

"Merciful gods——" Quintus whispered. Suddenly as he realized the incredible extent of the destruction and thought of the concentrated hatred that had prompted it, he felt a thrill of fear. But where *were* the Britons? Where had they gone after destroying Colchester?

This was the problem which also occupied General Petillius. Nor was it answered for some hours. The general drew up his legion beside the river Colne, away from the city, while he sent men to search amongst the ruins for any sign of life. They came back with tales of frightful death. Every inhabitant of Colchester had apparently been slaughtered and the place was full of bones and half-burned corpses. At length they found an old Roman shopkeeper, who crawled trembling out of a cellar near the river when he saw the legionaires. They took him to the general, who conferred with him beneath a tree on the riverbank. Presently, Quintus, to his amazement, received another summons from his general, who greeted him without preamble, or apparent memory of Quintus' disgrace, and said, "This old man thinks the British forces have withdrawn to the north where they are making plans to march next to London. You are the only one of my legion who has recently covered that road to Iceni country. Can you remember a likely encampment for their forces?"

Quintus thought a moment and said hesitatingly, "Well, sir, there were some earthworks and a hill up past the river Stour. The British use that sort of thing for a fort."

The general nodded. "We'll go after them at dawn. Take them by surprise, I hope."

That night was a tense one for the Ninth Legion as they listened to the measured footsteps of the sentries or snatched what sleep they could. Even the war-scarred veterans of many a battle were keyed up and jumpy, more so than Quintus who had never seen actual warfare, or Lucius who got thoroughly drunk even under Flaccus' watchful eye. No matter the circumstances, thought Quintus, Lucius always managed by devious means to gratify his own desires. Flaccus grew more and more gloomy, his long Spanish face set in grim furrows. He pointed out that the waters of the Colne had suddenly turned blood-red as the legion camped beside it. Nobody else had noticed but Flaccus said it was so, and he went to pray to Mars once again at the little altar which they had set up in the camp. And Flaccus said he heard the shrieks of spirits issuing from the burning Temple of Claudius, where some of the doomed inhabitants of Colchester had held out for two days against the Britons.

Quintus did not hear the ghostly shrieks, but as he

forced himself to shut his eyes and relax his body as Roman soldiers were taught, he heard something else—something from the dark woods across the Colne; the sharp yelping of foxes, and more distant answers. And he thought that there was little chance of surprising the British forces, for there were unseen eyes watching every Roman move.

The Ninth Legion marched at dawn, heading north for the Stour. They marched in close formation ten abreast with the cavalry at the sides, as usual in times of danger, though they did not expect to find the British forces for many miles. It was a gentle summer dawn. There was no sound but the rustling of the trees. It seemed impossible that the peaceful day could hide any threat. I don't believe they're up this way at all, Quintus thought, looking at the blue sky—and as he thought it, the quiet air exploded with blood-curdling war cries. They heard before they saw, for the pandemonium of hideous sound came from all around them.

The legion had marched into a pocket encircled by slopes, and over the brow of these slopes, on every side, poured masses of yelling frenzied Britons—thousands of them. The legion's shields clanked together, forming the solid battle fence they were trained to make, but the attack was so sudden and they were so grossly outnumbered that the whirling chariots, the shaggy British war ponies, the hate-driven howling warriors mowed them down in the first minutes. While the cavalry galloped to protect the infantry's flanks, General Petillius shouted the order to charge. They could not charge. The Britons with their blue-painted faces and flying gaudy tartans were on top of them, while from a war chariot high on the hillside a woman yelled hoarse orders—Queen Boadicea, a spear in her hand, her long golden hair flying as she shouted encouragement to her army. Behind her were clustered other women and her two daughters.

Quintus fought as in a nightmare, slashing with his sword, seeing blood flow, yanking Ferox away from the darting British chariots, dodging spears, protecting, as long as he could, the standard of his cohort until it was knocked from his hand. Unbelieving, dazed, Quintus saw the main body of the legion, the foot soldiers, fall. The little valley was a sea of thrashing bodies that grew quiet, and a sea

61

of Roman blood. Through the roaring in his ears, and the spine-chilling whoops of the victorious Britons, Quintus heard the command of his own general. "Retreat! Retreat! —Make south for London."

Quintus turned blindly to obey, but his forehead was gashed so that blood and sweat ran into his eyes. He did not see a huge Icenian sneak up behind him. His sword was flung from him. The Icenian seized Ferox's bridle and the horse plunged and snorted, unseating Quintus, who fell to the ground on one knee. He knuckled the blood from his eyes and saw the Icenian pick up the sword and turn to raise it high with the point toward Quintus' throat. Quintus floundered frantically and could not rise, for his leg had twisted under him. Helpless, he looked up into the murderous eyes.

But the gleaming sword did not descend. Someone had grabbed the Icenian's arm, someone gave a sharp command and then ran back toward the sloping hillside. The huge British warrior threw down the sword and suddenly scooped Quintus up, flinging him over his shoulder like a sack of grain. He strode out of the melee and dumped Quintus on the ground beside the chariot of the warrior Queen.

Boadicea did not see Quintus as she leaned far over her chariot and called in a great harsh voice to her men below, "Kill! Kill!"

"We *have* killed, Your Majesty!" came a mighty roar in answer from the multitude of Britons, "Look how *well* we have killed!"

"Andraste! Andraste!" shouted the Queen exultantly. "The sacred hare prophesied this when it ran toward the sun! Oh goddess of victory, we thank thee!" She raised her powerful arms toward the sky. Her body trembled. Her face was white and glistening with triumphant tears.

Quintus, too dazed to think or speculate why he himself was not yet dead, tried to ease his leg and struggle to his feet. The Queen's exaltation died. She lowered her head and saw the wounded Roman beside her chariot. "Why do you suffer this hell spawn to live?" she cried angrily to the warrior nearest her. Suddenly she peered hard at Quintus, "I remember him! This is one that came to my palace with the procurator. He watched them scourge me!" Her face convulsed. "Roman, Roman—it is well you are not yet dead. By Lugh, the sun god, and his

62

life sap, the holy mistletoe, I swear you shall suffer the tortures of——"

"No! No!" cried a terrified girl's voice. "My gracious Queen, do you not remember? This is the Roman I told you of. This is the one I stopped Murdoch from killing just now!"

Quintus turned and stared blankly at Regan's tense imploring face.

"Ah . . ." said the Queen. Her blue eyes lost their frenzied fire, they became cold. "Then I shall spare you for now, Roman," she said in Latin. "As you spared Regan here. Because *Icenians* pay their debts . . . and I shall pay my debt to Rome too, never fear——" Her eyes glinted with implacable meaning. "We will rid this country of you, every one of you. Do you see my people——?" She waved her arm toward the plain below. "A few are dead but there are still fifty thousand of them—Icenians and their allies—Trinovantes, Coritani, Parisii—soon *all* the tribes of Britain will be with us—and do you see *your* proud legion, Roman?"

Quintus looked down at the acres of mangled Roman bodies, the blood encrusted shields, helmets, eagles glinting in the sunlight. His throat choked.

"Aye," went on the Queen with a terrible laugh, "there *is* no more Ninth Legion, is there! And now you see how it will fare with all Romans everywhere." She turned from him contemptuously. "The Roman does not speak. Bind him, Murdoch. *He* shall see what if feels like to be a slave."

The huge Icenian yanked off Quintus' helmet and threw it away. It rolled and bumped down to the hollow below, where it stopped near all the other useless helmets of the dead. He bound Quintus' wrists behind his back with leather thongs. He snapped an iron collar around Quintus' neck, jerked him to his feet, and hauled him along by a chain. The twisted ligaments in his leg throbbed violently, but Quintus did not feel them. He tried to calm the panic in his head, to think collectedly, as he stumbled along amongst all the triumphant Britons who were heading back to their fort. They passed the edge of the battlefield, and Quintus, whose forehead wound had stopped trickling, suddenly saw a familiar breastplate amongst a heap of corpses. Beneath a battered centurion's helmet he saw Flaccus' pallid face, the eyes wide open as though they still could see the blue sky above. Bitter fluid rose in Quintus' mouth; his stomach heaved; he turned away. May Charon give easy passage across the river Styx to poor Flaccus, he prayed, and to all these others.

But the general had got away, and some of the cavalry. Quintus had seen that, though in all the turmoil and confusion, the Britons had not noticed.

I must think coolly, repeated Quintus to himself. I must make a plan for escape. Just think of that, nothing else.

Yet there was no possible escape for a chained Roman amongst fifty thousand enemies. Except Regan. She had saved his life, it was true, but after pleading with the Queen, she had not looked at Quintus. She had gone back to the princesses and the other women, and they had all disappeared, riding on ahead in their chariots.

Regan has paid her debt, he thought. There will certainly be no more help from her. He clenched his jaw and tried not to give way to fear.

They marched two days before they reached the great ring of earthworks that circled the Icenian fort. The Britons started at once on a victory feast. They lay on the ground guzzling great skinfuls of their heather mead. There were whole oxen roasting at several fires. Murdoch wished to be rid of his captive. He chained Quintus to a small oak tree outside the earthworks and there left him. Night began to fall and Quintus grew faint from hunger and thirst. Nobody came near him. He groped on the ground behind his back until he found a sharp stone and tried to rub the thongs that bound his wrists against it. But the stone slipped away. He crouched on the ground beneath the tree, and his chin fell forward on the iron collar. He thought of his mother and Livia at home. He thought of Gaius, his ancestor, and of the quest which had seemed to promise nothing but adventure. Gaius himself had been captured like this and got free, for a moment, anyway. Ah, but Gaius had not been put in chains. The Britons had learned much from the Romans in a hundred years. From inside the earthworks the sounds of revelry grew louder. They were chanting triumphal songs, wild barbaric chants. The lights of their bonfires turned the sky red.

An hour passed. Quintus dozed from exhaustion and jumped as he felt a touch on his arm.

"Sh . . ." whispered a voice in his ear. "Don't speak!"

A strand of silky hair blew against his cheek as he

looked dully up into Regan's shadowy eyes. The warning pressure on his arm increased, and she shrank behind him. He saw then that where she was looking—on top of the earthworks—a tall man's figure was dimly outlined. The man peered down for a few seconds toward the oak tree. Then the tall figure disappeared.

"It's Navin, chief of the Trinovantes," Regan whispered. "I heard him arguing with our Queen. She wants to torture you tomorrow for a sacrifice, the torture of the——" She used a Celtic word he could not understand, and shuddered. "It's horrible," she whispered.

Quintus swallowed hard. "What did Navin say?" he whispered back.

"He said that because you had once befriended him, you should not be tortured, only killed quickly. She would not agree."

"I shall try to die as a Roman soldier should," said Quintus grimly. "But then why did you save me today, Regan? I'd rather have died with my men."

"I know," she whispered, "I did not think the Queen would be so—so cruel. I too hate Rome—I have tried—but I cannot—quite hate *you*. I've brought a knife," she added very low. "Lean over so I can cut the wrist thongs."

"May the divine gods bless you!" he muttered through his teeth, as Regan sawed away behind his back. The thongs fell apart and without thought he raised his freed hands and, pulling her face to his, kissed her fervently. She stiffened and pushed him back but for a moment he fancied he had felt her soft lips yield.

"Fool!" she whispered breathlessly. "I do this only out of justice, and you're not free yet." She fumbled with the clasp of his iron collar. "Here, like this," she said, guiding his fingers behind his neck, "it's too stiff for me."

They struggled for agonizing seconds until the clasp loosened. "Now go——" she whispered, while he eased the collar and chain soundlessly to the ground. They uprooted a small bush to place it by the tree so it might look, from the ramparts, like Quintus' crouching figure.

He took a step and limped so badly that she gave a smothered exclamation. "Wait," she said. "They've put your horse alone over by the grove of our goddess Andraste, for the sacrifice tomorrow. I think I can get it." She disappeared while he waited feverishly. The instant he saw her appear between the trees with Ferox he whistled very

65

low, and the horse responded at once, trotting to him. Ferox was still saddled. Quintus mounted and leaned over. "Regan—someday we'll meet again. I know it, and I'll tell you—tell you——"

"Hurry——" she said. "Go quickly, quickly—may the gods of my people forgive me for what I've done this night." She ran, light and silent as a moth, back toward the fort.

CHAPTER IV

IF QUINTUS had any remnants of softness, he lost them on the desperate flight from Boadicea's camp. He had no weapon with which to kill game, no means of making fire. He lived on berries and a tiny raw fish which he caught with his hands by great good luck, as he forded the river Lea. Ferox did better, for he could crop the sweet wild grasses, but Quintus dared give the horse little time to graze. He followed the road only at night; by day he slept in snatches or pushed his way through the forests, listening every moment for unusual sounds, and wondering— whenever he heard a badger call, or the scream of a wild-cat, or the bark of foxes.

At times he thought about Regan with warm gratitude. But then he would think of Colchester's destruction, of the slaughter of the Ninth, of Flaccus' dead eyes staring up into the sky, of the hideous torture Boadicea had decreed for himself. And he hardened his heart against all memory of Regan, who had paid her debt to him but who was still an enemy.

On the third night he staggered into London and found it a city of dread. Knots of white-faced Roman citizens were gathered on the street corners, whispering to each other. The shopwindows were barred. A hush of uncertainty hung over the town—which Quintus did not understand, for as the poor lathered Ferox dragged him haltingly toward the center of town by the Wal Brook Quintus saw that Governor Suetonius must have arrived. The royal eagle flag was flying from the government house, and in the encampment by the Thames he saw a crowd of pitched tents, with emblems of the Fourteenth and Twentieth legions.

Thanks be to Mars! Quintus thought hazily, we'll be all right now. He managed to reach headquarters and give his name to the startled sentry at the gate, but then, to his humiliation, his brain began to swim, the sentry's face wavered in sickening circles.

Quintus stumbled off Ferox, tried to speak again, and slumped instead to the pavement.

When the black mists cleared, he knew he was lying on a couch. He felt the pressure of a cup to his lips and found that he was swallowing strong wine with a stimulating herb in it. He opened his eyes and saw who was holding the cup. Petillius Cerealis, his general. But the general was dreadfully changed, so haggard and drawn had his face become. And the hazel eyes looked down at Quintus with a terrible sadness.

"He's coming around," said Petillius quietly to someone behind him. "Here, Quintus, drink—don't try to talk yet."

As Quintus drank, he saw another face swim up next to Petillius'. A square, florid one above a bull neck. Crisp graying curls beneath the elaborately embossed helmet of the governor. The gilded helmet was dazzling, and Quintus shut his eyes.

"This lad's in pretty bad shape—loss of blood—exhaustion," he heard his general say in a tone of bitterness, "but at least *he's* alive."

"You were a madman, Petillius," said the harsh voice of Governor Suetonius. "A dangerous fool. Pushing up into enemy country, letting yourself be ambushed. May the gods forgive you, for you've cost us a legion."

"By all the spirits of my ancestors, Excellency——" cried the general violently. "Don't you think I am tortured by that night and day? The shame will never leave me. I did not guess Boadicea's numbers, nor judge their fury. I've resigned to you my command—the disposition of my life—or death—is in your hands, yours and our august Emperor's."

There was a heavy silence, while Quintus felt a stinging behind his closed lids. Petillius had said "or death . . ." with unmistakable emphasis. Yes, as every lowliest auxiliary knew, death was the most honorable course open to a Roman soldier who had bungled. The quick self-driven sword thrust was the end of shame to a Roman general who had lost his legion.

"You know I would have joined in death my legionaries who lie rotting up there to the north—before this, Excellency," went on the sad, bitter voice, "except that you have said you need me and commanded me to stay with you."

Again there was silence and the sound of the two men's breathing. Then Suetonius said, "Aye, it is so. I need you and every help I can find. You've been a fine general, Petillius, and will redeem yourself. You shall continue to command the remnants of the Ninth and help me with the other legions."

Suddenly Quintus heard the sharp slap of sandals on the pavement as Suetonius began to pace the floor. "But *where* is the Second Legion?" the governor said as though to himself. *"Where*, where? I sent to Gloucester for them ten days ago. Why haven't they come?" Then with a change of tone, as though he had remembered the unhappy general beside him, "Oh, I understand the fatal error that you made, but by the GODS, Petillius—there must be no more errors! Everything must be sacrificed—*everything*—to one aim." His voice trumpeted out, "We must vanquish that she-devil of a Queen!"

Later when he had eaten and recovered some strength, Quintus told to Petillius the story of his capture and escape from Boadicea, and learned that a couple of hundred of their cavalry had indeed managed to get back to London and had now been quartered amongst the two legions Suetonius had brought from Wales.

And it was then that Quintus finally nerved himself to ask the question which had been occupying his mind for days. "What happened to the Optio, Lucius Claudius Drusus, my—my friend, sir? Did he get away?"

"He did," said the general grimly. "In fact he got away some time before I gave the order to retreat."

Quintus reddened slowly as he took in the meaning of this. "You mean, sir——"

"I mean that Lucius Claudius turned tail and fled in that first moment when the Britons leaped upon the infantry. I saw him gallop off." He added quietly, looking at Quintus' shocked face, "Yes, panic is a fearful thing to some men—those who haven't learned to control themselves."

    Quintus moistened his lips and said, "Where did he go, sir?"

The general shrugged wearily. "I don't know. We've not seen him here. It may be that he escaped to Gaul by ship, as has the procurator, Decianus Catus. Ah, trust the procurator to save his worthless skin and leave us to the terror he brought on us!"

Quintus bowed his head and stared down at the mosaic floor. So the procurator had fled to safety across the water. That was not surprising but——

"I don't think Lucius has done that too, sir," he said unhappily. "He wouldn't really desert you and our legion."

"Yes, you are loyal, Quintus. Foolishly so, I think. As I also think it was not *you* who visited the Parisii village that night back in Lincoln. I want the truth this time. Was it you?"

"No, sir," murmured Quintus. "But Lucius would have confessed, he——"

The general raised his hand and let it fall as though he cut something in two. "In the light of what came after, and what is still to come, that incident is trivial—forgotten. Lucius Claudius is not the first young aristrocrat I've had sent to me for schooling, nor the first to break under discipline and fear. We've no time to waste on such weaklings now. Go to the barracks and get some rest. The next days will be grueling if Boadicea's forces get here before our plans are complete."

The next days were grueling not because of battle but because of uncertainty. The governor had made a terrible but inevitable decision. He would not try to defend unfortified London. He explained this to a hushed populace from the rostrum before Government House. Until the Second Legion from Gloucester joined him, his entire army consisted only of the Fourteenth and part of the Twentieth. Less than nine thousand men. He must play for time until the Second came, and a few cohorts of raw auxiliaries who had been sent for from the north—if indeed these could get through the enemy lines, or did not turn traitor to Rome themselves and join the British forces.

He was therefore, said the governor, abandoning London, and fast. Such refugees as could keep up with the army would be taken along. They would march south to

70

Chichester in Sussex where the Regni tribe was still loyal to Rome. But he warned them that there was little surplus food for them. The army provisions must be hoarded, not wasted on non-combatants. And he was leaving at once. That night. After the army had crossed the Thames, the bridge would be burned.

The Londoners received this ultimatum with weeping and protestations. Some of them made ready to leave, and it was the duty of Quintus and other junior officers to shepherd these evacuees across the river and start them on the road south to Chichester. But many more begged for time to secure their property first, to find means of transporting those too small or old or sick to keep up with fast marches. While many others simply did not believe that there was danger: they preferred to stay in their own homes and take a chance. Surely, they said, Boadicea would not bother with women and children and sick people. She would pursue the Roman army, if indeed her greed for vengeance had not already been satisfied by the havoc she had wreaked in Essex.

Suetonius was unmoved by any arguments. That night the legions marched across the Thames and the last men of the last cohort fired the city-side end of the bridge as they passed over it. Soon the whole wooden bridge was burning, while dimly through its flames the legionaries could see the anxious faces of those who had remained in London.

May Vesta, goddess of the hearth, somehow preserve the poor things and their homes, Quintus thought. But he had seen the ruins of Colchester, while the Londoners had not. Yet Suetonius was undoubtedly right; it was better to abandon one town rather than risk the certain loss of a province.

The Romans marched some miles to a great open heath. Here they could camp in comparative safety, since there were no trees near them to harbor enemies and a loop of the wide river protected them on two sides. Suetonius' forces had had no proper rest for days, and the general decreed a six hour respite.

Quintus wolfed down his scanty ration of food—he had still not made up for the days of hunger—tethered Ferox to a bush, lay down on the ground, and instantly went to sleep.

He was roused by a commotion near him, and shouts of "We've got him! We've *got* him—the filthy Icenian!"

Quintus jumped up and, drawing his sword, ran toward a group of struggling figures. "What's going on?" he cried, seeing two Roman sentries dragging a man's figure between them.

"It's a Briton, sir, an Icenian by his tartan. He was sneaking around the edge of the camp. In broad daylight too, the stupid fool, he might know he'd be caught!" answered the excited sentry.

A spy? Quintus thought, puzzled by something familiar in the big red-haired Briton's sulky scarred face. The Briton let loose a flood of expostulation in Celtic, seemed to be explaining something, then suddenly came Latin words, "Quintus Tullius—I look for Quintus Tullius."

The sentries tightened their grasp on the man's arms and cried sneeringly, "Well, you're *looking* at him, you pig of a Briton. Though how'd you know his name?"

"Quintus Tullius——" repeated the captive with a sort of angry despair.

"I——" began Quintus, peering harder at the scarred face, when suddenly he recognized it. "Pendoc, the potter!" he cried, remembering the little hut he had taken Regan to, after the outrage on Boadicea.

Pendoc nodded with relief and nodded again as Quintus finished by saying, "*I* am Quintus Tullius." Pendoc had not known him. During the excited moment he had seen Quintus before, he had not examined the face of the helmeted young Roman.

"Amicus!—friend!" said Pendoc, pointing to himself, and frowning over the Latin. "I have—message—Quintus Tullius." He fished around in a deerskin bag he carried slung on his belt and held something out on his palm. Quintus stared and flushed brick red. On the great callused palm lay a lock of soft curly chestnut hair. "Regan," said Pendoc, "wants—you."

The sentries gaped at Quintus' astonished red face.

"Where *is* Regan?" said Quintus, recovering and watching Pendoc closely. This might well be a trap, and this villainous-looking Briton did not inspire much confidence.

Pendoc jerked his head backward toward the river. "Hiding in a coracle. Come," he said in Celtic which Quintus understood.

Quintus thought for a moment, then turned to the sentries. "I'm going to see what this is all about."

"Not *alone*, sir!" cried one of them.

"No. That'd be foolish. You continue patrolling. I'll take some men with me." He roused three foot soldiers and explained briefly. With swords drawn and tense watchfulness they followed Pendoc down to a little bay in the river where reeds grew high.

Pendoc gave a high whistling cry, like a curlew, and was answered by the same sound from the reeds, which quivered and parted.

Regan stepped up onto the bank and looked at Quintus with anxious uncertainty. Her small face was pale and bruised. Her lovely hair was tangled. Her violet tartan was torn and dirty.

Before Quintus could speak, she shook her head, signifying her understanding of the three other soldiers and the wary looks they gave her. "No—no," she said. "There's only *us*, Pendoc and me. I—I have come to you—for protection." Tears filled her gray eyes and the trembling of her proud little mouth showed the effort it cost her to say this.

"You've run away from Boadicea?" Quintus asked in amazement. "You want *ROME'S* protection?"

She bowed her head, while a long sigh that was half a sob shook her. "Quintus, could I speak with you—alone?"

He hesitated yet a minute, then said to his three men, "Stand over there—keep a sharp lookout." As they obeyed, he turned back to Regan. "Tell me," he said gently, "what's happened to change you like this?"

She found it very hard because she was frightened and ashamed. She spoke in a mixture of Latin and Celtic, but as he helped her with questions he began to understand.

Regan's part in his escape from the British camp had been discovered. Suspecting something was amiss, Navin had not gone back to the victory feasting after they had seen him on the ramparts that night. He had crept down behind them and watched.

"But why didn't he stop me from escaping?" Quintus cried.

"Because he thinks you are a good man though a Roman. He did not want you to be tortured."

"But then why did he tell Boadicea what you had done? Why did he capture *you*?"

"Ah," she said with a bitter sigh, "that is different. I'm a Briton. I was betraying my people and disobeying my Queen. He felt I must be punished, though not——" Her voice sank, and terror thickened it as she went on very low, "Navin did not want me to suffer in the way Boadicea commanded I should."

He saw how painful all this was to her but he felt he had to know exactly what had happened. As they stood there by the river reeds, the three soldiers watched curiously. Pendoc squatted on the ground and chipped at a flint spear point, while Quintus continued his questions. He was appalled at her answers.

When Bodicea had heard from Navin how the girl had managed Quintus' escape, the Queen's anger had been fiendish. All the maternal kindness she had previously shown to Regan had vanished in an instant. She had called the girl dreadful names of which "hypocrite" and "traitress" were the least. With arms upstretched to the skies she had cursed Regan, and she had decreed that since Andraste, the goddess of victory, had been defrauded of her rightful sacrifice, Regan should take Quintus' place in the sacred grove. There would be first the torture of the hooks, and then of fire. Andraste's victims were enclosed in wicker baskets and slowly burned alive on her altar.

Quintus stopped the girl violently when he heard this. "That's enough," he cried. "It's past, you're safe now. Don't think about it! But how did you get away?"

She moistened her lips and said, "Navin. He's not quite like the Icenians, not so fierce and cruel. Boadicea put me in his charge, and he called Pendoc, who was my father's friend. Navin found us a coracle and let us go. He didn't care where we went, or even if we drowned, but he gave me a chance to live. I couldn't think where to go—we came down to the Thames seeking you, for I have no other friend now. From the river we saw the legions camping. I sent Pendoc to try and find you."

Quintus was silent, thinking of the girl's extraordinary story, the days of sailing down the coast in the coracle, of the horror she had escaped, and of Navin, and his savage code of retribution, which was tempered and civilized by the years he had spent in Rome. And yet Quintus knew that in actual battle Navin would show no mercy. Then a

74

new thought struck him. "What will happen to Navin, since Boadicea must suspect he let you go?"

"Nothing, I'm sure," she answered. "Navin will give some excuse that she won't dare question. Navin is chief of the Trinovantes and commands many thousand fighters. She needs his support."

"Ah," assented Quintus, "I see. Is Boadicea still planning to march on London?"

"Her forces must be nearly there now," said the girl with a frightened glance down the Thames. "They were to start right after the—the sacrifice to Andraste." She had been answering him steadily, but now she swayed and gave a little gasp.

"Poor girl—you're exhausted," said Quintus remorsefully, steadying her. "Come, we'll go up to the camp. I'll take care of you, Regan. You need fear nothing any more." A brave promise that he prayed he could fulfill.

During the next days, while the legions in full retreat marched south, Quintus caught only occasional glimpses of Regan. She and Pendoc had been put amongst the London refugees and everyone's private emotions were swamped in the physical strains and necessities of reaching the fertile lands and friendlier people along the Sussex coast. The Regni tribe under their King Cogidumnus was a small, peaceful one, close-knit with Gaul across the water, and more Romanized than any of the other tribes. The Regni welcomed the legions as best they could and provided them with grain and fruit and flocks. But obviously this situation could not last indefinitely and the army was cut off from all its usual supplies by Boadicea's forces to the north.

There were two small trading ships in Portsmouth, the harbor. Some of the refugees sailed for Gaul on them, and the governor sent desperate messages asking for reinforcements to be sent him. But he knew it must be weeks before help could possibly arrive.

In the meantime Boadicea and her growing army could —and doubtless intended to—massacre them all.

The morning after the Romans arrived on the coast, the sun rose broiling hot in a hazy coppery sky. The men were restless, anxious, reflecting the uncertainty felt by their superiors. Quintus spent some time with Ferox, currying him and removing a stone from his hoof, then,

75

there being no orders or special duties to stop him for the moment, he yielded to a desire he had been suppressing on the march.

He walked from the camp to some little bark-and-leaf shelters that the remaining civilians had set up in a corner of the ramparts Here he found Regan on her knees by a large mortar, pounding wheat with a stone pestle. Pendoc was near her, shaping flint into spearheads. She looked up as the young Roman approached and smiled politely though her eyes were shadowed and heavy from weariness.

"It's hot, isn't it!" said Quintus inanely, suddenly embarrassed. He had thought a lot about her. His heart swelled at the thought of how she had fled to him for help. As he looked at her now, she seemed grateful, but ashamed and unhappy too—probably torn by a feeling of disloyalty to her own people. Despite her smallness and softness there was always a shell of reserve.

"It is hot," she agreed, continuing to pound the grain. She was flushed; damp tendrils of hair stuck to her forehead, but she looked extremely pretty. Were it not for the watchful Pendoc, Quintus would have taken the heavy pestle and crushed the stubborn grain for her himself. But a Roman standard-bearer would look ridiculous doing menial woman's work, and Regan probably would not admire such softness—although it was hard to know what she thought. And the more he looked at her, the more he wanted to know.

"Can't you stop that, for a moment?" he said imploringly. "Walk down to the beach with me—there's a breeze, and——" Quintus broke off as a trumpet blast resounded through the fort.

He jerked around and listened carefully to the call. "That's assembly," he explained to Regan. "The governor's going to make some announcement, I guess. I'll have to go." He heaved a sigh, as the realization of the Romans' grave predicament returned. "I'll see you later?" he asked with unmistakable longing. She gave him only a dark, unencouraging look, and bent to her pounding.

So she *doesn't* like me! Quintus thought hotly, as he walked away. Well, what of it? She had had a right to his protection and she was safe enough now, as safe as any of them in this menacing country. He certainly was not going to force unwelcome attentions on her, attentions, moreover, that were forbidden by Roman law. She is nothing but an ignorant little barbarian after all, remember that, Quintus told himself, and stalked on to the parade ground.

The officers were assembling; the prefects, the tribunes, the centurions; the lowlier standard-bearers and Optios. They formed a semicircle in front of the striped tent that was topped with a gilded eagle. The governor stepped out. Behind him were the generals of the Twentieth and Fourteenth legions, and Petillius Cerealis, who no longer had a legion.

Suetonius climbed into a chariot and began to talk earnestly. Beneath the glittering helmet, his heavy red face was drawn with fatigue and worry.

"Roman officers," he began to the tense listeners, "I shall speak frankly. We are in a tight and shameful situation. We've retreated as far as we can without quitting the island completely, which is, of course, unthinkable. Rome has never tasted total defeat nor will she now. But we are not yet nearly ready to engage the British forces." He paused. "I have just received terrible news. The spy I left on the southern bank of the Thames has just come to me." He stopped again and wiped the sweat from his forehead. "Boadicea has totally destroyed London," he said in a harsh dragging voice. "She massacred all those we left behind. When the spy left, the Queen was apparently bound for the town of St. Albans, where she will doubtless do likewise."

Suetonius shut his eyes for a second and clenced the rim of the chariot. A choked murmur came from the ring of officers.

Suddenly Suetonius raised his head and shouted as though up into the sky, "By Mars, by all the sacred gods of Rome—WHERE is the Second Legion? *Why* does it not come!"

The hot sun beat down on the silent group in the fort. A bee hummed lazily and winged off over the ramparts.

The governor continued on a lower note, "When in Wales I first heard of the revolt, I sent a trusted messenger straight down to Gloucester. I sent another before we left London. And we've heard nothing. It's true the legion *may* be on its way. I propose to march north cautiously and try to intercept it. And yet I feel there's something wrong. I've called you together because I need a volunteer. No wait——" he added sharply as several hands went up. "This will be a mission of great danger. The man must travel secretly direct from here over a hundred miles of unknown country. We've built no roads through that land and the Belgic tribes there have never been tamed. It will mean traversing the sacred places of the Druids. True, I've exterminated most of that filthy priesthood on the island of Anglesey, but not all, I fear. I think some still lurk near the monstrous ring of stones to the west. This mission is one of almost certain death—I know a Roman will not cringe from this, but I need other qualifications as well as sheer courage, or it will be the waste of a man. . . . Who volunteers . . . ?"

Hands were raised again, more slowly, but Quintus broke ranks and stepped forward eagerly. "*I* do, sir. Quintus Tullius Pertinax, standard-bearer, third cohort of—of the Ninth!"

The governor's heavy-lidded eyes roamed over the faces of the other volunteers, then returned to Quintus. Suetonius leaned over and whispered something to General Petillius, who nodded and sent a quiet smile of recognition to Quintus.

"And why," said the governor, "are you so eager to undertake this mission?"

Quintus could not say that he was hurt by Regan and eager for any action, nor explain at this inappropriate moment about his quest—his heart had jumped when he realized that this mission might take him through the very place he had longed all his life to reach. But there were other reasons and he told them.

"I've seen something of the Britons, sir, and have plenty of personal reasons for hating them—besides wishing to avenge the Ninth. I speak and understand some Celtic and I think I could get through to Gloucester——"

He saw from the general's face that he was not convinced. The pondering gaze turned again toward an older man, a tribune, whose hand was raised.

Suddenly a girl's clear voice rang out. "O Roman Governor, may I speak?"

The astonished officers made way, as Regan walked through with perfect composure and stood before the governor's chariot.

"What's this?" growled Suetonius, frowning at Regan. "One of the refugees?"

Again General Petillius explained in a quick aside, for Quintus had earlier reported Regan and Pendoc's arrival to his general.

"Oh," said Suetonius with heightened interest, "you're the girl who fled from Boadicea? Well, what is it, maiden?"

"I have understood most of what you said, O Governor," said Regan carefully. "But not Quintus Tullius, nor any-one, will ever get to Gloucester in the way you ordered."

"Why not?" said the governor sharply. "How do you know?"

"Because no Roman could. There are trackless forests —there are strange things that happen——" she broke off suddenly. "It was once my country—I was born in the sacred plain to the west—so I know."

So that's where she came from! Quintus thought, amazed, and was more astonished as her quiet little voice went on.

"But we will help. Pendoc and I. Quintus shall dress as a native. He is dark so we will say he comes from the land of the Silures across the mountains in Wales. We will speak for him. And we will"—she hesitated—"we will set him on his way. I will not harm my own people, but I will do *this* much for Rome."

"Well, I'll be——" murmured the governor, looking down at the small resolute figure with a certain admiration. Regan's clear gray eyes looked back at him steadily. "If she weren't a Briton, I might—— It almost seems like a sensible plan. . . ."

"Yes, Suetonius, I think so," said General Petillius gravely. "Our need is too desperate for quibbling. Quintus Tullius, come here." When Quintus had obeyed, Petillius said in a low voice, "Do you trust this girl completely?"

Quintus answered from deepest instinct. "Yes, sir. There's much she doesn't say, but what she does say is true."

Petillius nodded. "These Britons keep the most extraordinarily exact moral balance sheets. They pay back precisely each good or evil done them. You rescued the girl in the Icenian city, so she saves you from Boadicea. You shelter her from Boadicea, so she will guide you to Gloucester. They're all like that—and if"—his face darkened—"that thrice-cursed fool of a procurator had

79

not committed those outrages on the Icenians, we wouldn't be in this fix now."

"No, sir," agreed Quintus, and he glanced toward Regan who was conversing with the governor.

Petillius saw the look and said half sharply, half smiling, "Here now—you haven't got any unduly tender feelings toward that little British savage, have you?"

"If I had, sir, you may be sure they'd not be returned. She operates only, as you say, from a strict sense of justice."

"Quintus," said his general, laying a stern hand on his arm, "I needn't tell you that the success of your mission is of supreme importance, that the whole fate of Rome here may depend on it—that no sentimentality must be allowed to intrude for a second. . . ."

"No, sir," said Quintus, solemnly tightening his square young jaw. "You needn't tell me."

An hour later, a party of three nondescript Britons trotted out of the fort on shaggy little native ponies— Pendoc first, his gangling feet almost touching the ground beneath his shaggy plaid trousers, his coarse sandy-red hair blowing around his shoulders in the sea breeze that had cut the heat; then Regan in her violet tartan tunic, her head and lovely hair all hidden by a rough linen scarf; and Quintus last. If the situation had not been so grave, Quintus would have been laughing wryly at himself, and there had been a momentary twinkle in his general's eye as he gave Quintus a folded, sealed parchment, the official message from the governor to General Valerianus of the Second Legion, and then rehearsed last instructions.

Regan had done a thorough job of metamorphosing Quintus from a Roman officer, by commandeering a few garments from the Regni village outside the fort. Quintus now wore long dirty wool trousers, fastened at waist and ankle by thongs, and a plaid cloth tunic so faded and soiled that the pattern was unidentifiable. A point Regan insisted on. Most Britons could recognize many tartans as belonging to this or that tribe, and Quintus, posing as a Silure from far distant Wales, must provoke no doubts. She finished his costume with an ancient cloak of mangy otter skins, held at the neck by a spiral iron brooch. His weapon was a clumsy spear tipped with one of Pendoc's flint heads. Regan spent several concentrated moments on the problem of his short hair and clean-shaven face,

80

which were so unmistakably Roman, and solved it by means of a horned British helmet to which she stuck wisps of black horsehair. "That is all right," she said critically, surveying her achievement. "The Silures have strange customs which no one quite knows. But your *face!* All Britons have beards." She frowned a moment, then seized a charred log from the hearth fire. She rubbed the charcoal on his chin and upper lip. "That's better, as though you were growing it, which you must. Try to keep your face hidden in your cloak."

"Don't worry," Quintus had said dryly, staring at himself in a polished shield. "You've done a perfect job. My own mother wouldn't know me."

"Your mother?" said the girl quickly, as though startled from the business-like efficiency she had been showing.

"Yes," said Quintus with faint irony, "I have a mother —in Rome—a very dear and good one. Also a little sister, Livia."

"Is it so . . . ?" said Regan with sudden gentleness. "I had not thought of you as—as—of your life before you came here. *My* mother died when I was ten, just before I went to Boadicea—sometimes I have so longed—I thought Queen Boadicea . . ."

She snapped the sentence off, the soft look left her eyes. She turned briskly to speak to Pendoc, who had gathered in the ponies.

Poor little thing, thought Quintus, this time understanding her cool abruptness, she's had a hard time. But in pursuance of his promise to Petillius and also of a vow he had made to Mars, Quintus resolutely shut his mind to tender thoughts of Regan. He would treat her like a boy, on this wild mission to the west.

CHAPTER V

WHEN THEY HAD LEFT THE COAST and the pastures of the Regni, they plunged into a great forest, and Quintus soon realized how impossible it would have been for him to make any time at all without Pendoc's and Regan's help. Pendoc, who lost most of his sulkiness once they were away from the Roman fort, was particularly helpful and by means of an occasional grunt, or the twist of his scarred lip that passed for a smile, even showed pleasure at being back in his own country, which he had not seen since he had been sent to the Icenians with Regan six years before.

The trails through the forest seemed absolutely invisible to Quintus, but Pendoc knew what to look for—a tiny spot of blue woad on the directional side of an oak trunk, or three pebbles arranged like the huge stone dolmens they sometimes passed. These dolmens consisted of flat table stones supported by upright stones, and Quintus asked Regan about them.

"I don't know," she answered, hesitating. "They were of the old, old time, longer back than memory."

"*Druid* stones . . . ?" he persisted. "Like the great circle at Stonehenge—is that what you call it?"

The girl turned around on her pony and looked at him. "Romans understand nothing about the Druids," she said quietly. "Your governor, Suetonius, has tried to kill them all . . ." She started to say something else but seemed to change her mind. "Quintus, why are you interested in the Druids?"

Following Pendoc, they jogged along in silence amongst the great trees while Quintus considered. The feeling between them was more natural, less tense and, now that he was no longer garbed like a Roman soldier, Regan had lost much of her defensiveness. They seemed very close and he decided to tell her of the quest later, when they stopped to eat and rest.

That evening just before moonrise they camped by a brook, under an enormous ash. Pendoc lit a small fire and they heated a stone for a griddle. They had ground wheat in their leather pouches, which Regan mixed with water and baked in cakes on the stone. Pendoc disappeared downstream to spear a fish. And Regan suddenly repeated her question. "Why do you ask about the Druids?"

"It is because of my great-grandfather, Gaius Tullius," Quintus began slowly. "I can't manage the Celtic words for such a long story . . ." he added thoughtfully.

"No," she said with a faint smile. "Though we are each learning the other's language fast. Tell it in Latin, I think I can understand."

"It was in Julius Caesar's day," he began. "You know who he was?"

He heard her sigh. "Yes. The *first* Roman general who came here to conquer us. Oh, *why* can't we all live in peace! Why did Rome want our island too when it has all the world besides!"

Quintus was taken aback. For a moment he could not think of the answers to that, so natural did it seem to him that Rome must rule everywhere. Then he took a deep breath and explained to her the benefits the Roman Empire brought to conquered nations, the more advanced education, the prosperity that came from increased trade with other countries, the better health everyone would have because of Roman cleanliness and sanitation, the social justice meted out by wise Roman law, and the advantage of a strong overrule in keeping the tribes from warring amongst themselves.

She listened patiently awhile, not quite understanding the complicated words he had to use to explain these things; then she said with a small rueful laugh, "Yes, well —I suppose there must be fighting, because men have always fought. It's true our tribes here fight each other. I see that you believe in what you grew up to believe. It is so with us all. Tell me of your great-grandfather, Quintus. . . ." She put her arms around her legs, rested her chin on her knees, and gazed up into his face while the firelight flickered over them.

He began the story which had always so fascinated him and she listened quietly until he came to the place where Gaius tore down the mistletoe, and trampled on it. Then she gave a gasp and cried, "Ah, it's no wonder the Druid priests killed him! Oh, Quintus, don't you see—I don't know your Roman gods, but they are sacred to *you*—if someone profaned them, trampled on them—wouldn't you be afraid and want revenge to appease the angry god?"

"But a plant is not a *god*," objected Quintus.

Regan frowned and wrestled with the problem of expressing her belief. "No, but the mistletoe is sent from heaven to rest high in the great oaks which make our temples. The mistletoe berries are the life sap of our great god, the sun. Lugh is his name, and without him we should all die."

For an instant Quintus smiled at what seemed to him such foolishness; yet Romans too had a god of the sun, Apollo, and the thrill of conviction in her low voice touched him. "We may not agree on that," he said gently, "Yet Britons believe in proper funeral rites as Romans do. You must see why my family is sure that Gaius' fate has given us bad luck for years and why I'd like to find the spot where he lies."

"Yes," she said after a moment, "I see that. It would be the same for us. And wherever this sacred oak is on the plain ahead, you may be sure he will be there still—the Druids would not touch him."

He glanced at her curiously. "You seem to know a lot about the Druids, Regan. I mean you speak with such certainty."

The moon suddenly topped the trees and shone down on them. It dappled her face with silver as she turned and answered, not in the reserved way she usually did, but in a rush, mixing Celtic and Latin words together. "I want to tell you something! This trip Pendoc and I are guiding you on, it isn't only because I—I wanted to help you. You will not be harmed—I gave you my word on that. And I will show you how to get to Gloucester, if you really wish it. But first——" She stopped and began pleating the folds of her tunic, back and forth. "First you must go to my grandfather."

"Your grandfather! But, Regan, I thought you had no people left now in the world."

"None but my grandfather. He will be at this time in the Great Temple of the Stones. In Stonehenge."

"WHY?" asked Quintus, astounded. "I don't understand at all."

"Because my grandfather is the Arch-Druid of Britain," she said solemnly. "He will be at Stonehenge for these days of Lugh's festival."

"Jupiter Maximus . . ." whispered Quintus, gaping at her. "You really are the most extraordinary girl. Just as I begin to think I know you, I find out something new and startling."

As though telling him her secret had relieved her, Regan gave a sudden smile, cocked her head and—as nearly as he could be sure in the moonlight—looked at him mischievously. "I have heard," said Regan in a demure voice, "that a little mystery makes a woman more attractive."

Quintus, with a shock, rearranged all his thoughts and burst out laughing. That little flash of feminine coquetry startled him as much as her previous revelation, and it delighted him. Too much so, he realized at once, remembering his vow to Petillius and Mars. Sitting in the secluded forest moonlight with a girl like this was dangerous. He discovered that he had quite unconsciously moved nearer to her, and it was with relief that he heard Pendoc crunching through the bracken behind them. The potter dangled three fish from his spear and threw them down triumphantly on the moss beside Regan.

Regan pulled her reserve over her at once like a cloak and with her little iron knife set about cleaning, scaling, and then broiling the fish.

They ate in hungry silence. After a while Quintus, throwing the fish spine over his shoulder into the forest, said, "Regan, why do you insist upon taking me to this Arch-Druid. It'll delay me, and——" He did not like to seem to doubt her word that he would not be harmed, but she might very well be overestimating her influence with her grandfather.

"Because," she answered, "he is very wise and powerful. And because"—she hesitated—"we do not know the way further north toward Gloucester." Again there was the curious pause before she said slowly, "Conn Lear must tell you how to go."

"WHO——?" cried Quintus. "Conn Lear—that was the name of the Druid priest we met on the road the first day in Britain. Is *that* your grandfather! But Suetonius ordered him captured; he sent one of his tribunes!"

"Nobody can capture Conn Lear," said Regan, wiping her knife and putting it in her pouch. "He is a magician, he can see things—and do things that others can not."

Quintus thought of the strange power of Conn Lear's eyes, of the numbed helpless way he had let the old man escape, and he fell silent trying to rally his courage. He tried to remember what the Arch-Druid had said that day —that the omens and auguries were bad for the Romans, that he came only to warn. Well, the omens were right, so far—Quintus thought of the slaughtered Ninth Legion, of the massacre in Colchester and London. While he had been talking with Regan, the seriousness of his mission to Gloucester had been submerged in other thoughts, but now it stabbed him with fierce reality again. His mind darted here and there, exploring the possibilities of stealing off from Pendoc and Regan; beating his way to Gloucester alone somehow. And he knew that it would be foolish. He trusted Regan and had committed himself to her guidance. He must continue to do so. But when the three of them had wrapped themselves in their cloaks and curled up beneath the tree, Quintus' brief doze was an uneasy one.

They left the camping place while the dawn light was still gray. The shadows were weird and wavering beneath the great overhanging branches, and as they emerged into a clearing they heard the long-drawn howl of a wolf. Quintus' shaggy pony snorted and trembled, its ears pricked forward. He soothed it as he would have Ferox, whom he greatly missed. Pencoc made a queer sign with his fingers to ward off evil, and Regan said, "The wolf howls with joy that he won't be sacrificed on this day, as he would have been in the old times."

"Sacrifice of wolves?" asked Quintus, glad enough to talk, for the uneasiness was still with him.

She nodded. "Once many beasts were burned in wicker baskets—and not only beasts but humans too, like—like ——" She stopped and shut her eyes.

Quintus knew she was thinking of Boadicea and the terrible rites for Andraste.

Then Regan went on with her usual composure. "My grandfather does not believe as Boadicea does though he put me in her care because she has much learning and was a cousin of my father's. The Icenians are not of the true religion—nor were those wild Druid folk that your governor, Suetonius, killed on the far isle of Anglesey. Conn Lear is merciful."

"Well, I'm glad to hear it," said Quintus as lightly as he could, and would have asked more questions, but Pendoc suddenly reined in his pony and said "H-sst!"

The three of them grew very quiet—listening. There was a confusion of guttural voices up ahead. Pendoc's eyes narrowed and he indicated by a gesture that they should move cautiously to the right and slip by unobserved. Quintus nudged his pony with his knee, but unfortunately the little beast scented a mare in the group ahead and let out a loud whinny of greeting.

Instantly the voices were stilled. "Hide your face," whispered Regan to Quintus, who pulled up his cloak. And the next moment a dozen British warriors galloped through the trees with spears drawn.

Quintus wheeled his horse in front of Regan and clumsily drew his own spear, wishing passionately that he had his familiar sword. "Wait!" called Regan in Celtic to the warriors. "Wait! We are friends, we go like you to the Feast of Lugh. Lugh, god of light!" This was a shot at random since this Belgic tribe, which she recognized by the tattooings, might be only a band of wandering marauders, in which case nothing would stop them from stealing the ponies at least. The leader of the band had a swarthy vicious face, with blue stripes on his cheeks, and he held his spear high aimed at Pendoc.

"We *kill* strangers who seek to spy upon our sacred feast . . ." growled the leader, but his spear arm dropped. His little red-rimmed eyes shifted from Regan to the two men. "You are not of our tribes. Your clothes are strange!" he said uncertainly.

"But we are not strangers!" cried Regan. "Look at this brooch! Look well——" She pointed to the bronze and enamel pin that held her mantle. "What do you see?"

The little eyes peered warily, then the horn-helmeted head jerked up. "I see the mark of the ruby serpent,"

muttered the man with a touch of awe. "It is a Druid sign."
He bowed his head in a gesture of reverence. His companions crowded around gaping at Regan. Then suddenly the leader raised his spear again.

"But how did you get this?" he cried. "Perhaps you've stolen it! And this man . . ." Quick as light his spear darted out and tore the folds of cloth down from Quintus' chin. In the same stroke he tipped the British helmet off Quintus' head. It rolled on the ground, the long tresses of horsehair trailing.

"Sure, this is no *Briton!*" shouted the warrior staring at the clean-shaven face and short curly black hair. "By the sacred fires of Beltane I think it is a——"

"A Silure from Wales," cried Quintus, feigning outraged dignity, and praying that his Celtic was recognizable. "You have insulted a Silure!"

"Yes," cried Regan quickly. "Is this the hospitality Conn Lear teaches you? You should be ashamed to mistreat those who come in peace to worship at the Feast of Lugh."

Above the long dangling mustaches and wisps of matted beard, the tattooed face looked perplexed. Regan gave him no time to think, but said, "We go straight to Conn Lear now. Follow if you like," and dug her heels into her pony's flanks. The three started forward. The band of Belgics let them go, then closed in behind them, muttering to themselves.

"Whew," breathed Quintus, "that was close." And still is, he thought.

It was hard to act confident when there was the continual mumbling behind them, and the spot between his shoulder blades tingled with awareness that a whistling spear might land there any minute.

"Don't speak," said Regan through the side of her mouth.

He nodded. All these Britons had ears keen as bats, and a knowledge of woodcraft like the wild things. Pendoc, don't get lost! Quintus implored silently, for the Belgics just behind watched the potter's every move as he led the two others. It was obvious that this was a test. No stranger could have found his way through the forest toward the great plain. If Pendoc hesitated, it seemed certain that Quintus would end up in this country in much the same way Gaius had. And that, thought Quintus grimly, was definitely not my plan.

At last, and suddenly, they emerged from the forest and looked down a slope toward a winding blue river. "Avon," grunted Pendoc pointing. "The river." His scarred lip lifted, and he turned squarely on his pony to face the Belgic leader. He pointed again across the river. "Beyond that hill is a ditch," he said, "and a village called Og, and many long earth tombs made by the people of the past, and further toward the west there stands the Great Temple of the Stones."

The Britons consulted sourly amongst themselves, then the leader spoke. "It is so. *You* at least are not a stranger." He darted one more suspicious look at Quintus, ignored the girl, and signaling to his band, trotted down the slope toward the river.

"That's the last of them, I hope," observed Quintus as Pendoc led them on upstream toward the ford.

"I think so," Regan sighed, her tense fingers relaxing on the bridle. She glanced back across her shoulder at the sun which had climbed halfway up the eastern sky. "Hurry," she said. "We must reach Conn Lear before the ceremony starts at midday."

They had not many miles to cover, and it was easy riding over the rolling fertile chalk plains where tracks were plainly marked. They passed earthwork forts, villages, and dozens of turf-covered mounds, which contained ancient burials. Soon after they crossed the river, they entered an avenue of single stones mounted on high banks on either side of them. And now they were no longer alone. Increasing hordes of people were trudging or riding along this processional way that led to their temple. Each man, woman, and child held in his hand an offering of growing corn or wheat or flax. Their mood was quiet and reverential. There were a few curious glances, but nobody molested the three who rode on silently until they topped a hill and looked down to the plain below, then Quintus let out a cry of wonder. He had expected a few crude stones, dotted helter-skelter like some rings he had seen up north. He had expected to be much amused at the contrast between this savage temple and the magnificent buildings he had known in Rome.

But there was nothing amusing about Stonehenge. It was awe-inspiring in sheer monstrous bulk. Thirty stone megaliths stood in the outer circle, each one as high as three men, and each pair topped with great flat boulders to make a continuous roof. Within the outer circle, Quintus could see other rows of stone, tons of them—a forest of stone—but more massive, and even in the full noon light, more sinister and brooding, than ever a tree forest grew.

"But how *could* those enormous things be upended and then made to support others?" Quintus cried. "And where could they have come from?" he added, staring around the barren grassy plain.

"Ah, I don't know," said Regan smiling, though her eyes were misty from the joy of seeing again the temple of her childhood memory. "This place has always been here—always. No doubt in the beginning of the world, Lugh built it for himself—with magic. That is what Conn Lear used to say. I only know that the ancient folk worshiped here as we do now."

It must certainly be some sort of magic that set these great stones here, Quintus thought as they approached. He tried to count the silent looming megaliths—ninety, a hundred—two hundred? His eyes swam, and not entirely from the sun. There was a strange sensation that flowed out from the forest of stones.

"Yes," said Regan watching him. "You feel the enchantment. It is always so here. We must walk now," she added on a brisker note. They had reached a fence of wooden posts set across an opening north of the great ditch that surrounded Stonehenge. Regan and Quintus dismounted, tethering the ponies by a pen full of small, sacred white bulls. They returned to join the people who were, one by one, filing through a gate, and passing a flat stone within the posts, which they touched. They began to chant.

"Lugh!" the people chanted on two notes, "Lugh—give blessing!" They raised their faces to the bright sky and walked thus with arms outstretched amongst the great stones.

A tall young man dressed in a leaf-green robe stood by the entrance, watching the crowds go in. He held a silvery birch wand in one hand, and a small harp was slung over his shoulder.

"Ah, that's a Bard," said Regan with glad recognition. "I must speak to him."

The Bard, who belonged to a minor class of Druid,

smiled and touched Regan's hand in greeting, as she showed him her brooch. Timidly she asked for the Arch-Druid and the Bard frowned a little.

"Conn Lear," answered the Bard, bowing at the name, "is in his secret retreat, preparing for the ceremony. You can not disturb him now, nor until sunset when the rites will be over." He spoke a very pure and solemn Celtic, because like all Bards he had been trained for recitation.

Quintus followed the Bard's words anxiously and was so dismayed that he cried without thinking, "But Regan, I can't wait that long, you know I've got to get on my——" He bit off the last word, while fiery heat rushed over him in a wave of shame. For he had spoken in Latin. And the young Bard had turned lithely like a cat and was surveying him with a detached chill gaze.

"This is a strange language to hear at our temple gate," the Bard said quietly. We do not welcome Romans here—no matter how—artfully—disguised."

You fool, you *blasted* impulsive fool! thought Quintus to himself. He knew there was no use pretending he was a Silure now. This Bard was obviously highly intelligent and in a subtle way more threatening than any band of savage Belgics. The Bard turned his cold considering eyes on Regan, who was also flushed and frightened. "You, maiden," said the Bard, "I find it most peculiar that you should bring a disguised Roman here—that you should ask for Conn Lear—I'm not unmindful of what has been done to Druids throughout the land—by Romans—nor that there has been treachery and spying——" His suddenly menacing glance swung on Pendoc who was standing a little way off, then moved to a group of fully armed men who were clustered outside the gate. Quintus with a sinking heart saw that the Belgics had arrived and were amongst them.

"You are wrong, O Bard—in your suspicions!" Regan cried at last in a shaking voice. "Take me at once to Conn Lear, for I am his granddaughter."

The young Bard's lips thinned; he looked at Regan's Icenian tartan. "I have never heard that the Arch-Druid had a granddaughter," he said imperturbably. "Nobody can disturb Conn Lear now. I think it safer that you never see Conn Lear at all. I think——" He glanced again toward the party of warriors and raised his wand.

He's going to put us under guard or worse! thought

Quintus, while Regan, realizing the same thing, suddenly grabbed his hand. "Run, Quintus!" she cried. "Run—INTO the temple!"

Before the startled Bard could stop them they darted past him, and Regan, dragging herself and Quintus to the "Heel" stone that guarded the temple gate, cried "I claim protection! The protection of Lugh!"

The Bard ran up to them, and stopped.

"You can't touch us!" cried Regan, panting.

"I see you know the ancient law," answered the Bard, frowning. "Go then to the stone of safety and stay there without moving—or—you know the penalty?"

She bowed her head and silently walked forward a little way with Quintus, until they entered the edge of the great outer ring of megaliths. Here there was a boulder, different from the others in shape and color. And a branch of mistletoe lay on it. "We must stay here," she said to Quintus, sinking down on the stone. "We're safe for as long as the ceremony lasts."

"And then?" said Quintus.

"And then we MUST get to Conn Lear."

Quintus tightened his lips and glanced back through the posts where he saw Pendoc's sandy-red head towering amongst the horned helmets of the Belgics. They've got Pendoc under guard, he thought.

"Regan—there's no use saying it—but when I think how I've run you into danger—why I didn't keep my cursed mouth shut—how I could forget—I'm always acting first and thinking afterward——" He pounded his clenched fist on the stone.

"Never mind," she whispered gently. "It's done. It'll be all right—as—as soon as we can get to Conn Lear."

Quintus thought a moment. "The Arch-Druid must be going to officiate, isn't he? When you see him in there"—he indicated the dim place of the altar through the concentric rows of megaliths—"can't you run to him, tell him who you are?"

She shook her head and gave a quivering sigh. "Look over behind that stone, and *that* one."

Then he saw that half hidden by the shadows stood two figures in white robes, silently watchful—and beside each figure there was the gleam of a golden spear. "They'd not let me run far," said Regan grimly. "Those are Druids-of-Justice. This stone of safety where we are sitting used to be called the Slaughter Stone. It might become so again."

The gods be merciful to us, Quintus thought. He did not invoke either Roman gods or Celtic gods; it was a general fervent prayer for help. The sun beat down on them. From inside the stone circle, where the people were all crowded, there came the rhythmic chant to Lugh. The Bard in green walked by without looking at them, while he strummed harsh monotonous notes on his little harp. He passed into the temple. The Belgic warriors filed in, all but those who had remained to guard Pendoc outside. Then Quintus and Regan were alone except for the white figures in the shadows. If it had not been for them, Quintus would have taken her hand and held it close in his. He could no longer deny tenderness for her, mingled as it was with shame that his own stupidity had brought them to this. She seemed very small and helpless as she sat there beside him on the stone, her head drooped, while the sunlight struck gleams in her soft curly hair. Despite all the dangers they had passed through, he had never seen her lose courage, but he could tell from the strained look around her lovely eyes and the tightness of her red mouth that she was trying to hide fear now.

"*Cara*——" He whispered the little Latin word for "darling," but so low she did not hear. "You mustn't be frightened," he said more loudly. "We've both got out of far worse troubles than this."

"I know," she said, trying to smile, "but it's so frightening not to be able to get to him—you see *he* is merciful, but the Druids-of-Justice are not. I think they won't touch me, because of this brooch, unless I try to leave the stone, but *you*—the minute the ceremony is over——" She twisted her hands together and was silent.

Yes, Quintus thought, they'll finish me off. Roman eyes would certainly not be allowed to see the sacred rites and live. A fine secret agent *you* turned out to be! said Quintus to himself. The mission to Gloucester! He had been so confident of success when they left Chichester—when?— less than two days ago. It seemed like months. And he was only halfway now—if indeed there was ever to be any more journeying for him.

At a stir in the temple, he roused himself from his black thoughts. Wild and strident music burst out, the clamor of bagpipes, and harps, and voices.

"Look!" whispered Regan, straining forward. "There is Conn Lear!"

Quintus followed her gaze and saw between the stones, far on the other side of the temple, that a procession was filing in through the sacred Druid entrance. There were barefoot, white-robed priests waving branches of mistletoe and oak leaves. There was a white bull with a garland of wheat around its neck, its horns tipped with gold. And at the end there walked a strange impressive figure, also in white. On his head there was a golden crown set between gray feathers like wings.

The Arch-Druid's arms were raised in invocation, his face was turned up to the sky while he marched steadily toward the center of the temple and the altar stone.

The music grew louder, as the Arch-Druid passed amongst the stones. The people nearby fell to their knees crying, "Lugh—shine on us. Lugh! Lugh!" The sun beat down upon the altar where had been placed corn and wheat for blessing. The white bull was led beside the altar, and two of the Druids held it by the horns.

The ancient ceremony began, solemnly. And it went on a long time with complicated ritual, of which Regan and Quintus could see little from their stone. But there was one moment when Quintus saw the flash of a golden sickle in the Arch-Druid's hand, and saw it descend swiftly toward the bull. The bull fell without a sound. The blood from its neck dripped on the altar, and the people cried out in ecstasy. This was not very different from the sacrifices to the gods in Rome, and Quintus recognized the rites of blood to purify the land and make it fertile for the coming year. But there were other parts of the ceremony he did not understand. Strange dances with mistletoe and with oak leaves, and hooded women in black who circled the altar and gave forth wailing cries.

The ceremonies went on until the sun had slanted toward the west and touched a stone which had been in shadow before. Then the Arch-Druid stepped up on this stone and began to speak to the hushed people. Quintus could hear his deep resonant voice, but not what he was saying, yet the voice seemed to exert a heavy thrall. Quintus grew drowsy, almost lulled. He ceased to fear the watching figures; he ceased to thrash and plan and worry over his chances of getting away. He glanced at Regan and saw that she too was calmed, the strain had left her listening face. It was exalted.

The hours passed until sunset, and Quintus, suddenly awakening from his dream, saw that the time of their safety was nearly over. The red light was dying and only a half circle of sun showed above the hill to the west.

The Arch-Druid ceased talking and pointed toward the sun. At once the thousand voices renewed their frenzied chant and fear came back to Quintus. He saw that the procession was beginning to form, and that it would take the Arch-Druid back the way he had come, far away from them. He saw the Bard in green suddenly appear between the nearest stones and look at them with steely eyes. He saw the white Druids-of-Justice move their golden spears from the left hand to the right.

Regan saw all these things too, and she saw Conn Lear turn his back to go, but the fear and confusion which had paralyzed her, melted away. Just as the sun dipped out of sight, she seized the sprig of mistletoe from off their stone of safety and, standing on the stone, raised the mistletoe high above her head, so that the waxy white berries and pale green leaves caught the last sunray. And she cried out with all her might, "Conn Lear! Conn Lear! Come to me! It is Regan, daughter of your daughter, who calls!"

The Druids-of-Justice lifted their spears, while Quintus held his breath. It seemed the girl's voice could not reach that distance through the chanting. For one moment the Arch-Druid did not move, then he turned slightly in their direction. Regan stood with her arms held out to him.

Quintus' heart thundered in his chest, and he took a deep breath. For slowly, slowly, with ponderous steps, the Arch-Druid walked from the sanctuary and came toward them.

Conn Lear moved through the maze of megaliths toward the stone of safety, and the people made way for him on either side. At last he stood and looked at Regan, then he smiled a little. His piercing hypnotic eyes softened.

"You have been frightened, poor child," he said in a deep tender voice. "You did not trust my powers? Yet you have been protected in all your journeying. I knew that you were here, and no harm could have come to you —or"—he turned his wise old face toward Quintus—"or the Roman you have brought—a young man I have met before."

Regan knelt down at the Arch-Druid's feet and placed her cheek against his hand. "I was frightened," she whispered, "for we seemed surrounded by enemies, and I could not get to you."

"It was written that way in the omens and in the stars," said Conn Lear solemnly. "Through fears and evils you must win to safety. As," he added, "much else is written for the future too, which will in time come to pass."

The Bard had crept up behind, afraid to speak but listening intently. The two Druids-of-Justice also had come near them, and one now spoke, saying "Great Master of Wisdom, this Roman—he has watched the sacred rites, he must not be allowed to go from here—alive. Great Master, do you not remember the dream? That a traitor would come to us in disguise—a Roman soldier who is on his way to summon other Romans to be our enemies!"

The Arch-Druid held up his hand, while his face grew sad and his eyes looked toward the sunset as though seeing something in the sky. "I remember the dream, and the prophecies too, Druid-of-Justice. Nevertheless, I say this Roman shall live, and *shall continue on his way untouched*—— Enough!" he cried in a voice of absolute command, as the Druid-of-Justice seemed about to protest. "I have spoken."

Under the impact of the fierce burning gaze, the man turned pale, and bowing, slunk away.

"Release my granddaughter's man, Pendoc," said Conn Lear to the Bard, then turning to Regan added, "Come, I will now talk to you—and the Roman."

CHAPTER VI

THE ARCH-DRUID LIVED in a circular stone house in a large grove of ancient oaks to the north of Stonehenge. There were other buildings in the sacred grove which contained a sort of college where Druid priests lived and instructed those who aspired to join the order. There was a school for the green-robed Bards, where they were taught the poetic branches of Druidic lore, while another school taught more practical learning to a different rank of Druids called Ovates.

While Quintus and Regan followed Conn Lear they saw various members of the priesthood walking back and forth conversing earnestly. There was a hushed feeling in the grove, where twilight made mysterious shadows amongst the darkening oak leaves. The dread of violence fell away from Quintus. When they actually entered the Arch-Druid's strange home, all turbulence gave place to awed quietness.

Quintus found himself in a large round room hung with woven cloth on which were painted trees and symbols. There were five-pointed stars, the sun, the crescent moon, a cup that glowed red as rubies, and balls of mistletoe. These symbols and many others were so artfully painted that the great room really seemed to be in the open amongst the trees; while the stars, the mistletoe, and all the other objects on the branches seemed as real as the bright fire that sparkled on a little hearth near the door. And the room smelled of incense, a pungent woodsy perfume that drifted in blue smoke from a bronze brazier. There were a few wooden benches and a table and couch, dimly visible by the light of flickering lamps, but it certainly was not these, nor even the tapestries, that gave the room such an odd feeling. It was the huge column in the center, and it took Quintus several moments to realize that the column was a living tree. An enormous oak that grew through the Arch-Druid's house and spread its leaves high above the thatched roof.

"O Conn Lear" cried Regan, clasping her hands. "I remember this room of the sacred tree and this lovely smell, though it was so long ago—and the painted forest too!" She walked to the tapestries and touched them softly with childlike pleasure.

The Arch-Druid's austere face relaxed as he looked at her. "Aye, little one," he said, "you have been a long time in the fierce land of the Icenians—it was necessary—it was your destiny. But now you shall stay with me awhile."

Quintus felt an unjustified pang as he saw the leap of delight in the girl's eyes. What better provision than this could there be for Regan? And what right had he to feel bleak disappointment that he must leave her now and go on with a Roman soldier's mission, alone.

"Sit down, Quintus Tullius," said Conn Lear suddenly, in Latin. "Indeed," he smiled, seeing Quintus' surprise, "I can speak your language when I *wish* to and I remember your name from our meeting last autumn upon the Kentish road."

"I'm sorry, sir," said Quintus uncomfortably, as he thought of his futile attempt to capture this same priest then. "I was but following orders."

"Even so," agreed Conn Lear calmly.

The Arch-Druid had removed his gold and feathered crown to reveal his head half shaven in the Druid's tonsure. Beneath his gray beard, Quintus could see hanging the mottled stone like a serpent skin, suspended on gold wire—but Quintus felt no impulse toward ridicule as he had on their first meeting.

Conn Lear—even seated on a simple wooden bench, in this queer stone house in the wilds of Britain—was the most majestic figure that Quintus had ever seen. Far more so than Governor Suetonius—or, thought Quintus, startled, than the *Emperor*, than the great Augustus Nero, whose plump dissipated young face rose in his mind. At once Quintus checked this treasonable thought. He rose and, slightly ashamed of having been led into such an unpatriotic comparison, cried sharply, "I can't stay here, Conn Lear. I must be on my way. Your granddaughter has promised."

He stopped as Regan gave a little moan and running to the Arch-Druid, knelt at his feet. "Yes, it's true," she cried, "my worshipful grandfather. And forgive me that I brought the Roman here. But *you* will know how to persuade him and turn him from his purpose! You have arts, Conn Lear, that will make him see that what he's going to do is terribly wrong."

Quintus gasped. And then he frowned. *"Regan!* You promised me! I trusted you. Because you speak so fast in Celtic, do you think I don't understand what you're saying? You promised that you'd set me on the way to Gloucester!"

She raised her head and stared at him. Her face had gone white as the Arch-Druid's robe, her lips trembled as she answered fiercely, "Yes, I promised—*IF* you *wished* to go on."

"But you thought I wouldn't *wish* to? You meant all along to get Conn Lear to—to hypnotize me—I suppose, as he did on the Kent road—to change my mind! Regan, now I see that, coming of different races, you and I, we think differently. I've been a fool to trust you." He gulped and turned his angry gaze from Regan to the Arch-Druid, whose mouth curved and who stood up, separating the two excited young people, and said, "Peace!—Quintus Tullius, you shall go to Gloucester, as my daughter's daughter has promised!"

"But Conn Lear——" cried Regan desperately, turning on him. "You don't know—Quintus goes to summon a legion, he goes to add to this killing—this torrent of violence and blood. Conn Lear, make him see that Romans have no right in our land. Make him see they must go back to their own place. Don't let him add yet more to the misery that's come to us—and that has turned—my foster mother, Boadicea—into a—devil!"

She crumpled suddenly and, hiding her face in her grandfather's robe, burst into tears.

Conn Lear bent down. His long wrinkled hand stroked her head gently. "Poor child," he said. His old face became very sad, the piercing eyes were veiled, as though they looked inward and had forgotten Quintus, who stood by uncomfortably while his anger ebbed. Yet Quintus refused to let himself feel pity for Regan, as he held sharp and firm to his purpose. He watched the Arch-Druid warily, guarding against any magical spell.

After a moment Conn Lear sighed and straightened up; sternness tinged the sadness of his features and he spoke in the chanting voice he had used in the stone temple—the voice of prophecy.

"It will be as it will be, Regan," he said solemnly. "I have consulted all the sacred oracles. They have spoken. There will be blood and yet more blood—there will be anguish —for our people—and in the end . . ." He shut his eyes, and when he opened them, looking directly at Quintus, he did not finish in the same voice, but in a lower more normal tone. "And you—young Roman soldier—you will go to summon the Second Legion from Gloucester, as it is your destiny to do, *but*——" He shook his head, a peculiar smile flitted across his eyes. "No matter," he said, "you will find out for yourself."

Quintus' relief almost made him dizzy. "Then I'd like to leave at once—Conn Lear," he cried. He heard Regan give a stifled gasp and he kept himself from looking at her.

"You shall leave when you have eaten," said the Arch-Druid. "My own servant will guide you. There is but one stipulation. Your way for some miles west will pass through a land of holy wells and groves where the sacred plant is. There are things there you may not see, nor do I wish you to remember what you have already seen this day. I am going to give you the herb of forgetfulness."

"No!" cried Quintus, starting back, all his fears aroused again. "So after all, you'd trick me into forgetting my mission!"

Conn Lear's mouth tightened. "You are stupid, Quintus Tullius! Do you think I could not make you forget your mission without warning you? Do you dare think I lie when I say you will get to Gloucester? This drug will dim your memory of only this *one* day. No more."

"And if I refuse to take the drug?"

"Then you will remain here until you do."

Quintus set his teeth. He had no alternative except to trust the old Druid, and indeed he instinctively did so. But Jupiter Maximus, Quintus thought, the weird and unpredictable things that kept happening to him in this country! And with the thought came remembrance of the quest that had first brought him to this land.

"Conn Lear," said Quintus suddenly, "perhaps I've taken the drug of forgetfulness already, for all this day I've not thought of the reason I so wished to see your Great Temple of the Stones."

"And what *is* that reason?" asked the Arch-Druid rather absently, leaning his head on his hand.

"A hundred years ago, my great-grandfather, one Gaius Tullius, a Roman who came with Julius Caesar, was killed near here by——"

"Stop!" thundered Conn Lear. He rose and drew himself to his full great height. His eyes flashed blue fire at the astounded Quintus. *"Say no more,* or I shall forget my mercy and my kindness! So it was YOUR ancestor who first invaded our peaceful plain here, whose filthy bones did desecrate our holiest place! By Lugh himself, had I known this——" His hand moved to the magic stone on his breast, a dreadful stillness flowed over his tall white figure.

"Conn Lear!" cried Regan in fear, as she watched the change in her grandfather. "It's not Quintus' fault! He only seeks the bones of his ancestor to give them proper burial."

"And shall *never* find them!" The fierce voice resounded through the room. "That Roman brought a curse upon us. A curse——" he repeated. His long old body shuddered as though he suppressed the violence of his thoughts. But his hand slowly dropped from the serpent stone. Then he clapped his palms sharply together. At once a lad in a red tunic ran in carrying dishes of smoking meat and a jug of mead.

"Eat," said Conn Lear coldly to Quintus. "And drink!" As he said this he pulled from under his robe a little bag made from the gray furry skin of the sacred hare. He opened the pouch and took out a pinch of greenish powdered herb which he dropped in Quintus' cup. Then he poured the mead in. "Drink!" He held the cup to Quintus' lips.

Quintus drew back. "A moment ago you had hatred in your eyes, Conn Lear. Can I believe this is some simple herb of forgetfulness!"

"Grandfather——" whispered Regan, putting her hand

101

on his arm. "I too am afraid—don't harm him for I—
I——"

What was it she whispered lower yet so that Quintus
could not hear? Anger gradually left the Arch-Druid's
face and was replaced by the sadness. "Sorrow, sorrow,"
he murmured as though to himself. "Always *He* lurks in
waiting, the dark god of the shadows—whose name must
not be uttered."

He roused himself and turned impatiently to Quintus.
"Drink the mead in safety—O Unbelieving Roman—the
dark god will not come for you through me—and you
know in your heart that the Arch-Druid of all the Britons
does not speak with double tongue."

Quintus looked at Regan suddenly and caught on her
unguarded face a look of yearning directed at him. Her
lips formed the word "Please. . . ."

Quintus bowed his head and quietly began to drink.
The mead was sweet and cool, faintly aromatic. He
finished the cup and waited for some strange sensation.
But there was none. He heard Regan give a little sigh of
relief. She walked over and smiled down at him. "Now
eat," she said matter-of-factly, "and I will too. We've had
no food since dawn." She took her dish of meat, and sat
down by Quintus on a bench.

The Arch-Druid glanced once toward them, then
moved abstractedly to the other side of the great round
room to a window cut between the tapestries. For some
moments he sat at a table and seemed to be writing. Then
he went to the window. He opened it and stood gazing
out toward the stars, murmuring some brooding incanta-
tion. The huge oak trunk in the center nearly hid his white
figure from Quintus and Regan, and while they ate, a new
intimacy came to them. They sat very close together on
the bench. Quintus was intensely conscious of the warmth
of her slender body, and of the silken feel of her long
hair as it brushed his arm. He wanted to put his arm
around her. He felt a tightness in his throat as she looked
up at him sideways through her lashes. A dimple he had
never noticed appeared near her mouth, and she said,
"But *Quintus*, you're not eating! Don't you like the flavor-
ing of this roast lamb? Conn Lear's cooks are supposed to
be so good!"

"I think you know very well why I've stopped eating,
Regan," said Quintus, looking steadily into her face.

102

She colored and dropped her eyes, but the dimple was still there as she said, "Oh, I *do* hope it isn't the herb of forgetfulness that's spoiled your appetite! But truly if Conn Lear says it's not harmful it isn't."

"No," he answered, very low, on a harsh breath, "it's not the herb—*Cara*."

She had put her dish down and now her hands clenched on a fold of her robe. The dimple vanished. "Why do you call me that?" she whispered, and he felt her shoulder tremble.

"Because it means 'beloved.' I love you, Regan."

Her own breathing quickened. She held herself still and tight, but he could see the shaking of her heart beneath the thin wool bodice.

"You must not," she whispered at last. "It is forbidden. . . ." Her shadowed eyes moved to the distant figure of the Arch-Druid. "There can never be love between us, never——"

"But there *is!*"

She made a sharp sound in her throat, and slowly as though against her will she raised her face.

He kissed her, not in the quick and grateful way he had done when she rescued him from Boadicea's camp, but warmly, passionately. The hard kiss of a man, and she responded as a woman. To them their kiss lasted an eternity or a second, it had no dimension—except beauty; then realization crept in, and pain.

His arms fell from her, she turned away her face, which was wet with sudden tears. The Arch-Druid had not moved, he still gazed out toward the stars.

"*Cara*—my Regan—I'll come back to you. Wait for me here—I'll come back. I don't know how or where—but after——"

" 'After . . .' " she repeated in a despairing lifeless voice. "After you've done your duty as a Roman soldier—after your people and mine have slaughtered each other. It's no use, Quintus. Yes, I love you, but there can never be a future for us."

"How CAN you say that!" he cried. "When now we both admit the love that's between us, when we both knew as we kissed that we belong to each other! That's changed everything."

She shook her head, tears slipped down her cheeks, but she gave a weary little smile. "You won't remember what we've said, Quintus. Nor our kiss. Otherwise, I couldn't have let it happen."

"Not remember! You mean the drug? Why, that's impossible!"

"Conn Lear is never wrong," she whispered, "and yet— oh, may all our gods forgive me—I *want* you to remember someday. Remember a little." Her hand went to the brooch that clasped her mantle; the bronze brooch decorated with Celtic scrolls and the ruby enamel Druidic emblem of a tiny snake. "Quick, take it—and keep it hidden." She fastened it inside his woolen tunic next to his heart, while she glanced quickly toward Conn Lear's back. "At least it will help to keep you safe. And I'll pray—pray to Lugh for you."

"Regan——!" He seized her hands, so overcome with emotion that he could not command his voice. Nor did he ever say the things to her he wished to, because the Arch-Druid turned from the window and walked toward them around the great tree trunk. Quintus dropped Regan's hands and was silent.

"The Star of the North has mounted high in the sky above the Sign of the Warrior, Quintus Tullius," said Conn Lear, looking somberly down at the young people. "It is time for you to go." He raised his voice and called "Bran!"

A strange creature shambled into the room and, kneeling at the Arch-Druid's feet, made gobbling noises. In Rome Quintus had seen big apes that had come in the galleys from Africa. This creature was like an ape with its short body clothed in otter skins, long powerful arms and a round head covered with matted rusty-black hair. But between the flattened nose and the low jutting forehead the eyes were bright and intelligent. Conn Lear drew the creature to one side, handed him a large deerskin bag, and seemed to be giving instructions, though he spoke in a swift dialect Quintus could not follow, and was answered by inhuman gobbling noises.

"This is Bran," said the Arch-Druid, walking back to Quintus. "My servant. He belongs to the little people of the west who were here in the old, old days, even before my own race, the Celts, came to this land. He will guide you to Gloucester."

Quintus bowed. "Thank you, Conn Lear." Through the desolation in his heart and his consciousness of Regan be-

104

side him still, he tried to examine his peculiar guide. "Doesn't he speak?"

The Arch-Druid frowned. "He does *not* speak—because he has no tongue." He gestured, and Bran came to Quintus and opened his mouth to disclose a scarred and pulpy stump where the tongue had been.

Quintus drew in his breath, and the Arch-Druid went on coldly. "It was necessary, for once Bran talked too much. Those who know some of our secrets cannot be allowed to tell of them."

Quintus swallowed. Would this have been his fate too, if it had not been for Regan?

"Now GO!" said the Arch-Druid. He raised his arm and pointed toward the door, and as Quintus turned instinctively toward the girl, Conn Lear stepped between them, blotting her from Quintus' sight. "There is nothing for you to say to her, Roman!" added the grim voice. "GO!" The piercing blue gaze fastened itself with power on Quintus as it had on the Kentish road. But Quintus did not this time yield to the Arch-Druid, he yielded to reason. He dared not risk subjecting Regan to her grandfather's anger.

"*Vale,*" he said in a dragging voice, "farewell," and turned quickly.

But I will come back to her someday, somehow, he vowed, as he preceded Bran from the round stone room of the living tree.

Quintus slept a short time that night beneath a hazel bush and opened his eyes into a fine mist, through which the new-risen sun could not penetrate. An extraordinary looking man, like an ape, was squatting beside him, gnawing at a chicken drumstick.

"What in Hades are *you?*" cried Quintus, reaching for his spear, which lay beside him. The man put down the drumstick and made a chuckling noise. His hairy hand pawed around in a deerskin bag, and bringing out a large oakleaf he handed it to Quintus. There was some Latin writing crudely scratched on the leaf. Quintus scowled at it until he made it out. The writing said, "This is Bran who will guide you to Gloucester. Trust him."

"Bran?" said Quintus, frowning harder for he was exceedingly puzzled. The man nodded, pounded his chest, grinned amiably, and began to gnaw the drumstick.

"Where did you come from? Where are we?" said Quintus in painstaking Celtic.

Bran shrugged, opened his mouth to show Quintus he had no tongue and could not answer.

This happened before in a dream, Quintus thought; where did I dream it? He rubbed his eyes and stared again at Bran. But where is Pendoc, he thought, and the campfire we were sitting by in the forest last night when we broiled the fish? WHERE IS REGAN?

At this he was overwhelmed with a feeling of pain and loss, far greater than he could understand. For amidst the dream-like confusion, he had a certainty that there was nothing wrong with her. She was in no danger. Then she and Pendoc must have slipped away in the night, leaving him this extraordinary guide and the message? Could Regan write Latin? That was strange, and yet the only explanation. But then had Regan deceived him all along? Had she never intended to take him to Stonehenge and her grandfather at all? This thought hurt him, even while a part of him denied it utterly. He knew that Regan was trustworthy. And yet so many things were strange; faint dream memories slipped in and out of his mind, bright sun and huge sinister stones, angry voices, a room of mysterious shadows, many trees. And something lost. Something beautiful and very precious. I've had a fever, that's what it is, he thought. He touched his cheek and found it cool. Well, he was all right now, whatever had happened, and on his way to Gloucester. That was the important thing. His military mission. How long had he been delayed?

He read again the message on the leaf, then tore it into tiny bits. "Well, come on then, Bran! Hurry—on to Gloucester!" He reinforced his Celtic with gestures.

The man nodded and threw away the drumstick. He pointed toward two ponies Quintus had not yet noticed, though one was his own; the shaggy native pony, on which he had left the Regni fort. At least he was certain of *that*, Quintus thought slightly reassured. They mounted and Bran set off in the lead, as the mists lifted and merged into a gray sky.

They were in a fertile land of pastures, brooks, and fields of ripening grain, with here and there a prosperous looking native farmhouse. It's queer, thought Quintus, as the rough little ponies trotted along tirelessly. I wonder why we don't ever get to the great plain of the stone temple. The country isn't at all what I expected.

Despite a maze of crisscross tracks, Bran, never hesitating, went as fast as even Quintus could desire. After a while they came in sight of some foothills and a ridge beyond, where Bran turned north along a river which they followed for a long time until they struck off to the left up a hill. When they reached the top, Bran drew in his pony and, grunting, pointed down below.

Quintus peered into the cup-like valley and was startled. There was a large cluster of houses on the bank of a river, not the round British huts, but substantial stone houses and a white edifice that looked very much like a Roman temple. A cloud of steam rose into the air from near the temple.

Surely those were hot springs down there, Quintus thought, and remembered that poor Flaccus had once mentioned hearing of healing springs in the west country. Could this possibly be Gloucester, though there was no sign of a fort?

He said the word for "Gloucester" questioningly to Bran, who shook his head vigorously and pointed further north. Then, by gestures of sleeping and eating, conveyed to Quintus that they would spend the night down below.

Quintus nodded reluctantly, anxious to press onward to the end of this difficult journey. But he was aware of badly needing sleep and food for they had finished the meat provided by the deerskin bag as they rode. During the last hour he had hardly been able to keep his eyes open, and his drowsiness extinguished curiosity as they entered the little town on a paved stone street which was lined with tiny shops and comfortable villas. Bran rode straight toward the temple, which, seen close, did not look quite as Roman, though it had rude columns built of whitish stone, and on the pediment above the entrance was a large sculptured face of an ugly woman, obviously some goddess, but none that Quintus recognized.

They dismounted and made for a sort of wooden shed from which clouds of steam were rising. Suddenly Quintus was jolted from his sleepiness by the sight of a Roman toga. In fact two of them! They were worn by very old men who were sitting on a bench beside the shed talking to an elderly woman in the draped blue palla and understola of a Roman matron. Quintus stared at her tiara of tightly curled gray hair, done in the fashion worn by his mother when he was a child.

"Why does that filthy Briton stare at us so, I wonder!" said the woman loudly to her companions. "And look at that ape man. Ugh! The most extraordinary people come to Bath. If it weren't for my rheumatism——"

It took Quintus a moment to realize that he was the "filthy Briton," and another to decide whether to disclose his true nationality. But after all there was nothing to be lost, and much to be gained by finding out what these Romans were doing in this remote spot and what they knew of the revolution that was shaking the east.

They knew nothing at all, Quintus soon discovered after he had addressed them in Latin, endured their incredulity, given explanations and received theirs.

The old men were time-expired veterans of the Claudian conquest, seventeen years ago. They explained that there were about a dozen others like them living here because the climate was gentle and the healing hot springs, called "Aquae Sulis," in which they bathed daily, kept them healthy. The Roman lady was a wife who had been sent for from Italy, during the peaceful years.

"Why no," said the matron, still eying Quintus suspiciously, "we've heard of no particular trouble. But the natives, you know, Standard-bearer—if you really *are* one—well, one has to really *understand* the natives. They don't bother us when they come here to the springs—and we let them keep their silly temple."

She pointed to the sculptured face. "That's their goddess Sulis, but we call her Minerva, and it doesn't matter."

A lot of things will matter to you, my dear lady, thought Quintus, exasperated—if Boadicea decides to include *you* in her plans. But he didn't say it. These people were old and incapable of understanding the situation. One could only hope for their sakes that their smug isolation would continue.

"Have you any knowledge at all about the Second Legion at Gloucester?" he asked.

But the old people shook their heads, without interest. "The prefect of the legion, Poenius Postumus, an enormous German he is, came here only last year to take the waters," answered one of the old men, "but he was a dull dog. Never spoke to anyone—ate too much—had some sort of stomach trouble."

"Oh no, Marcus," said his wife impatiently, "it was boils he had. You never remember anything right."

"My dear Octavia, I believe my memory is quite as good as yours, and am certain it was stomach trouble the prefect suffered from."

Quintus murmured hasty farewells and escaped, totally uninterested in whatever ailments had afflicted the Second Legion's prefect.

He found that there were rooms for travelers provided near the bath shed and, after gulping some food, fell dead asleep.

CHAPTER VII

QUINTUS AWOKE in the town of Bath to a familiar though long unheard sound—the clatter and a creak of a chariot on flagstones, like the sounds that had awakened him many a morning in his own frescoed cubiculum at his mother's villa in Rome. He jumped up and peered through the door of the wooden shelter to see the Roman couple, Marcus and Octavia, sedately rattling along toward the baths. Their large old horse—obviously a cavalry veteran—their bronze-studded chariot, the precise drapings of his toga and her stola, all looked so thoroughly respectable and commonplace that Quintus suddenly laughed.

Bran, who had slept on the floor, looked up alertly. "They might be my own aunt and uncle driving over from Ostia to spend the day with poor Mother, and scold her for household extravagance, or for spoiling Livia and me!" said Quintus whimsically to Bran, who naturally did not understand but grinned, then made gestures indicating that they should go.

"Yes, I know," said Quintus, sobering at once. "Get the ponies, buy food—here." He gave him some coins. "I'll be ready when you are."

While Bran nodded and went off to obey, Quintus ran to the baths. He had not washed properly in days and was delighted to find in this unlikely spot a fair example of Roman comfort and progress. The hot springs had been visited by Britons for centuries, and it had always been for them a sacred place of healing, under the protection of their goddess Sulis. But the few elderly Romans who had so far discovered the virtues of the spa had naturally

110

not been satisfied with a lot of steam and a muddy pool. They had begun at once to transform these into acceptable baths. Quintus, after he had soaked himself in the steam and heat of the shed which enclosed the springs, encountered Marcus and some other Roman gentlemen breakfasting on the edge of a great rectangular swimming pool made of stones bedded in "puddle" clay.

"Ah," said Marcus, who was sipping a cup of wine, "greeting, Standard-bearer, I must say you look more like a Roman without those ridiculous native clothes on! You see what we're doing here? Though it's slow work and we're extremely short of slaves. Every inch of lead for these pipes has to be dragged out of the Mendip hills, and we haven't even a decent tepidarium yet—fearfully hard getting anything done in the wilderness."

"Yes—I see," said Quintus politely, hurrying toward the stone step at the corner of the cold plunge, "but I think you've already done wonders."

"Did you get your massage?" called the old man. "We do have a slave who's good at oiling and scraping the skin with strigils."

"Haven't time, thanks," answered Quintus, diving into the chilly water. When he clambered out at the other end, Marcus was waiting for him on the brink.

"Have some of those wild eastern tribes really revolted?" the old man asked frowning. "You young people all exaggerate so."

"They *have* revolted, sir," answered Quintus shortly.

"Oh well . . ." Marcus said comfortably, as he wrapped a woolen robe around his skinny hunched shoulders. "Our legions'll soon deal with the trouble. Probably all over already. By the way, if the prefect, Postumus, *is* still at Gloucester, you might just find out if it was stomach trouble he came here for last year. I'm positive"—he glanced toward a small arcade at the end of the pool where Octavia's tiara of gray curls was bent toward that of another old lady—"POSITIVE it was not boils."

"I'll try to find out, sir," said Quintus with control. He made a hasty farewell and ran toward the vestibule, where he had left his clothes. He threw them on and hurried out to the court where Bran was just riding up with the ponies.

The dew was still on the grass when Bran and Quintus climbed out of the quiet cup-like valley where Bath lay;

and the last part of their journey was slower going than even the great forests had been because here they were in hill country. These Cotswolds were most lovely wooded hills through which the native track wound and climbed and dipped suddenly down to little brooks which the ponies stumbled and splashed through.

Though his anxiety mounted with each hour that brought them nearer to the goal at last, Quintus was aware of the special beauty of the country. Once when they paused to let the horses drink, Quintus looked down a small ravine that opened onto a view of hazy purplish hills beyond and thought that it would be a wonderful site for a country villa. There was ample water, shade, and lush meadows to turn into farm lands. And he discovered that in picturing his villa, which would be spacious, built of brick, well warmed, and decorated with fine mosaics, he was also picturing Regan there as the mistress of it. He had an image of her charming little face thoughtfully bent over the home fire, between two altars, one for household gods, the Lares and Penates, and the other for the gentle hearth goddess, Vesta.

A very silly picture, he realized impatiently. Regan had certainly emphasized her indifference when she had changed her mind about taking him to her grandfather, and instead deserted him in the forest and gone off with Pendoc. Also, if a young Roman soldier were to do anything as ridiculous as to build dream villas in the wilderness, and dream a wife to fit into them, let him at least dream the latter in the shape of a beautiful Roman girl, with neatly curled black hair, large melting eyes, lush olive skin. Like Pomponia, he thought, remembering the daughter of one of his mother's friends who had given him definitely languishing looks last year at a banquet.

But Pomponia did not seem in the least attractive now.

Quintus jerked his pony's bridle, and they started forward up the next hill. This time with Regan it's finished for good! Quintus thought in sudden anger, exasperated by the sick yearning and sense of loss that came to him when he remembered her, and which he could not seem to control—a baffling feeling as though something had happened that part of him knew, but that was hidden where he could not find it.

They rode and rode, and then they walked; for even the British ponies began to tire. It rained gently at times, at others the sun came out warm on their backs. But finally it set, sinking in a blaze of rose and violet beyond a broad estuary that they could see shining far below.

They trudged on through the long northern twilight, until the moon rose like a golden plate, above the distant Welsh mountains.

At long last they descended to an open plain, and Bran gave a grunt of satisfaction. By the brilliant moon's light, Quintus saw rearing up ahead the unmistakable ramparts and turrets of a large Roman fortress.

At *last!* thought Quintus exultantly. And as the fort seemed so quiet, he thought, They've gone, thanks be to Mars! He did not even feel disappointment that his long journey was for nothing, in relief that the Second Legion must now be united with Suetonius' forces. It might even be that the smug old Marcus in Bath was right, and the revolt put down by now. This gave him a pang, that the great final battle should happen without him, but he decided stoically that he would have to take what comfort he could from having faithfully fulfilled his mission.

As they got nearer he saw the dark shape of a sentry walking along the ramparts from turret to turret. Perhaps this was not surprising since they *might* leave some guard at the fort, though they shouldn't. Suetonius had ordered complete abandonment because he needed every fighting arm to help him. But then Quintus noticed something else.

The legionary flag was flying! It suddenly flapped and billowed in a gust of wind, and below the eagle on the pole Quintus saw plainly the curious capricorn badge— half goat, half fish—that denoted the proud royal "Augusta," the Second Legion.

So, after all, they were still there! A standard moved with the legion.

Quintus' heart began to beat fast. "Hold the ponies. Stay here! I'll arrange for you later," he cried to Bran, throwing him his horse's bridle. But the little dark man shook his ape head and gobbled something vehemently, at the same time pointing south the way they had come.

"You mean you won't wait?" Quintus asked, astonished. "But you must have food and rest."

Bran shook his head again and made it clear that he was leaving with the two horses.

"Well, I can't stop you," said Quintus ruefully, "and I

113

thank you for your guidance, but I wish I knew where you came from and where you're going."

Bran made the hoarse sound in his throat that meant a laugh, and even in the moonlight Quintus could see that the alert eyes were looking at him with a peculiar expression, as though he could have told some strange things if he could speak. Bran raised his arm in salute and, jumping on his pony, led the other pony rapidly off into the night.

Quintus had no time for conjecture. He called "Farewell, Bran," then ran toward one of the four portals to the great rectangular fortress.

The sentry had seen the shapes moving below and heard the voice. He leaned over, poised his spear, and called out a sharp challenge.

Quintus started to shout back his name and rank and legion, but before he could get it all out, the startled sentry at the gate rushed forward waving his sword and crying, "Silure! Silure!" as he lunged at Quintus.

"I'm not a Silure—you fool!" cried Quintus, jumping sideways and barely escaping the sword point. "I've a message from the governor!"

He yanked off his native helmet and shouted the universal Roman army password, "In the name of Caesar Augustus Nero!" at the sentry, who slowly lowered his sword, while the sentry from the ramparts ran down to join him, crying, "What is it, Titus? What've we caught?"

"You haven't 'caught' anything, my friends," said Quintus impatiently. "I'm as Roman as you are, a standard-bearer of the Ninth. Take me at once to General Valerianus!"

"Another one. . . ." said Titus slowly and cryptically to his fellow sentry. "I wonder what the prefect'll make of THIS one."

"Never mind the prefect!" said Quintus sharply. "Take me to the general. . . . Look men, here I have a message from His Excellency, Governor Suetonius Paulinus——" He held out the piece of parchment that he had been given at Chichester. "It's of desperate importance—desperate."

"Well," said Titus, shrugging, "desperate or not you'll have to take it to the prefect, Poenius Postumus, and I daresay you won't like the result."

"Why?" cried Quintus, ignoring the last words, which he did not understand. "Why to the *prefect?*"

"Because he's in command of the legion just now, that's why."

"But where's the general, Valerianus?"

"That," answered the sentry, with a puzzling blend of rudeness and hesitation, "is a matter for guessing, and not with outsiders neither, my lad." He made a quick sign with his fingers as protection against the evil eye, and added on a sharper note, "The general's gone away."

Quintus frowned, thinking—what's happening here?—something queer. Though the sentries did not meet his eyes, they seemed not so much unfriendly as ashamed, or anxious.

"Then take me to the prefect," said Quintus grimly. The sentry, called Titus, nodded and started in the army's formal quickstep along the Via Principalis, or Principal Street, which bisected the vast enclosure inside the walls.

As he followed, Quintus noted unconsciously the usual layout of a legionary fortress; the acres of barracks built in blocks, and the granaries, kitchens, stables, baths, parade grounds—everything for the care of six or seven thousand men. Ahead loomed larger stone buildings, which were of a type always built as the headquarters of a fortress, to house the staff, the treasure chamber, and administrative offices.

It was very late. There was no sound from the sleeping men; only a dog barked over by the north portal, and a whinny came from the stables.

As they drew near the heavy wooden door that led to staff quarters, Titus suddenly turned and said, "There you are! Old Jumbo Postumus is in there. Good luck and good-by. I don't suppose I'll be seeing *you* again."

"Why not?" snapped Quintus, staring.

"Because nobody's seen the other two, since we took 'em in here."

"Other two *what?*"

"Messengers from the governor. Leastways they said they were. I wouldn't know."

Quintus whirled and put a firm hand on Titus' arm. "Listen sentry! I can't make head or tail of this. If you've had two messengers, they came to summon the legion, as I do. And why hasn't it gone? What in the name of all the divine gods is the matter here?"

"I expect you'll find out," answered the sentry, with a tinge of sympathy. "Us, we're not here to speculate. We do our duty and obey orders." He banged the heavy iron knocker and called out a password.

After a moment the door swung open, a sleepy guard held up a torch and, peering at the sentry, said, "What's up, Titus?"

The sentry jerked his chin toward Quintus. "Messenger. Wants to see the prefect right now."

"Oh," said the guard without expression, inspecting the stubble of black beard on Quintus' chin, the tattered native clothes. "Pass in."

Quintus entered the sparsely furnished vestibule of the post commander's quarters and was faintly relieved to see the usual little altar to Mars in the corner. So peculiar had been his reception, that anything which indicated normal legionary life was reassuring.

The guard, who was a middle-aged man with shrewd gray eyes, put the torch in a bracket and said without interest as though he knew the answer, "You have credentials and indentification?"

Quintus held out the letter. "This is the governor's dispatch, under his personal seal. Arouse the prefect, Postumus, at once!"

The guard did not look at the seal; his eyes flickered over Quintus with the same mixture of embarrassment and what seemed like hidden sympathy that Titus had shown. "The prefect's not asleep," he said tonelessly. "It is seldom that he sleeps these days. Come with me."

In the next hall they passed the great iron-barred door to the strong room which was marked with a large "II Augusta" to show that there the legion's treasure was kept and its standards and emblems also, when they were not in use.

"Aren't there any guards in here by the strong room?" asked Quintus, in surprise.

"I—Balbo—am the guard," answered the man quietly. "The prefect doesn't want others around." He raised his hand to pull aside a heavy leather curtain that screened the commandant's private room from the hall and paused involuntarily as they both heard a strange sound. It was like laughter, peals of it, mirthless, high-pitched as a woman's and yet somehow masculine. It came from somewhere to the left and ended abruptly, as a heavy voice from behind the leather curtain shouted, "Stop it! *Stop!*"

Quintus' breath was cut short; he stiffened against the

shiver caused by that uncanny laughter, but Balbo gave him no time to think. He pulled the curtain roughly aside and said, "Poenius Postumus, O Exalted Prefect, here is a messenger!" Balbo dropped the curtain and disappeared.

A man sat at a table, alone in the room.

Quintus by now was prepared to be confronted with almost any peculiarity in the prefect. But he had not expected what he actually saw. An enormous man with a shock of flaxen hair was sitting at a completely bare table with his head bowed on his clenched fists. He raised toward Quintus a stolid peasant face from which round blue eyes stared out with an expression of ox-like misery.

"Messenger?" said the prefect in the thick guttural accent of the Rhineland troops. "I want no more messengers. Leave me alone!"

"Impossible, sir!" cried Quintus. "The whole east of Britain is in revolt, the governor is fearfully outnumbered by the native forces. He commands that your legion march this instant to his aid. Here is his dispatch." He put the parchment on the table in front of the prefect.

"It is perhaps a trap," said the prefect dully. "How do I know that it is not a trap!"

"By Jupiter Maximus, sir—READ IT!" Quintus cried. "And that is the governor's own private seal."

The big flaxen head wagged uneasily from side to side. "I do not know the governor's private seal. I will not read it—it is addressed to General Valerianus. So I must not read it. You see it's addressed to my general?"

This is incredible, thought Quintus, feeling as though he were fighting shadows in a nightmare. "By Mars, of course it is! But since you are in command, *you* must read it and act, now!" The big man hunched his massive shoulders, as though to shut out the voice of Quintus which cried out suddenly, "Where IS General Valerianus? I demand to know!"

Quintus knew that his tone was highly improper coming from a lowly standard-bearer to the commander of a legion, but he did not care what discipline might be given him if he could only penetrate this baffling fog.

There was a silence. The prefect stared at the dispatch with unseeing eyes. He seemed to have forgotten Quintus when suddenly there came a sound from the left—a snatch of song and a high laughing wail.

Quintus whirled around and gazed at a door covered by another leather curtain. "What's that?"

The prefect lumbered clumsily to his feet; a colossus, six and a half feet tall, whose tow head grazed the low ceiling. He thrust his underlip out and made a gesture to Quintus with a ham-like hand. He trod heavily to the curtain and raised it. "There," he said in a hoarse dragging voice, "is General Valerianus."

Quintus looked into a small room that was lit only by a tiny wall lamp. He saw a man in a white shirt crouching on a pallet. The man was pulling straw out of the pallet and arranging it on the floor in six neat little piles. He was emaciated; his cropped hair was grizzled on a knobby skull head. His hand, like a yellow eagle's claw, carefully placed the straw now on this pile, now on that.

Quintus' mouth went dry, for, in the second that he took in the scene, the man began to snicker. He flattened out a whole pile of straw and burst into a peal of metallic laughter.

"The gods take pity on him, he's mad," whispered Quintus, starting back.

The prefect dropped the curtain. "Not always," he said dully. "Only sometimes. The legion doesn't know. I tell them he's gone off to visit the western fort at Caerleon."

"They know, all right," said Quintus in a hushed voice. "Or at least they suspect. It's a terrible thing, and now I understand what was so puzzling—but Poenius Postumus, this tragedy does not affect THIS!"

He picked up the governor's message and thrust it at the prefect. "Don't you understand? Our whole army's in fearful danger. You've got about seven thousand men here, nearly as many as Suetonius' whole force, since my legion—the Ninth—was wiped out by Queen Boadicea. Your legion must start tonight, straight east, and pray we're not too late!"

He spoke vehemently but distinctly straight up into the huge ox-like face, trying to reach through the barrier of doubt and indecision.

It was no use. Apparently Postumus took in only one sentence, for he said, "Your whole legion was wiped out? —yes. You see? If this should happen to *us*—what could I tell my general when he is himself again? No, messenger, we stay here at Gloucester, as my general has ordered."

Quintus gasped. "But he ordered it before he knew this

—and he's mad——" he began, and stopped. The round blue eyes were blank as pebbles. There was no reasoning with the stubborn, closed, and obviously frightened mind behind them.

The tribunes! Quintus thought. The six ranking officers of a legion must be quartered somewhere near. Surely if he could get to them with the message, they would dare to override this dangerous fool with his misguided loyalty to a madman. Get myself out of here, somehow, find the tribunes, Quintus thought.

"No, no," grunted the big man, shaking his head as though Quintus had voiced his plan. "*I* am commander of this post. I know what to do. I will not be bothered all the time, worried, badgered . . . I have decided . . . Balbo!" he called suddenly.

The guard rushed in with his sword drawn, as though he had been waiting for this. "Yes, sir."

"Put him with the others."

"No!" cried Quintus. "I've imperial protection from the governor! You can't touch me!" and cursed inwardly that he had no sword, nothing but the native spear which he could not use at close quarters. It was hopeless. The giant German strode across the room and picked Quintus up as though he'd been a child. He pinioned his arms, tossed the spear in a corner, and carried him out to the hall.

Balbo pulled the bolt on the great oaken door of the strong room, and Postumus threw Quintus inside. The bolt grated back into place.

Quintus lay dazed for some moments on the stone floor. When his wits returned, he found that there was a light burning, and two men's faces were peering down at him curiously. Both were young, both were dressed in army fatigues, their leather jerkins bearing the number and emblem of the Fourteenth Legion. One was dark, short, and snub-nosed, with merry brown eyes; the other who looked older, about twenty-six, had freckles, crisp reddish hair, and a determined chin, also a deep half-healed cut across his cheek.

"I see you're coming to, after the prefect's truly hospitable reception," said the small dark one to Quintus. "Welcome to our select company. Have some wine." He held out a cup. Quintus drank thirstily and sat up, rubbing his head where a large egg was forming.

"Messenger from Suetonius Paulinus, no doubt?" stated the grave, freckled young man. As Quintus nodded, he added, "So are we. Dio here arrived first, about two weeks ago. The governor sent him off from Wales as soon as we got news of the rebellion. I was sent later when we arrived in London and there was still no sign of the Second. I had a spot of trouble getting through the Atrebate country—somebody's spear did this." He fingered the wound on his cheek. "But I made it. Five days ago. We've kept count." He indicated a row of scratches on the wall. "And here we are. Where'd you get sent from, and what's happened since we've been here?"

"Let him eat first," said Dio. "He's still groggy, and the gods know we have plenty of time." He held out a handful of hard wheat cakes to Quintus, who murmured thanks and started to eat.

"You from Rome?" continued Dio cheerfully. "I thought so, could tell from the classical way you muttered 'thank you,' though you sure aren't a very trim-looking citizen of the imperial city right this moment."

Quintus smiled faintly. He sensed that Dio was rattling on to give him a chance to recover, and he was soon to learn that a great deal of judgment lay beneath the young man's light manner.

"I'm from Naples," continued Dio. "I've got a lot of Greek blood. While Fabian"—he punched the other messenger affectionately in the ribs—"he's a blasted Gaul—but not a bad fellow for all that. We've come to know each other quite well."

"I should think so," said Quintus dryly. Looking around their prison, he noticed several iron-bound triple-locked coffers. Dio was sitting on one of them. As Quintus went over to examine them, Dio explained that they contained the legion's money, the imperial coins which paid the troops. The sacred emblems, flags, and standards were neatly stacked in a corner. There was nothing else in the way of furnishing in the small stone room, and no window. But fortunately there was a tiny grilled fresh-air shaft to prevent the accumulation of dampness. And there was a lamp beside the wheat cakes and wine.

"Balbo sees that we get light and enough food; as far as prisons go it's not so bad," Dio added. "We might have been thrown in the dungeon."

"Postumus couldn't do that without exposing the whole

situation to a lot of other people, I guess," said Quintus slowly. "I think in his own way he's as crazy as that poor general."

"No," said Fabian, his lean freckled face growing thoughtful. "The prefect's not crazy, but he's scared, scared of responsibility. It's a certain type of German mind. I've fought beside lots of them and seen it before—splendid at obeying orders *and* giving them, as long as there's someone over them to tell 'em what to do."

"Governor Suetonius *is* telling him what to do," protested Quintus.

"Yes, but Postumus has never seen the governor and has no more imagination than a bull. All he really knows and cares about is his own general and his own legion. He loves and is protecting Valerianus, who, I have heard, grew up in the same Rhineland village with him."

Quintus considered this and nodded. "That's all very well, and I think from the look in the prefect's eyes he's suffering in that stupid gnat-sized mind of his—but what are *we* going to do now—and more important—what will Suetonius be able to do without this legion?"

"That," said Dio, curling his legs up under him on the coffer, and quirking one eyebrow, "is precisely what Fabian and I've been wondering. But I'd suggest, before you join our fascinating and so far quite useless discussion, that you get some sleep, my friend!" He indicated a strip of stone flooring next to the pile of standards. "That elegant accommodation is—so far—unreserved. I say 'so far' because we never know, of course, when some other messenger from the governor may not arrive and be ushered into Postumus' unique hotel! Here," he said, interrupting himself with brisk practicality, "put my cloak under your head, which I see from the wince you just gave is still aching."

"And might stop aching if you'd stop babbling, you little southern wag-tongue," interrupted Fabian, grinning at Quintus. "I'm not the talkative type myself. . . ."

But you're both mighty good fellows, thought Quintus thankfully. This fact was the one ray of light in a decidedly grim blackness. For a moment before he fell asleep he pondered on the irony of his position. After all the dangers that he had already escaped—from the Britons, from Boadicea, from these last days of perilous journeying through enemy country—how dismal it was to end up now with a banged head, imprisoned in the very heart of what should have been about the safest place in Britain for him —the Roman fortress of the famous "Augusta" Second Legion!

It was midday when he awoke, but there was, of course, no light in the strong room except the lamp. Quintus raised his head, which felt much better, and saw that Dio and Fabian were playing checkers with different colored fragments of wheat cake. They had carved the board on the back of a coffer with the little eating knife which Balbo had allotted them after their weapons had been taken away.

"My game," said Fabian sternly, picking up and munching one of his men. "Now you owe me forty thousand sesterces. Mark it up!"

"Oh, but no, Fabian—you cheat yourself," protested Dio, solemnly scratching a row of M's on the wall. "It's forty-one thousand I believe; you forget the wager I lost on our fly race when my fly basely disappeared up the air shaft. . . . Hullo . . ." he added, catching sight of Quintus. "You finally wake up?"

"Uhmm" yawned Quintus, stretching, then gingerly feeling the bump on his head. "And delighted to find I've such rich companions. I should think you could've bribed Balbo and the whole legion by now."

"Yes—you'd think so," answered Dio, chuckling. "Only I'm afraid they'd not be impressed by airy numbers on a wall. Our actual material wealth amounts to four pennies between us. How about you?"

"A bit more than that. I was given a purse for the journey at Chichester, but I—I don't seem to have used much."

"Tell us your experience from the beginning," said Fabian gravely. "We've just been killing time till you woke up."

The two earlier messengers naturally knew the grim story of Roman misfortunes up to the time Fabian had been sent from London, and as they listened intently to Quintus' account of the forced march south to Chichester, the governor's speech to his officers, the massacre in London, and Quintus' appointment as messenger to Gloucester, even Dio's cheerful face grew long. "It sounds very bad," he said quietly. "Only the Fates know what's happened to

Suetonius' force by now. You say he was going to try and march north to the Thames and wait for the Second to join him? How long ago was it you left?"

"Well," said Quintus, counting, "I left Monday noon, and it's been—let's see—two and a half days. Today must be Thursday."

"But this is Friday," said Fabian, glancing at the scratches which counted the days.

Quintus stared at him dismayed. He drew his heavy dark brows together. "All along I've had the oddest feeling that I've lost a day somewhere. I can't understand it."

"Probably that bump on your head," said Dio kindly. "Makes one dizzy for a while. And it really doesn't matter."

Quintus knew it was not the bump on the head, but he let it pass. There were far more important things to be decided.

"What do you think the prefect's plans for us are?" he asked. "Just keep us here indefinitely until and if Valerianus recovers from this fit of madness?"

Both young men nodded. "That's my guess," said Dio.

There was a gloomy silence, then Quintus said, "If we could only get to the tribunes somehow with our messages. . . ."

Fabian shook his head. "I doubt it would do any good. Most of them are Germans like the majority of this legion. I don't think they'd disobey their commanding officer—not if Postumus told them he thought these messages weren't genuine, which I think in a muddleheaded way he's made himself believe."

Quintus sighed, depressed by the soundness of this reasoning. There was another silence. Then Quintus roused himself and cried passionately, "But by Mars and by the spirit of my beloved father, we've *got* to get out of here and back to Suetonius ourselves! We can't just sit here like toads in a hole when we know what they're up against. Your own legion needs you two, and my General Petillius needs what small help I can give. Why, they may be fighting Boadicea right now!"

"Exactly," said Dio, smiling a little as he tightened the thong on his sandal. "Fabian and I some time ago came to the same conclusion."

"Yes, of course," said Quintus contritely. He began to pace the tiny cleared space between the coffers. "What

123

about Balbo?" he said after a moment. "Couldn't he be overpowered when he puts the provisions in here?"

"We never see the guard," answered Fabian. "He shoves our food through that hole down there." At the bottom of the door there was a square of about eight inches filled with a block of wood which barred it from the outside.

"I see," said Quintus wearily. "Yes, of course, most strong rooms are built so they can be converted to temporary cells."

"There *is* one very feeble hope," said Dio slowly. "Friday's pay day. They have to get at the money to pay the troops and they wouldn't dare skip now when they don't want them suspecting anything queer. Last Friday, Fabian hadn't arrived yet and I was here alone when Balbo and Postumus rushed in here and counted out the coin they needed. They bound me, and you can imagine that with my size and unarmed, I could scarcely fight off that tow-headed elephant . . . but with three of us . . . and you, Quintus, are pretty big yourself . . ."

"Not *that* big," said Quintus ruefully, but his eyes suddenly shone. "Yet that's a great idea, wonderful, at least it has a chance . . ."

Fabian nodded, less impetuous than the two younger men, but no less excited in his quiet way. "We must plan this very carefully," he said. "Think of every possibility and try to be ready for it."

The hours dragged by. They had no idea what time it was but could at least tell that it was day by a faint glimmer in the air shaft. Dio thought it had been about sundown when they had come for the army pay before, and, as the glimmer grew fainter, the three of them grew tense and silent. They had made what preparations they could, which consisted chiefly in transforming Quintus back into something like a Roman, as the Silure costume could only be an embarrassment in a Roman fortress—though indeed none of them dared think how they would get out of the fortress even if, by a miracle, they got out of the strong room. They had hacked off Quintus' long native trousers, so that his knees were again bare, and covered his tartan tunic with Dio's mantle. It was during this process that Quintus had been puzzled to feel something hard in the breast of his tunic and discovered

Regan's brooch. He held it in the palm of his hand, and in spite of his tenseness, a feeling of extraordinary sweetness flowed over him—sweetness and reassurance. It was as though a shutter half opened, and, in the crack, he could see her face looking at him with love, and hear a low tender voice saying, "Yet—I want you to remember some-day—this will keep you safe."

"Quintus, Quintus," said Dio, craning over to see what Quintus was staring at, "surely not a lady's brooch . . .? And a British lady's brooch at that . . .? Though now I remember you made some offhand mention of a girl who guided you . . . surely our little blind god, Cupid, has not loosed a careless arrow?"

"Oh Pax, Dio—hush up!" said Quintus with an embarrassed grin, closing his hand over the brooch. "I'm mighty glad to have this brooch, for I've a hunch it'll bring us luck," and he pinned it back inside his tunic.

"Well, we need it," said Fabian somberly. "Nothing but the most extraordinary favor from Fortuna is going to get us out of this fix, and I hereby vow to build an altar to her if she protects us."

Quintus and Dio murmured agreement and fell silent. They waited.

Quite a while went by before their sharp ears heard a noise in the vestibule, then the slow grating of the bolt as it was drawn back.

The three young men instantly flattened themselves against the wall behind the door. Surprise was their only hope.

The first part of the plan worked perfectly. The door opened wide. Balbo walked in carrying a bunch of keys for the coffers. He was dressed in helmet and full armor, his sword gleaming. The prefect followed, his mammoth body also armored in ceremonial gilded bronze with red epaulettes, for he was to review the troops later. He wore no helmet, nor indeed would his head have cleared the ceiling if he had, and he had not bothered with a weapon, having perfect faith in the strength of his enormous hands.

"Now where are they?" he said to Balbo. The three had known that they could go undiscovered no more than a second, but it was that second which they counted on. They sprang around the door. Fabian, flourishing the little knife, leaped out sideways at Balbo, while Quintus and Dio made a concerted rush for the prefect's knees and, grabbing them, exerted all their combined force to jerk the big man off balance.

For an instant Quintus thought they had succeeded. The prefect tottered and, letting out a sharp grunt, he swayed, while Quintus with desperate strength pounded upward with his fist against the massive chin. The prefect's great head wove from side to side; astonishment, rather than Quintus' blows, stunning his slow mind. He tried to raise his arms but could not, because Dio was clinging to them like a monkey, while Quintus went on hitting.

Suddenly the prefect let out a bellow of rage. He shook Dio off and seized Quintus by the neck. We've lost! thought Quintus. Red mist swam in his eyes as the huge fingers tightened on his windpipe then he heard a resounding thwack, and the fingers round his throat went limp.

He blinked and staggered back to see with amazement that the prefect was clutching at the air, reeling. Then he sprawled face down over one of the coffers.

Dio sprang to Quintus' side and they stared at the fallen giant.

"What happened?" stammered Dio. They both swung around at the same moment, remembering Fabian.

Fabian was standing by the wall gazing open-mouthed, not at the prefect, but at Balbo, who was in the act of hurriedly sheathing his sword.

"HE did it!" gasped Fabian, pointing at the guard. "He knocked Postumus on the head from behind with the flat of his sword."

"Aye," said Balbo, "I did it, or you young fools'd have had every bone in your bodies broken. Now be off with you quick, before he rouses."

The prefect was already beginning to snort and groan.

"Be off with us?" repeated Quintus. So sudden was this reversal of their expectations that all three young men were having trouble taking it in.

"Back to your legions, back to the governor! May Jupiter Maximus get you there safely," and Balbo added on a lower note, "May the great god also take pity on this legion and commander which have disgraced Rome forever. Go out by the southern portal. Titus is on guard there. Tell him only that you're sent back. No more. And the password today is 'Gloria et Dignitas'—glory and dig-

126

nity are *brave* words for the *brave* 'Augusta' Second Legion, are they not?" He said with indescribable bitterness, "Go! Your weapons are in the corner of the hall!" He bent over the prefect.

The three young men obeyed, picking up their weapons and walking with controlled speed out of the staff-quarters door. Most of the legionaries were lined up in the forum waiting for their pay. No one noticed the three. They came to the south portal and gave the password as Balbo had told them. Titus, the sentry, let them through without comment, until Quintus, who was last, stepped through the gate. Then Titus whispered, "I'm glad you fellows are all right. What's been happening up there?" He looked toward headquarters. "Are we marching soon?"

Quintus dared not answer but hurried away after Fabian and Dio on a track that led toward the east.

CHAPTER VIII

THE YOUNG ROMANS marched for a long time without speaking: Quintus, a cavalryman, had not been as well trained as the two official messengers in the long easy stride that the legions were taught; a pace designed to cover a steady three miles an hour, no matter the conditions. But he was taller than the other two and had no difficulty in keeping up with them along the hilly trail. Fabian led because he had traveled this very route last week on his way to Gloucester from London.

The moon shone as it had the night before, so that when the sky suddenly clouded over, they had come a long way across several ridges, and through brooks and copses. It had begun to drizzle when they reached a clearing, in the center of which was an ancient burial mound, a long barrow surmounted by a cairn of stones. Here Fabian stopped.

"I think we should get some rest," he said. "I remember seeing a cave over there on that hillside when I came by before. I'm sure it was up here to the right of this cairn. We could keep dry in the cave."

They were in a deserted part of the Cotswolds and had seen no native huts at all since leaving the fort. The cairn and the track were evidence that Britons sometimes passed along here, but no Roman road had as yet been built in this direction.

"Well, I'd be pleased to keep dry," said Quintus, as they struck off the trail and began to climb the hill, "but I'd be a lot more pleased to have a square meal. Even those wheat cakes would help."

For some time Quintus had felt nothing but relief at

their escape from the fortress, but now it occurred to him that their present situation gave little cause for rejoicing. Ahead there was a four-day march, at best, to find Suetonius' forces, which they were not even sure of locating. Also they must traverse Atrebate country. Fabian's encounter with an Atrebate on the way west would indicate that that tribe too had revolted against the Romans. Moreover, their weapons consisted of but two swords and Quintus' clumsy native spear—hardly the most efficient means of killing game or defending themselves.

"But I've *brought* some food," said Dio unexpectedly, with his bubbling little chuckle. "I scooped it up from the table outside the strong room while we were getting our weapons. Guess what it is?"

"Wheat cakes!" cried Quintus, with resignation, and gratitude.

"Exactly. Our own daily allotment Balbo had ready to bring in to us."

"And mighty useful to have," observed Fabian approvingly. "I was so thunderstruck, when I realized that Balbo not only wasn't fighting me but was watching for a chance to bang Postumus over the head, that I didn't have my wits about me."

Nor I, Quintus thought ruefully, aware once again of his own lack of forethought as well as his inclination to blunder and blurt things and act on impulse. For an instant, there was again that queer little stab of half memory. Somewhere, lately, he had stupidly blurted out something that had led him into unnecessary danger. Led him and someone else—Regan? But how could it be? Like an image in a pool, he glimpsed the cold angry face of a man in a green robe, against a background of tremendous upended stones. The image dissolved as Fabian said, "Look, there's the cave!"

Ahead on the hillside amongst a stand of white birches, they could dimly see a pile of rock and a black opening in the pile which, they found when they got nearer, led into a cave quite large enough to shelter the three of them, crouching. It had an overhanging ledge and was dry.

They settled themselves comfortably against the rocky wall and began to devour the wheat cakes, which Dio produced from beneath his leather jerkin.

The army's standard wheat cakes might be monotonous fare, but they had been designed to be the best hungersatisfiers for the least bulk. They were made from crushed whole wheat mixed with fat pork and water, then baked into hard flat biscuits. Three of them apiece took the edge off their hunger but left nothing for next day.

"I wonder," said Quintus, "if I could possibly spear a rabbit for us with this thing." He balanced the spear on his fingers. "The Britons do, but I can't seem to throw it straight, though I've practiced plenty."

"Beaver maybe," said Fabian. "I noticed a dam on the brook below. We'll see if we can't get one somehow when it's light. Beaver's not bad eating, but I admit I don't much fancy it raw."

The making of fire was a difficult process so the Romans were accustomed to carrying only dried or cooked provisions with them. In emergencies they commandeered a live ember from some peasant's hearth.

"I watched Pendoc—that was the Briton I told you about—making fire with two sticks," said Quintus. "I could try. It seems to me that there are quite a few useful bits of knowledge neither my Roman school nor the army ever taught——" He broke off abruptly. "Listen, what's that?" he whispered. "Something's in the back of the cave."

They all stiffened, turning toward the small dark tunnel behind them, where there were faint scuffling noises mixed with higher sounds, like mewings or squeaks.

"Oh, bats, of course," said Fabian, who had had more varied experiences than the others. "They always live in caves."

The other two nodded. "Of course."

Dio yawned and said, "Well, I don't need a bat's lullaby to make me sleep. Call me when you've caught AND cooked that beaver, boys—and I'd suggest you add a little wine and truffle sauce to make it tastier!"

"Ha! You lazy lout," said Fabian sternly. "Every man to his own breakfast."

Dio snorted, Quintus laughed. There were good-natured grumbles back and forth as to the use of the cramped space for sleeping; each one of them aware that they were joking so as not to think too much. Finally the three of them curled up on Dio's mantle and spread Fabian's mantle over the top of them.

The white birches near the mouth of the cave cast faint

shadows over the sleeping three as the sky grayed into early dawn.

Quintus was sleeping heavily and dreaming of Rome. An extremely pleasant dream in which his mother was laughing with Regan, who was dressed in gorgeous clothes like those of Nero's beloved Poppaea—all peacock satins and cloth of gold, which Quintus had somehow provided for her.

He didn't know what the sound was that woke him, but he sprang up grabbing his spear. The other two woke at his jump, and without knowing what the trouble was, both backed against the wall and drew their swords in one motion.

For a second, between sleepiness and the uncertain light, they could not see anything, but then the sound which had awakened Quintus came again. A low snarling growl that raised the hairs on his neck. He had never heard that sound before yet he knew what it was, even before Dio whispered, "Wolves."

Then Quintus saw two huge shapes slinking toward them through the birches.

"Shout!" cried Fabian. "Make a noise! They'll go away, they can't be hungry this time of year."

The young men shouted and yelled until the cave reverberated behind them, but the two sinister shapes behind the birches did not retreat. They stopped and watched, their cruel yellow eyes glinting with menace.

"Jupiter Maximus——" groaned Fabian suddenly. "I know what it is—this is their lair and those were wolf cubs we heard in the cave. They're going to attack us!"

The great gray wolf and his mate had started to move forward again. They drew slowly nearer, and the horrible low growling grew louder.

Quintus' hand clenched around his spear. The mouth of the cave was too low. He couldn't straighten up to aim. He began to edge outside, until his head cleared the rock ledge.

"No, don't——" whispered Fabian. "If you miss him we'll have lost the spear. Get behind us, we've the swords——"

Quintus did not hear. His heart was pounding, but his mind was cool and alert as he carefully counted the distance between him and the larger wolf, who kept advancing. Quintus drew his arm back and waited. He saw the

131

white fangs bared, the slobbering red tongue. He saw the fur on the shoulders stiffen and rise, as the great beast tensed for the spring.

Quintus drew a rasping breath and waited yet another second. The instant the wolf lunged, Quintus hurled the spear straight at the lighter fur on the chest. There was a fountain jet of blood as the spearhead pierced to the wolf's heart. The wolf fell from midair into a twitching heap on the ground. And the other wolf, snarling and panting, stopped her stealthy advance and stood irresolute, the yellow eyes glaring at the heaving body of her mate and at the blood that spurted once more—and stopped.

"Bravo, Quintus!" cried Dio. He and Fabian rushed together toward the she-wolf. But she was too quick for them. She doubled back and flattening herself belly-to-ground ran past their drawn swords straight into the cave.

"Whew——!" breathed Quintus, looking down at the dead wolf. "Thanks be to Diana, to Fortuna, even to the Celtic gods, that I've finally learned how to throw that thing."

He hauled and tugged until the spear came out, dripping red. He examined the flint head, which was undamaged. Even the rawhide which bound the flint to the shaft had not loosened.

"Here, quick—help me," grunted Fabian, who was on his knees beside the wolf, expertly carving out a piece of haunch with his small knife. "Get a stick."

Quintus found a long pointed one, and he and Dio skewered the hunk of meat on it. Dio hoisted the stick over his shoulder. "Interesting change of menu," he said. "Wolf instead of beaver, one never knows. . . ."

"And one doesn't know what that she-wolf intends to do either," interrupted Fabian curtly, with a glance over his shoulder at the cave.

"Won't she stay by her young?" asked Quintus.

"Probably, or by the body of her dead mate, but——"

"We'd better be going," Quintus finished the sentence.

They started down the hillside with considerable haste, crashing through the thickets and brambles until they reached the barrow with its cairn of stones, and the overgrown rutted track. They started east again along the track and had gone a few yards when Dio, shifting the heavy hunk of skewered meat from one shoulder to the other, said, "You know, it suddenly occurs to me that

132

we've left our mantles and helmets behind in the cave, Fabian."

"Yes, it occurs to me too," said Fabian grimly.

"Also," continued Dio, "that returning for them doesn't appeal to me. Madam Wolf is in full possession, and for all I know has summoned all her relatives by now."

As if in answer to him they heard a sound floating down from the hillside behind—the long mournful howl of a wolf.

The three paused and listened, then walked on silently.

"So now we are in the same boat as Quintus," observed Dio after a while. "And there's nothing to show definitely that we're Romans, except the Fourteen on our jerkins, which can be hidden."

"And your swords," said Quintus a trifle enviously, but not as he would have said it yesterday. He now clasped his spear with confidence.

"And our swords," agreed Dio. "Though I hope we'll have no use for them—until the big battle. I find that my adventures of the last fortnight have left me with a—shall we say—disinclination for more excitement right away. I find myself shamefully thinking of a good bed, of sweet Neapolitan sunshine and music, of gentle smiling girls, and soft living generally."

"Go ahead and think," said Fabian dryly, striding ahead and lacing the top of his jerkin, for a cold wet wind had sprung up.

But Quintus was startled by something reminiscent in Dio's chatter. "I had a—a friend, in the Ninth, who used to talk like that," he said hesitantly, though realizing at once how little Dio and Lucius really resembled each other. Dio's rueful complaint had been humorous, unresentful. For all his light manner, Dio had a tremendous loyalty to his job, and a strong sense of duty. While Lucius——

"Something queer happen to the friend?" asked Dio, looking up at Quintus. "Your voice was funny."

Quintus wished that he could confide the pain and disillusionment that the thought of Lucius gave him. But he couldn't bring himself to say, "I was awfully fond of him and *thought* he was a friend, but he let me down once; and far worse than that, when all our men were being slaughtered around us, he ran away." So he nodded briefly instead and stared ahead at Fabian's shoulders.

"That's too bad," said Dio gently, thinking that the friend had been killed in the disaster to the Ninth, and he changed the subject. "How long are we going to lug this blasted hunk of wolf meat, Fabian? I'm hungry enough to eat it raw."

The elder messenger turned around. "I hope we won't have to. There's a native hut there in the valley; perhaps they'll let us use their fire."

They looked down at an isolated little British farm. Behind a paling there was a round wattle-and-mud hut thatched with reeds.

From the circular vent on top of the roof, smoke was curling upward. They descended the hill and approached the stockade of saplings that enclosed the barnyard. From inside, a dog barked savagely, a goat bleated, and pigs snorted alarm. The three Romans stopped outside the barred gate.

"I'll try," said Quintus. "I speak enough Celtic." He raised his voice and shouted, "Greeting! Greeting! We are friends, will you talk to us?"

The dog lunged against the gate snapping and growling, but there was no other answer.

"Better get that spear ready, Quintus," said Dio, chuckling. "This dog is as fierce as the wolf."

"I'm sure there's someone in there," said Fabian. "Isn't that a baby crying?"

Quintus nodded and tried again. "Greeting friend! All we want is a bit of your fire. We can pay."

At that an old woman stuck her head around the deer hide that served for a door. She had long tangled gray hair, and a fat stupid face. She inspected the three men and spoke to the dog, who stopped his furious barking. "What is it you want?" she quavered.

Quintus explained again, and the old woman disappeared, but in a moment she waddled out into the yard. "You can *pay?*"

As Quintus assented, her pendulous lips parted in a silly gratified grin. She unbarred the gate. "Where do you come from?" she asked, as they threaded their way between sheep, goats, and pigs, while the dog sniffed suspiciously at Dio and jumped toward the wolf meat.

"From the north," said Quintus vaguely.

"Oh," she said, "that's why your speech is not much like ours. You're off to fight the Roman swine too, I suppose!" She walked into her hut as Quintus grunted something that might be agreement.

"She thinks we're Britons, be careful," he whispered hastily to his friends before they stepped into the hut.

When their eyes got used to the smoky darkness, they saw pallets of animal skins stretched along the walls, and a huge loom at which a young woman was weaving lumpy gray strands of rough wool, while she nursed a naked baby on her lap. She was a handsome girl with the dark hair and greenish-hazel eyes of the western tribes. She turned her head as the three men came in, and giggled, blushing a little

"Cook your meat there," said the old woman, pointing to the fire. "It's good to see visitors. My daughter and I are lonely since our men all left to join the great Queen of the Icenians."

The girl sighed and murmured, "It is so. They've gone far away."

Quintus, looking at them, realized that they were both simple women without guile, who had probably never traveled three miles from their home. Maybe I can learn something, he thought with sudden hope.

"When was that?" asked Quintus casually, kneeling beside Dio, who was broiling the meat, while Fabian sat down on a pile of skins and watched Quintus, knowing that something important was afoot but unable to understand what they said. "When did your men go?"

The old woman shrugged. "Long time. I don't know. Some days——"

"It was the day Mog here got his tooth," said the young mother eagerly, forgetting her shyness. "His father felt it with his thumb before he left. This many days——" She held up three fingers.

Not so long then, Quintus thought, with growing excitement. "And where were they going to find Queen Boadicea?" he asked. "We want to be sure we know the way."

But the two women looked blank. "Over there somewhere——" said the old one, pointing toward the east. "Past the Great White Horse, then along the ancient road of the little people, and far—far toward the rising sun."

Quintus hid his disappointment at this vagueness by poking an ember under the broiling meat.

"Why don't the *others* speak?" asked the girl suddenly,

135

casting curious looks from Dio's snub-nosed merry face to Fabian's grave, thin, freckled one.

"Well, you see, they come from a far country over the mountains," said Quintus hastily. "Their tribe has a different language."

The women were satisfied by this, and Quintus was astonished at their naïveté until he realized that they had doubtless never seen a Roman, certainly not one without the full panoply of flashing armor. As for him—by now, with a week's stubble of beard, the spear, and the increasingly dirty tartan tunic he must make a fairly convincing Briton.

The girl left the loom and put the baby carefully down near Fabian who recoiled from it in dismay. She went to a large pottery jug and poured its contents into a clay cup. "We have goat milk," she said shyly to Quintus. "Have some."

"Not unless they pay," said the old woman quickly.

Quintus reassured her again though wondering how much the greedy old woman would demand. He accepted the milk with thanks. When they had all drunk and choked down great hunks of the rank wolf meat, Quintus knew they must be going, but tried once more for information.

"Have all the Atrebate men left to join the war against the Romans?" he said, putting his cup down and smiling at the girl.

"The *Atrebates?*" she repeated, with some surprise. "Perhaps. We don't know. They live yonder in the country of the Great White Horse. WE are Dobuni," she said proudly.

"Oh, I see——" But Quintus was dismayed. So the revolt had spread to still another nation. How many tribes had Boadicea amassed by now? Where WERE her forces? Did these women know anything at all? It seemed unlikely and yet an intuition told him to keep on.

Dio was staring at him, obviously wondering why they were delaying but afraid to ask in Latin. Fabian had risen from the skins and was waiting by the door.

Quintus made them both a quick quelling gesture and shook his head. Both men instantly understood and nodded. They turned their backs and negligently pushed aside the deerhide curtain as though considering the weather outside, thus leaving Quintus a free hand.

"We have traveled a long way to do battle," said Quintus with perfect truth, "so far that we've become fearful that we may have missed the fighting. Do you think that perhaps there has been a great battle already between the Britons and the Roman governor's army?"

The women looked at him intently, willing to answer, but comprehending neither his thought, nor the way he had expressed himself in his halting Celtic.

He tried again, more carefully. The old woman hunched her shoulders and, losing interest, stirred a mess that bubbled in an iron pot over the fire.

But the girl, who was pleased with this break in her monotonous life, finally got the gist of his meaning and shook her head. "I think not. The runner who came to call my husband and brothers, he said the great Queen would wait until so many tribes had joined her that the land would be black with warriors as far as eye could see. And women too will fight," she added wistfully, "but my husband would not let me go. 'Tis not the custom of the Dobuni."

"I should hope not," Quintus murmured, and was forming another question when the girl picked up her baby and, holding it to her breast, cried, "Andraste, the glorious goddess, will give us victory, yet I grow a little afraid when I think of the many, many Roman monsters, so many—like pebbles in a brook."

I wish there were, thought Quintus ruefully.

"I have never seen a Roman," continued the girl. "I've heard they have tusks like wild boars, and claws like bears, and heads made all of gold that gleams in the sun. The Icenian runner said that when he passed near their camp on his way here, he saw one watching from a mound who had a red horse's tail growing from his head and who flashed in gold all over."

Quintus put on an expression of horrified interest and held his breath as he said, "Where was this camp where the runner saw the Roman in gold? Did he say it was near a river? Near a town?"

She looked puzzled. "He did not say—except it was a place the Roman beasts had always used, since the first one came."

"The *first* one? Did he say the name? Was it Julius Caesar?"

"It might be—yes. I think he used some sound like
137

'Caesar.' Why do you care so much?" she said curiously.

"Simply," answered Quintus, "that I and my friends would like to look at the Roman monster too, before we meet it in battle. . . . Good wife, you've been most kind, you and your mother. We thank you and must go."

"The payment——" whined the old woman, looking up from the pot. "For the fire—for the goat milk!"

"Yes. Yes." Quintus reached into his pouch. "Shall we say three pennies?" Which was generous recompense. He held out the coins. They were, of course, Roman coins stamped with the head of Nero, but he thought he could invent some story to explain that to these people, if they happened to notice.

"What are *those*?" cried the old woman contemptuously. "Little thin bits of metal! You promised to *pay*."

"I *am* paying," protested Quintus. "This is good money. It's used all through the land."

"That's no *payment!*" The old woman's fat face grew suddenly purple. She knocked Quintus' hand viciously, so that the coins scattered on the trampled clay floor. "You are lying thieves——"

"Here, wait a minute!" cried Quintus between anger and astonishment, as Dio and Fabian, seeing trouble, came silently to stand beside him. "I don't understand——"

"Why, Mother wants an iron bar, of course," said the girl frowning. "A small one."

"A large one!" screamed the old woman, shaking her fist.

"Small or large, I don't know what you're talking about," snapped Quintus, when he felt a tug at his tunic and saw Fabian make a motion of the eyebrows. "I must speak to my friend a moment."

By the door Fabian spoke in low rapid Latin. "These backward tribes use iron bars for currency—that's the trouble, isn't it? They've never seen coins."

"What'll we do?" breathed Quintus.

"Talk yourself out of it, somehow."

Quintus turned back to the women and tried. The girl soon accepted the fact that the tribe these three came from did not have iron bars and that the coins on the floor were ample payment, but the old woman did not. Her bleary eyes were sparked with fury. "Liars! Thieves!" she

138

kept shouting. "Pay me! Pay me!" And she hopped up and down angrily.

There was no use arguing. Quintus sent the girl an apologetic look and turned hastily to go with the others, whereupon the old woman, in a frenzy, grabbed the ladle from the iron pot and flung it straight at Quintus. The pot contained some sort of stew and the ladle carried a portion through the air in a boiling spatter. Quintus ran, and the others with him, pelting ignominiously across the barnyard, while the old woman yelled insults after them, and the dog snapped and bit at their heels.

They vaulted over the gate, thus getting rid of the dog, and ran down the road until they were out of sight, when Dio took a good look at Quintus and burst into a roar of laughter. "Stop! Stop!" he choked. "Let us take count of our wounds after this shameful defeat. Let us at least cleanse Quintus from beans—and yes"—he reached up and removed something from Quintus' hair—"and pieces of stewed rabbit."

Quintus scraped beans off the back of his neck in disgust. "That blasted stew was *hot!*" he said angrily, then suddenly joined Dio in laughter. "We're a fine dignified credit to the legions! Routed by a pot ladle!" Even Fabian chuckled as he said, "And a mangy little dog who's made off with some of my sandal."

"As long as he didn't take part of your ankle too," said Quintus who spied a brook and sluiced his head and neck in it until all the old woman's stew was off him. He came back to the others and said, "No, but listen—I *did* get some information, I'm not sure just how useful. Is there any place that's called 'Caesar's Camp'?"

"But, of course," said Fabian and Dio together. And Fabian continued, "It's a British earthwork fort, which Caesar is said to have used. We camped there with Suetonius on the march down from Wales. It's this side of the Thames and southwest of London. Why?"

"Because I think that's where Suetonius is now," and he told them what the girl had said.

Fabian nodded. "That seems very likely. At least we know where to strike for. What else did she say?"

"I tried to find our where all the tribes were convening with Boadicea, but all they knew was something about 'beyond the White Horse and then the ancient way of the little people, and far, far toward the rising sun'—doesn't make any sense."

"Yes, it does," said Fabian thoughtfully. "I know their Vale of the White Horse, in fact we'll be there ourselves tomorrow, and the ancient road would be the Icknield Way, which leads northeast from there though I'm not sure how far. At any rate Boadicea is apparently somewhere near her own East Anglia."

"I wonder what she's been up to since you last heard of her, Quintus?" said Dio, all the laughter gone from his face.

"To no good for us, that's sure," answered Quintus. "Boadicea is a terrible woman with the heart of a lion—of a wolf——" he added somberly, thinking of the wolves that morning, and their fury to protect and avenge their own.

As they strode along, he thought of Regan and the unspeakable torture she would have suffered from Boadicea if she had not escaped. His hand went of itself to feel the outline of the brooch Regan had given him which he still wore inside his tunic next to his breast. A piece of sentiment he hoped the others hadn't noticed. Perhaps, if he had shown the brooch to the old woman in the hut, she might not have been so furious at not getting her iron bar; the Druid sign on it seemed to work miracles with the Britons—— But wait a minute, he thought, so startled that he stopped dead on the road, how do I know that little red enamel snake is a Druid sign? Did Regan ever say so?

"What's the matter, Quintus?" asked Dio. "Something bite you?"

"A thought," said Quintus, starting to walk again.

The little Neapolitan chuckled, and the three of them marched on. But all the rest of that day, as they cautiously skirted the Dobuni capital of Cirencester, which was hardly larger than a mud village, and came down out of the hills to the banks of the infant Thames, Quintus kept mulling over the puzzle. He rehearsed every word that Regan had said to him that night by the campfire in the forest. There had been no mention of the brooch. Yet he was convinced that he had been present when that brooch had been shown to hostile people, and that they had looked on it with respect. When the three young Romans paused to drink from the river, Quintus suddenly said, "Do you believe in spells? I mean do you think something could be done to make one forget a day in one's life?"

Dio laughed and said he forgot things all the time, but Fabian answered gravely. "That depends—I have seen magic things in Gaul. I know it's possible. Why?"

"Because I think it's happened to me. But the memory of that day is coming back a little."

"Is it important?" asked Fabian. "Does it affect our mission, or Rome?"

"I don't think so. It feels"—Quintus' tanned skin flushed, and he gave a lopsided smile—"like a private matter. . . . a very strange one."

If Regan did *not* really desert me, he thought, if after all she was with me on that day I think I've lost—— A feeling of exquisite relief came to him, and a rush of tenderness which was cut short by a cry from Dio. "Look! Dinner—ahead! Just as I was offering up another vow to Fortuna!"

A hundred yards away on the riverbank a man sat by a roaring fire turning a large pig on a spit.

Quintus sniffed at the intoxicating odor of roast pork, then saw beyond the fire an even more alluring sight.

"Horses!" he breathed, his eyes sparkling. "That's better than dinner!"

"We will hope to get both," whispered Fabian, drawing his companions behind a large hazel bush, "by fair means or foul. But let's be sure he's alone."

They couldn't see the man very well, because he was sitting on the other side of the campfire, but he seemed to be large, with a mane of shaggy blond hair, drooping yellow mustaches, and a plaid mantle of a type Quintus had seen on Britons in the towns. Behind him was a native two-wheeled cart with an ox between the shafts. Around the cart were seven rough-coated ponies tethered and grazing on the lush grass.

"He seems to be alone. Let's try our luck. Quintus, let loose your best Celtic again."

The three walked out from the hazel bush and advanced with their arms high in token of peace while Quintus called out a friendly greeting.

The man gazed at them through the smoke of the fire. "Oho!" he called in a deep bass voice. "And what do you want of a poor unfortunate, who is protected by the gods?"

Now what does he mean by that? Quintus thought, not sure he had understood. But as they walked nearer, he and the others paused in consternation.

In the face the man turned up to them, one eye was gone. Where it had been, there was a shriveled pit, while the same blow had sliced off half his nose. Nor was this all, for on the ground beside one long tartan-covered leg, there was a stump bound neatly with the rolled up trouser. "One leg, one eye——" whispered Quintus. "He says truly that he's unfortunate."

The three looked at each other with the same dismayed thought. They needed food and wanted the horses and had planned to help themselves if the man resisted, but this was different. The man was a cripple.

"Who are you and where are you going, friend?" stammered Quintus.

The man flicked off a piece of crackling from the pig, ate it, and licked his fingers. The one eye peered at them sardonically. "I am Gwyndagh, a trader in horses. I travel where I wish, no man molests me."

Which would be as true for Romans as it was for Britons. In both countries cripples such as this were considered to be under direct supervision of the gods who had punished them, gods jealous of their rights, and who would send fearful wrath on a person who mistreated one of their chosen.

"We need to eat, O Gwyndagh," said Quintus, sighing and glancing hungrily at the roasting pig. "And we badly need horses to carry us on a journey of great importance. Can you think of any way we can get these things?"

It was hard to be sure, but it seemed that beneath the greasy yellow mustache there was a smile. The shrewd eye roamed calmly over each of the young men.

"Come here—all three of you," said the horse dealer at last. They came slowly and stood close to him. He raised his hand and pointed a finger at Dio. "Say the words 'Caesar Augustus Nero, Emperor of Rome,'" he commanded. Dio was so astounded to hear this come out in passable Latin that he stifled a gasp and looked for help to Quintus, who did not know what to make of it either.

"*Say those words*," repeated the cripple sternly, "or you have no chance of help from me."

Dio swallowed and said, "Caesar Augustus Nero, Emperor of Rome," very fast, while Gwyndagh listened critically. "Now you," he said, turning to Fabian, who hesitantly complied, and then Quintus.

"So," said Gwyndagh. "I thought so. You are Romans, though you try to hide it—legionaries too. I see by the shape of the swords."

"You see a great deal with that lone eye, good Gwyndagh," said Quintus, still trying to brave it out. "But how can you be sure? My friends may have stolen the swords."

"That might be," agreed Gwyndagh, twirling the spit nonchalantly. "But there is *no* way to steal the true accent of a Roman when he salutes his Emperor!"

So that was that. And no more use pretending.

"Well . . ." said Quintus uncertainly, for he could not tell how this revelation of their nationality affected the man. "You are right. But we still need meat and horses. We have some money—Roman money, but not enough to pay you fairly."

"You are honest," said Gwyndagh, breaking off another piece of crisp pork skin. "It is not believed by many of my fellow Britons, but some Romans *are* honest. I might trust you with three of my horses. I might trust you with half my pig, except that you will soon fight the British forces and will certainly be killed. Then I would be quite out of pocket."

Quintus translated this to Dio and Fabian, while Gwyndagh listened intently. He understood much Latin, having lived in London and purveyed horses to the Roman government.

"Then there's nothing for it," said Fabian to Dio and Quintus, "but to pay for the pig and take three horses, whether he likes it or not."

"And brave my curse? The curse of the gods? Of the all-powerful Lugh who rules the earth and skies?" cried Gwyndagh in a great solemn voice.

"I'm sorry," said Quintus, "but we must chance it. And the curse of Lugh will doubtless not affect a Roman."

Gwyndagh considered this in silence, then appeared to make up his mind. "Very well," he said. "Give me what money you have, and do as you like. In truth I am pleased to ill serve the Icenians since it was an Icenian chariot of the whirling knives that did this," he pointed to his face, "some years ago. This"—he pointed to his am-

143

putated stump—"came from another cause we won't go into."

"Many thanks," said Quintus fervently, and the other two echoed him.

Gwyndagh shrugged. "If you are not killed—which, I repeat, seems improbable—I'll find you again some day, never fear. And get back my horses."

"You shall have them!" cried Quintus. "And a pouch of gold as well. We promise you!"

Fabian made a grimace at this exuberance, but he said nothing. They sat down beside Gwyndagh and since the pig was roasted, split it carefully. They ate a portion of their half, stowed the rest in their bags, paid Gwyndagh all their coins, and departed with the three likeliest ponies.

The last they saw of the horse dealer, he was clambering into his cart, managing skillfully on his one leg. He saw them looking after him and raised his arm in a philosophic wave, that showed he bore no resentment.

"I think our luck has turned," said Dio. "And now we can really hurry—thanks be to Fortuna!"

CHAPTER IX

AFTER LEAVING THE HORSE DEALER, the three Romans forded the Thames and slept a few hours in the Vale of the Great White Horse, within sight of that strange chalk beast, big as a village, which the ancient people had long ago carved out of the green hillside.

The white horse with its long spindly legs and snaky head was worshiped by the Atrebates, and this was the heart of their country. The three young men, therefore, proceeded with great caution, but they had no further adventures. They climbed to the Ridgeway track which they followed for some time. It was almost deserted. The natives they did pass occasionally were old or very young, and incurious. It was clear that the vigorous portion of the Atrebate population was not there, and all too easy to guess where they had gone.

Calleva, the Atrebate capital near Silchester, also seemed deserted, a circumstance which Fabian found sinister. He told the others that once there had been a Roman camp adjoining the British town, where for some years following the Claudian conquest, the Atrebates had lived on friendly enough commercial terms with their conquerors. But now the Roman camp was as abandoned as the town seemed to be, though the three young men dared not investigate closely.

But they found mute testimony of what must have happened as they picked up the road again the other side of town and nearly stumbled over the body of a man in a Roman jerkin. The jerkin was marked with the sign that showed him to be a veteran of the legions. The Roman sprawled face down as though felled in a frantic rush to

145

escape. The back of his head was crushed in; the blood-stained slingshot stone which had crushed it lay beside him.

"There were sights like these along the way when I marched down from Lincoln with the Ninth," said Quintus grimly, turning from the dead Roman. "And we dare not even take the time to give him burial rites."

"No," said Fabian.

Nobody spoke again for a long time. They followed the good road that the Romans had built, and the next noon came upon a milestone that said "A Londinio XX." The milestone had been overturned; filth and the half-burned entrails of some animals were scattered on it.

They gazed at this small senseless expression of hatred, then Fabian said, "Twenty miles to London, or what was *once* London, but 'Caesar's Camp' is considerably nearer. We'll soon know now if Suetonius is there."

They kicked the horses' flanks and broke into a rough gallop.

The sun came out from behind clouds. It shone upon the loops and windings of the Thames and it shone—after they had struck through forest and emerged onto a broad heath—upon the sight they had all prayed to see. Above strong circular ramparts made of earth and timber and stone, the eagle standard reared itself proudly and the imperial flag was flying!

They dismounted by the great ditch which was the outer ring of fortification, and suddenly all three of them looked at each other, and joined hands in a firm quick clasp. They needed no words to seal their friendship; the recognition of all they had been through together, and of what was still to come, was enough for each of them.

Leading the horses, they strode to the first sentry post. The lookout on the ramparts had already seen them and recognized Dio and Fabian.

Here there was no difficulty, no mystery as at Gloucester's fortress. Here they were received with shouts of joy, and backslappings, and a chorus of eager excited questions. "Where's the Second? Are they just behind? We've been watching for days!"

The questions were soon repeated by the governor himself, for they were ushered at once to Suetonius' red and white striped tent in the center of the fort. He got up to receive them, his heavy-jawed ruddy face alight with relief. "Welcome! Welcome, imperial messengers!" he cried. "You *too?*" he added, recognizing Quintus with a smile. "So you are all together. Ah, this is good news. Where's General Valerianus and the Second? Are you much ahead of them?"

"Your Excellency," Fabian dropped to one knee, and, fixing his eyes on the governor's gilded sandals, continued very low, "we bring bad news. . . . The Second Legion has not left Gloucester."

"Not left Gloucester! But this is monstrous. I can't delay battle much longer. It'll take at least five days' march to bring the whole legion. What's the matter with them? When are they starting?"

Fabian grew very pale. He cast one quick glance toward Dio and Quintus, then raised his eyes resolutely to the governor's empurpling face. "They are not starting, I'm afraid—Your Excellency."

The governor's harsh breath rasped through the tent. "Have they been slaughtered? Has the fortress fallen? By all the gods, what *has* happened?"

"Nothing has happened to the legion, Excellency, they're all right—I—we——" Fabian looked beyond the governor to the officers and guards clustered around the back of the tent and the entrance.

"For the honor of Rome, Excellency, it is better that we tell you alone," he said very low.

It looked as though the governor's ready and violent temper might get the better of him, but he restrained it and made a signal. The other men left the tent, all but the general of the Fourteenth, and Petillius Cerealis of the Ninth, who had greeted Quintus with a quick look of welcome. These two stood behind the governor as Fabian explained what had happened to the Second.

"You mean," roared Suetonius, banging his fist on the table, "that because Valerianus is a madman, and the prefect a coward, the Royal 'Augusta' Legion refuses to obey my orders? You mean that half of Rome's military force in Britain is bottled up useless on the other side of the island, while the Britons are preparing to massacre us all?"

"It is so, Excellency."

"Do you two say the same?" said the governor looking at Dio and Quintus.

They bowed their heads. "It is so, Excellency."

147

Suetonius slumped heavily onto his chair. Beneath the brilliant gilt of his cuirass, his shoulders sagged. The thick fingers of his right hand drummed slowly on the table top, while he stared, frowning, at the wooden floor. "Leave me alone, all of you!" he muttered. "You'll get your orders later."

Silently, the two generals and the three messengers filed out of the tent.

General Petillius put his hand on Quintus' shoulder as they started across the parade ground. "Come with me—I want to talk to you."

In Petillius' quarters, Quintus enjoyed the first full meal he had had in days. His general sent for a flask of Gaulish wine and indulgently watched Quintus drink and eat, forbearing as yet to question him.

"You don't eat too, sir?" asked Quintus timidly, after a bit.

"No, I'm not hungry," said Petillius briefly, though his tired eyes smiled. Quintus saw that there were new grooves in Petillius' thin cheeks; he no longer seemed like a very young general. Suddenly Quintus guessed.

"This is your own supper I'm eating, isn't it, sir?" he said unhappily. "Food *must* be getting very low in camp."

"We'll hold out a few more days," said Petillius. "Boadicea's forces too are short of provisions. They've descended like a storm of locusts on all the country north of the Thames. And they sowed no crops this spring—so certain were they of victory."

"I wonder they haven't crossed the Thames and attacked us," said Quintus, putting down his wine cup. "We—Dio, Fabian, and I—were dreadfully afraid of that during these days we were struggling to get here."

"Boadicea is so confident that she's been in no hurry for the final showdown. These three weeks since the sack of Colchester, and our"—Petillius paused and went on through tight lips—"the disaster to the Ninth, she's been fully occupied, burning and plundering—London, Colchester, St. Albans. She's managed to torture and kill about fifty thousand civilians as well. She has—as I say—been busy."

Petillius' dry understatement awakened Quintus to the immediate gravity of the crisis. He felt a thrill of hatred for the Queen, a thrill intensified by the memory of her behavior to Regan. And yet in justice he could not help saying, "Boadicea was terribly wronged, sir, in the beginning. I was there and I saw. I saw her while Catus' slave flogged her. I heard the two princesses screaming when Catus' men——"

"I know." Petillius cut him short. "Rome has made a series of incredibly stupid blunders, of which my own is not the least. We have through our own folly let loose a monster of death and destruction. But this monster must be cut down so that peace can return to Britain."

Peace here? Quintus thought—and could not imagine it.

"Sometimes the sword is the only way to peace, Quintus," said his general quietly. "Now I want you to tell me in detail exactly what has happened to you during these seven days since I saw you last at Chichester, when you were disguised as a very peculiar Silure, jogging on a native pony between a villainous looking Briton, and an extremely pretty girl!" The twinkle flickered briefly in Petillius' hazel eyes.

"Yes, sir," said Quintus, coloring a little. "But, sir—I don't suppose you'd know about it, but I've been worrying a bit about my horse, Ferox. Do you suppose he was brought here from Chichester with the other cavalry horses? He's an awfully good mount, sir," Quintus finished quickly, loathe to have his general suspect sentimental fondness for the horse.

"Your Ferox is here," said Petillius, smiling. "I saw to that myself."

Quintus sent the general a look of passionate gratitude and launched at once into a carefully unemotional report of his journey.

Petillius listened without interrupting, and at the end he nodded. "Yes, there're some bits of information here which'll be useful, however disquieting. So the Dobuni and Atrebates are also joining Boadicea?—well, at least we've got the Regni with *us*."

"As auxiliaries, sir?"

"Yes. The old King Cogidumnus let us have a couple of thousand men. They're not up to our regulars, of course, but they'll fight all right."

"How many are we altogether, sir?" asked Quintus. He had been speculating anxiously on this question with Dio and Fabian and was not sure he would be trusted with such an important military secret. But Petillius had throughout

149

this interview been treating him without consciousness of rank and he answered at once.

"Our force consists of the full Fourteenth, six thousand in all, a third of the Twentieth, plus the Regni and a sprinkling of Cantii warriors from Kent. We have altogether a bare ten thousand."

They were both silent, thinking of Boadicea's forces, which now numbered sixty thousand at least—probably more.

"Yes," said Petillius, reading Quintus' expression. "It is not a very bright picture." He made a sharp dismissing gesture with his hand and changed the subject. "All that Druid business you told me is interesting. So you think you have forgotten a day, do you?"

"Yes, sir. I'm sure of it. I'm beginning to think I got to Stonehenge, for I keep remembering little bits. I think I met the Arch-Druid too—he was Regan's—that's the girl —Regan's grandfather."

"Aha," said the general thoughtfully. "I met Conn Lear once—a remarkable man. I don't agree with our governor that all Druids should be exterminated—but that's neither here nor there. Tell me every single thing you can remember about the Druid stronghold."

Quintus complied, and the general listened carefully. Then he said, "Quintus, you had some special reason for volunteering to take that mission to the west, didn't you? I could see that."

"Yes, sir, to find the bones of my ancestor, Gaius Tullius, who was killed there by the Druids during Caesar's campaign."

"And did you find them?"

Quintus shook his head. "I'm sure I didn't. I seem to remember speaking about it, and that someone—Conn Lear, I think—grew frightfully angry."

"And was the girl angry too?—ah, never mind, I shouldn't have asked that," Petillius smiled. He started to say something else, but they both turned as a messenger ran into the tent and, kneeling, murmured to the general. Petillius rose. "This is what I've been expecting. The governor has decided on a course of action. He'll speak to the troops at sunset."

"What course of action, sir?" asked Quintus quietly.

"Do you need to ask?" The general looked into Quintus' earnest face, then glanced toward the pegs where his own magnificent armor hung, the crested helmet with the red horsehair fringe, the ceremonial shield, and gilded sword. "We fight."

"Thanks be to Mars," Quintus murmured, and meant it. Soon now the long-drawn-out suspense would be ended. Yet deep within him, for the first time he was aware of cowardly shrinking—a hollow feeling. On the plank floor it was as though he saw Flaccus' dead eyes staring up at him. "I'm young, I don't want to die yet." The sentence flashed through his mind as though someone else spoke it, but his face showed nothing as he stood respectfully awaiting orders.

"Before we go out to hear the governor," said Petillius after a moment's silence, "there's one—ah—detail—to be attended to."

"Yes, sir," said Quintus, and waited. His general walked to the camp table and picked up a square of parchment and a white staff about two feet long.

"For you," said Petillius, handing the parchment to Quintus, who looked down to see his name jump out at him in heavy black script. *"Quintus Tullius Pertinax,* standard-bearer to the third cohort, Ninth 'Hispana' Legion of the imperial troops. . . ."* There were a lot more words that Quintus skipped over in a daze, because all he could see were the last ones that seemed to ring out like a shout. *". . . from this time forth is promoted to CENTURION."* He read them three times, and his face and neck flamed.

"For *me. . . ."* Quintus whispered, staring at the parchment. "Oh, General Petillius . . ."

"For you, Centurion," said the general in a carefully light tone. "You're very young and sometimes foolhardy —but you have courage, intelligence, and leadership, and you've shown a remarkable amount of ability in dealing with the Britons since you landed. I wish you to be one of my officers. Here's your badge of office." He handed him the centurion's staff. "Apply at once to the quartermaster's department, for the proper helmet and shield. AND," he added sternly, cutting across Quintus' excited stammers of thanks, "I believe my men refer to me as 'old fusspot' —nevertheless, I command that you have a shave, a bath, and a haircut before I have to look at *you* again. HURRY UP!"

"Yes, sir," breathed Quintus gratefully and ran.

It was certainly the sprucest, shiniest young centurion in all the legions who emerged from the barracks just before Governor Suetonius mounted the earth platform to address the troops.

The portions of Quintus' old uniform which he could still wear had been brought from Chichester and cleaned and polished by one of the auxiliaries. The crested helmet and the shield with its great murderous boss in the center were issued to him by the quartermaster. They had belonged to some other centurion whose use for them was over, but Quintus did not let himself dwell on that. His own sword hung again at his belt and he carried the deadly Roman cavalry lance in one hand, his staff of office in the other. There hadn't been time to greet or saddle Ferox before Quintus strode across the parade ground with the proud long step of the Roman legionary, his tall figure followed by many approving eyes. Quintus had been popular in the Ninth, and the remnant of that demolished legion, now temporarily merged with the Fourteenth and Twentieth, had spread news of him. Dio and Fabian had been forbidden to tell the true story of their trip, but there were many who knew that, though the dangerous mission to Gloucester had somehow ended in failure, it had been gallantly carried through nonetheless.

Quintus had not yet been told what "century" would be assigned to his command, so he walked over to join Dio, who was standing near the altar to Mars.

"Well!" cried Dio, bowing and saluting with excessive ceremony. "Will you look at what's happened to our shabby little Silurian friend from the back hills! I tremble with awe. I am blinded by the glory." And Dio covered his eyes with his hand.

"Oh, don't be an ass," said Quintus, grinning and striking down Dio's hand. "I'm the same simple boy at heart, no matter how gorgeous I may appear."

"Don't you believe it," Dio snorted. "There never was born a sweet simple boy who was also a Roman of Rome. Masters of the Earth, you people are, and now you *look* it too."

For an instant of dismay, Quintus thought that Dio was jealous of his promotion, and was hinting that it had come from the usual preference shown by the High Command for officers actually born in the imperial city.

Dio sensed this and his sparkling eyes softened. He

shook his curly black head as he took Quintus' hand in a warm grasp. "My silly jokes! Quintus, I congratulate you with all my heart, and so will Fabian when he knows. We expected it. And I'll make a prophecy. You'll be a tribune some day, and then a general yourself. A good one!"

Quintus returned the handclasp, much moved by this generous extravagance and feeling guilty that he should be eligible for promotion when his two friends were not. Official messengers such as they were attached to a legion's staff and bore no special rank, though they were very well paid.

"I wouldn't have got this," said Quintus soberly, "if my legion weren't so short of officers . . . and there weren't considerable doubt as to whether . . ." He did not finish the thought aloud—whether any of us lives long enough for a promotion to matter one way or the other —but Dio understood, nodded quickly, and said, "Here comes the governor."

Suetonius' approach was heralded by solemn horn blasts. He was a majestic figure as he mounted the platform and stood beneath the huge standard of imperial Rome—a solid silver eagle. Behind him were grouped the smaller standards of the legions represented here tonight, the Twentieth, the Fourteenth, and the Ninth.

A spontaneous cheer broke from the packed troops below as Suetonius looked down on them, and the governor's heavy face lightened into a smile. He raised his arm slowly in acknowledgment.

When the outbreak had died down, Suetonius leaned forward and began to speak in a strong, confident voice which gave to the troops no inkling of the shock and dismay he had shown earlier in his tent.

They would wait no longer for the Second Legion, said Suetonius. It was unfortunately delayed. But they could manage very well without it! One thoroughly trained Roman soldier was worth a dozen scatterbrained savages. They all knew that. And they had but to remember the many glorious Roman victories in the past when a handful of legionaries had easily vanquished a whole host of the enemy. Besides, it seemed that the British forces included women, and were led by a woman!

"Almost," cried Suetonius with infinite scorn, "am I ashamed to command that we do battle with such a weak

153

and miserable foe! Yet too long this silly painted people, this woman-led rabble, has been allowed to have its head. Yes, there have been unfortunate incidents, it's true. There have been disasters you all know of—to one of our legions—to the towns of Colchester, London and St. Albans—but we must forget these! Nor consider that they represent anything but temporary setbacks!"

"H-mm," whispered Dio to Quintus, "Brave words . . ."

"And much needed . . ." nodded Quintus, himself impressed by the powerful assured voice, and wholeheartedly admiring the governor as he never had before.

"You must not think of past disasters," the voice continued, "EXCEPT as they fill your heart with zeal to fight and avenge Romans who have been slaughtered, and other innocent people who have suffered hideous fates, deaths inflicted by these unruly hordes who are little better than beasts—and here, there's one thing I must warn you of! Like wild beasts these barbarians whom we shall fight make howlings and shriekings and fearful noises when they do battle. To this you will shut your ears, each one of you in grim determined silence performing your appointed task—as it shall be allotted to you!"

Then Suetonius spoke to them in some detail, telling them the general plan he had made. They would march in the morning, cross the Thames, and take up a position north of it in Epping Forest, a position which he had chosen after long consultation both with maps and with some of the London refugees who knew the terrain well. He had reason to believe that Boadicea's forces were on the move and would arrive at that spot in about two days; then they would fight. More than that it was unnecessary for the legions to know. Their officers would acquaint them with special orders.

In conclusion, Suetonius suddenly turned, and grabbing the great silver eagle from the chief standard-bearer, held it in the air and cried, "As our imperial eagle rises high above our heads, so will the winged Victory soar above us! And we shall win through to law and justice, win through to honor, win through to the greater glory of our beloved and eternal Rome!"

"Ave! Ave! Ave!" thundered the troops. "Salve! Roma! Roma Dea!" Then they cheered the Emperor and the governor, and clashed swords on shields in their exuberance.

The enthusiastic cries resounded for some time unchecked, while Suetonius, with the two generals and his staff officers, walked back to his tent.

"That was a good speech," said Quintus on a long shaky breath. His eyes shone. "I'd no idea the governor was such an orator. He manged to remove all the qualms I confess I had. But how do you suppose he knows when Boadicea's apt to turn up at the place he's picked?"

"Cantii spies," said Dio, who had been talking with his friends during the time Quintus was cleaning up and dressing. "Several of them have been sneaking around up north keeping track of Boadicea's forces. They tell me one of our spies got back here just before we came."

"Oh," said Quintus thoughtfully. "And I suppose Boadicea has spies watching *us*?"

Dio nodded. "It seems they caught two Iceni in that wood over there the other day. One wouldn't tell anything even under torture, but the other admitted Boadicea's forces were almost out of food, and she was on the march preparing to wipe us out and overrun the south, where she must think we've left more food than there is."

Quintus would have conjectured further as to the exact site Suetonius had chosen and the military tactics involved, but an orderly came up and, saluting, inquired if this were the centurion Quintus Tullius Pertinax? Upon receiving Quintus' rather flustered assent, he announced that the new centurion was to report to headquarters for orders.

The next morning at dawn when the Roman army marched from camp, Quintus rode on Ferox at the head of the century of ninety men that had been assigned to him. His company was composed of auxiliaries—all of them Regni from Sussex, on their native ponies, except for three men of the regular cavalry who had belonged to the Ninth, part of Quintus' original cohort.

Quintus was proud of his first command. The Regni were a tall fair Belgic tribe, much Romanized, as their Sussex coast, like that of the Cantii in Kent, had always been in close touch with Gaul across the water. They were fine horsemen, already well trained in the use of cavalry weapons, and were pleased to have been assigned to a real Roman who understood much of their language. They showed this by extra smartness and co-operation

155

as the legions marched along the broad road, then forded the Thames at Chelsea.

Ferox leaped up the far bank of the river in one great bound. The horse had had no exercise in days and was, moreover, so glad to see his master that he was prancing with excitement and had to be continually curbed.

"Quiet down, you black imp," Quintus whispered affectionately. "I'd like a tearing gallop just as much as you would, but we're not going to get it!" He patted the gleaming black satin neck, and Ferox slewed a bright eye around and wuffled as though he had understood.

Quintus reined to one side on the bank, carefully watching the remainder of his company splash through the ford, and found himself near one of his men, a stocky little Italian called Rufus, with whom he had played many a ball game in the garrison at Lincoln.

"Ferox is so mettlesome today," remarked Quintus amiably. "I'll bet you he could beat your horse by a mile, pig or no pig!" This referred to a race he'd run against Rufus in Lincoln, which had been a standing joke in the garrison because of a pig which had entangled itself amongst the contestants. Rufus had never before failed to hotly defend the merits of his own horse, and Quintus was startled to have him smile politely and say, "Yes, sir. No doubt."

Jupiter, thought Quintus, he answers me the way we did Flaccus! A gulf had opened; he had become a thing apart, an officer. It was a rather lonely state, and Rufus had quite rightly reminded him of it. Quintus soberly counted his company, saw that they were all there, and gave the order to proceed.

Ahead and behind Quintus' century, the legions marched, four abreast, like a broad shining ribbon of gold unrolling under the hot late August sun.

They advanced along the river road until they came to an island in the Thames on their right, the marshy Isle of Thorns, where there were a couple of native huts raised on piles, with blue curls floating up from the smoke vents.

Governor Suetonius, with most of the legions, had already marched past the island, to the rhythmic pounding of sandaled feet, and Quintus' company had reached a point near the island when he thought he heard a voice calling his name. He couldn't be sure above the clop-clop of the horses, but he looked around startled.

"Quintus!" cried the voice again—a man's voice—and suddenly out from behind a thicket on the bank there rode a familiar figure. It was a Roman legionary on a drooping mud-caked horse, a legionary in tarnished armor. The face was half hidden by the helmet and chin strap, but before the horseman got near him, Quintus recognized the arrogant set of the head, and in the repetition of his name he heard a defiance not unmixed with nervousness.

"So it is you—Lucius Claudius," said Quintus tonelessly, as the newcomer wheeled his horse into step beside Ferox. "What do you want?"

"The legions are on the march again." said Lucius, his handsome face bent down, not quite looking at Quintus. "I saw Suetonius pass some time ago. I waited until you came along."

"You saw from where?"

Lucius hitched his shoulder backward. "From there, the Isle of Thorns, where I've been—been—staying."

"You found natives to receive you—Lucius? To keep you in safety, even though Boadicea's forces must have overrun this bank?"

"No—not here. She turned north for St. Albans before she got here. I found a British woman, a Catuvellauni, who has given me shelter in her hut."

A woman, of course, Quintus thought. So that's where he's been this three weeks!

"Then you had better go back to her, Lucius Claudius. You'll have more need of her protection than ever, since we are going to fight, and Boadicea's forces have grown immeasurably since that disaster to the Ninth, *part* of which you may remember."

Lucius caught his breath, his knuckles whitened on the bridle. "What's happened to you, Quintus!" he cried sharply. "You were my friend. Oh, I see they've made you a centurion, and I suppose it's gone to your head. But you've no right to speak to me like this! You *all* retreated. It was every man for himself!"

Not until our general gave the command, Quintus thought, and as it happened *I* was captured—but he rode on in silence for a while, somewhat ashamed of the bitterness with which he had spoken, aware of the bond between them, the old friendship Lucius had invoked. And yet unable to really trust again.

"Why have you come out of hiding, Lucius?" he said at last in a cold voice.

"I'm sick of the filthy natives and that mud hut. I want to get back where at least I can hear my own language," said Lucius flippantly.

"Then gallop up ahead until you find General Petillius. Report to him. He's a just man. He'll decide what he wants you to do."

Lucius reached over and put his hand on Quintus' arm. His lazy persuasive voice held all its old warm charm as he said, "Why can't I ride along with you, Quintus? The High Command'd never know. You're an officer, you can do what you like. I'll fall behind amongst your men. No one'll notice. By Mercury, I've missed you—my old comrade!"

Quintus felt a sinking in his chest. He remembered the cowardly thoughts he had himself suffered yesterday. He remembered all the loyalty he had once felt for Lucius. He thought that perhaps if Lucius was really ashamed and wanted to make amends, he should be spared further ignominy—until after the battle. But—Quintus forced himself to consider the other side, for he was an officer now with full responsibility—the legions depended on discipline. They were going forth to a great battle in which no individual's private feelings should count. And Lucius was—quite simply—a deserter. The decision could not be Quintus'.

"I'm sorry," he said at last. "You can't hide here with me. If you want to rejoin the legions, you must report to our general."

"He hates me, Quintus, he always has—he'll put me in irons—he'll have me flogged—I won't——"

"Then go back to the Isle of Thorns—where you can skulk the rest of your days. I'll not give you away."

Lucius gave him a strange look. There was hatred in it, and yet there was appeal. The slack-mouthed young patrician face for a moment showed a sort of confused despair. Quintus set his jaw and turned his head.

Lucius slowly pulled up his horse's reins and rode out of the column. He stayed a moment by the roadside, then disappeared into the trees, in what direction Quintus could not see. And Quintus was miserable.

Soon, on the march, they forded the little Fleet River and passed the ruins of London—acres of black rubble and ashes, a devastation even worse than Colchester had been.

The faces of the legionaries grew pale and set as they remembered the thriving little town as it had been so short a time before, and remembered the thousands of wretched people who had stayed there to be slaughtered.

The legions turned north and marched some miles along the ancient British trackway until, in the heart of Epping Forest, they reached the strategic spot which had been previously picked by Suetonius. It was a funnel-shaped ravine, with just room enough for the disposal of the Roman forces at the narrow end, which was backed by dense underbrush and forest. The steep-sided funnel opened out onto a gravelly plain, also enclosed by rolling banks and forest.

Quintus at first did not understand the special advantages of this site, until the governor ordered his whole force into battle formation, and they practiced over and over throughout the remaining hours of daylight, and on into the night, until every man knew his place and exact part. The foot soldiers, each armed with two javelins or pila, a light one and a heavy one, were wedged in the center, thick and deep, for a thin strung-out line could not hope to hold against Boadicea's immensely superior force. The cavalry were placed on the flanks which meant riding the lower rises of the ravine. The legions were not to move as the Britons came into view. They were to wait with their shields above their heads to form a roof, until Suetonius gave the signal to throw the first barrage of the deadly Roman javelins. Suetonius himself enacted the part of Boadicea's force in these grim rehearsals, galloping from the north along the trackway into the plain in front of the ravine, judging the exact distance necessary to be kept between the two armies, scrutinizing the placement of all his troops, and finally watching the exact effect as he gave the signal for action.

At midnight the troops were permitted to rest. Each man munched the dried beef he had brought with him and drank brook water. Quintus did the same and after presenting Ferox with a small bag of oats, went to find General Petillius.

The generals and tribunes were in conference with Suetonius beside a small campfire on the edge of the ravine. The army had traveled unencumbered; not even the governor had a tent. Quintus had to wait some time before Petillius, with a grave nod of agreement to the governor, walked away from the fire, and saw him.

"Well, Centurion, what's the matter? Trouble with your new command?"

"Oh, no, sir. They're a fine bunch. Forgive me for disturbing you, but—did Lucius Claudius Drusus find you today?"

"Lucius Claudius Drusus?" Petillius frowned. "You mean that Optio who deserted? Certainly not. What do you mean?"

"This, sir," said Quintus unhappily, and told the story of his meeting with Lucius though he did not say where it had happened or reveal Lucius' hiding place. "I don't know if I did right. He—I think now that he was desperately ashamed—underneath. I think he wanted to fight, and we need every man we can get—but——"

"But he has a rotten streak. It's the curse of aristocratic Rome nowadays and even our Emperor Nero——" Petillius checked himself. "No, you did right, Quintus. If he had come, I wouldn't have been too hard on him. Forget it, and go get some rest."

CHAPTER X

SOME OF THE SEASONED LEGIONARIES slept a little that night of waiting in the ravine, but Quintus was amongst those who did not. He sat down near Ferox with his back against a rock; and, staring into the night, thought long thoughts. He thought about his mother and his sister in Rome, and about the quest which had brought him to Britain in the first place and which had once seemed the most important thing in the world. Then he thought of Regan. He wore her brooch still, pinned now to his white linen tunic beneath the shining centurion's breast-plate—Regan, far away on the other side of Britain in the Arch-Druid's weird house of the living tree. It was there by the tree that he had kissed her, there they had both admitted the love between them.

"You won't remember this, Quintus—or I couldn't have let it happen . . ." But he *did* remember now! Suddenly, as he sat there in the ravine waiting for the battle, the last mists lifted. The herb of forgetfulness had ceased to cloud that strange day's memory.

"Regan," he whispered, sending her a prayer of longing so strong that he felt it must reach her. Then he got up abruptly for the soft pink dawn was breaking through the trees. He examined Ferox in detail, his hoofs, his saddle, bit, and bridle, before he moved amongst his men, rousing those that were asleep, telling them all to check their own horses and weapons again.

He said good morning to Rufus, who saluted and said, "Looks like a fine day, sir."

"It does indeed," answered Quintus, turning to see Dio and Fabian behind him.

161

"Fine day for walloping queens?" chuckled Dio. "We came to breakfast with you, a sentimental gesture. *Viva* the wheat cake!" He crunched one between strong white teeth.

Fabian gave Quintus his slow smile and said, "Dio's only concern is his stomach, as you may remember."

"I remember," Quintus grinned back, deeply glad to see them, knowing, though neither of them gave any indication of it, that they had wanted to say good-by—in case. "Where've you two been placed?"

"In the middle of the Fourteenth, fifth cohort, just behind the shock troops," said Fabian. Both young messengers were dressed in full legionary armor today, carrying the light and heavy javelins and the short sword. Their oblong shields hung ready on their backs.

"I, in fact, am in a superb position," announced Dio airily. "It's a handy thing to be somewhat small—by scrunching a bit I find I can keep myself thoroughly hidden behind the enormous Gaul in front of me—most convenient."

Quintus and Fabian, who both knew Dio's courage, ignored this nonsense, and Quintus said, "I wonder what time we may expect to be honored by Boadicea's arrival."

"Not long after sunrise, I should think," answered Fabian. "One of the Cantii spies was sure she camped this night at Braughing."

As he finished speaking, a trumpeted "alert" sounded through the ravine. "Well, here we go on our merry way," said Dio, clapping Quintus on the shoulder. "Good hunting!"

"And to you," answered Quintus. They shook hands all around. As Fabian and Dio sped back down the sides of the ravine toward their posts, they each paused at a rude little stone altar to Jupiter that the men had set up. They touched it reverently in passing.

Yes, thought Quintus, who had made vows at that altar earlier. May the great supreme god have Rome in his keeping this day. . . . He turned to make sure that each of his men had mounted.

The sun rose brick-red over the forest top. Its rays slanted briefly into the ravine where the legions waited, but then clouds gathered and the sky turned pearl gray. A cool breeze began to blow from the north. Still nothing happened. The horses moved uneasily, now and then nibbling at the sparse grass. The men murmured to each other in subdued tones. There was a break in the tension when the governor rode up on his huge bay horse, while Quintus and his company snapped smartly to attention.

Suetonius ran his eyes over the men's positions and equipment. "Repeat your orders, Centurion," he said to Quintus.

"Wait. . . . Don't move while the legions make the first onslaught after your signal, Excellency. Then charge here"—Quintus pointed right along the slope—"following General Petillius Cerealis around our own men below and veer down amongst the enemy to meet our left cavalry wing behind enemy lines."

The governor nodded. "A pincer action. General Petillius will decide when to veer." He jerked his bridle and rode off to inspect the next centurion and company behind Quintus. In two hours Suetonius had checked on all his troops and returned to a place in the center rear of the foot soldiers.

This is a dream and nothing is ever going to happen, Quintus thought after a while, when like all of them he had repeatedly strained his eyes toward the far end of the gravelly plain outside the ravine. There was no hint of sun now, nor any rain either, only the murky gray sky and the fitful breeze.

It was the breeze that brought them the first warning, just as Quintus had tested for the twentieth time the sharpness of his lance's nine-inch iron point and shifted the weight of the heavy shield on his forearm.

A quiver ran through the silent massed legions as they heard a distant hullabaloo, a confusion of rumblings and shoutings from the north. The governor's trumpeter let out a low pulsating blast.

As one man, the legions behind the front row raised their shields and clanked them into place above their heads to form the famous Roman "testudo," a metal roof impervious to falling spears, arrows, or stones. And they waited. The sounds to the north grew louder, but there was still nothing to be seen.

Quintus, concentrated on watching the plain ahead, did not hear rolling pebbles and stumbling hoofs behind him, until Ferox shied as another horse's nose hit his croup. Quintus turned sharply and saw Lucius looking at him

163

with the same expression of uncertain bravado he had had when he appeared by the Isle of Thorns.

"What in Hades——" breathed Quintus. "How'd *you* get here?"

"Followed the legions, waited through the night—came along the trail—down the side of the ravine."

"Well, get over there, out of that man's way! Don't raise your lance or move, until you see me move. Watch General Petillius up ahead on the white stallion for the signal, d'you understand?"

Lucius swallowed. "You despise me, Quintus—don't you—I mean, 'Yes, sir, my Centurion, I understand,' " he added bitterly, but obeying, he moved up the slope to the place indicated by Quintus.

Then Quintus forgot Lucius, forgot everything but the far end of the plain, as thousands of howling British warriors galloped into sight through the trees.

The plain rapidly blackened with advancing figures brandishing clubs and spears and small round bronze shields. Here and there Quintus discerned an archer, and then he saw, thundering behind the mounted warriors, a line of war chariots, the murderous curved knives flashing around on the hubs of the wooden wheels.

The Romans did not move. They made no sound. The Britons could have no idea of their numbers, because the funnel-shaped site disclosed only the point of the legionary wedge.

The Britons, gazing down the plain toward the ravine, let out yells of triumph and paused well out of range apparently waiting for something. Quintus had a good view from the slope and soon saw what they were waiting for —when a large war chariot lumbered into view. There was no mistaking its occupants.

Boadicea, tall as any of the chiefs in the chariots near her, was shouting and brandishing a spear. Her masses of tawny yellow hair whipped in the wind. On her head was a bronze helmet; on her chest, the gleam of the royal golden gorget. Behind her crouched the two redheaded princesses, clinging to the chariot's high sides as their mother lashed the horses and drove frenziedly amongst her suddenly quietened forces.

Quintus could see that she was shouting to her troops, and he caught isolated phrases. "Avenge!" "Rid our land of the hated tyrants!" "Kill them all—no mercy!" As she shouted this she reined in her horses and shook back a fold of her streaming mantle. A small animal jumped out and leaped to the ground.

Quintus saw long ears on the little beast. Their sacred hare, he thought, as the Britons let out a wild tumult of exultation, for the hare had turned and darted away to the east.

"Victory! Andraste! Andraste! The hare runs toward the sun for victory!" The Queen's harsh cry of triumph could be heard over all the rest.

They were drunk, Quintus thought, drunk with confidence as well as the heather ale they had undoubtedly been swilling all night. They seemed unaware that the Roman forces might have charged, by now, so absolutely certain of invincibility had the Britons become through their recent unchecked conquests. No doubt they thought the Romans held back from fear. But they were advancing now, the Britons, in a great disorderly mass, pushed forward by arrivals at their rear. There were wagons, hundreds of them, wagons apparently filled with women and even children; Quintus could see long flying hair.

By Mars, and are they as sure as *that!* he thought with dismay that changed to anger. They had brought their families as spectators to watch the massacre of the Romans, as one might go to the Circus Maximus to watch the punishment of slaves.

And there were so many of them! It was true then that half the British tribes had joined Boadicea, for there were many thousands of warriors in that packed advancing horde, not counting the civilians drawn up in wagons on the far side of the plain.

Now it's coming, Quintus thought, and a thrill ran through him though he felt no fear, only a cold calculating expectation. Boadicea's chariot had disappeared back into her ranks while mounted tribal chiefs took her place. Toward the right, opposite Quintus' position, he recognized Navin by the Trinovante helmet. "And so the time you prophesied is here, Navin, and we meet as enemies," Quintus murmured grimly to himself.

The British front line was quickly forming. It was composed of archers, as the Romans had expected, and stone throwers. Quintus glanced at Petillius' erect back on the white stallion and then involuntarily behind

165

at Lucius. The young man's face was a glistening putty gray, sweat was pouring down it into his chin strap.

"Good luck," said Quintus softly, with a prick of pity, and never knew whether Lucius heard him or not, for the air exploded into a pandemonium of war whoops and battle cries, of twanging bows and the hiss of slingshots, followed by the harmless clatter and thump of the arrows and stones on the roof of shields above the legions.

The instant after, came the Roman trumpet blast and Suetonius' shout, "Legions *charge!*"

The shields came down again as in one motion, the flying wedge ran forward and as it ran discharged the light pilum, the snake-thin, razor-sharp javelin that could fly as far as an arrow.

The oversure Britons were taken by surprise. The archers and slingers, with no chance to rearm, staggered back under the onslaught and went down beneath the javelins. The Roman wedge broadened, the heavy javelins followed the light ones. They penetrated to the line of wildly plunging horses. At this moment General Petillius shouted and put his stallion to the gallop. The right-wing cavalry streamed after him along the edge of the tumult. A spear whistled past Quintus' ear, but he ducked his head unnoticing, watching the general, who raised his lance in signal and veered left, straight down into the middle of the enemy amongst the milling horde of British chariots and foot soldiers.

The left-wing cavalry met them there, and the Britons, utterly bewildered found themselves battling enemies on all sides—enemies whose management of the lance, the short slicing sword, the bossed shield, far surpassed the Britons' skill with cruder weapons. The heavy Roman armor turned blows for which the British had no protection.

Quintus had lost all awareness of himself. He had become a machine that cut, thrust, sliced, parried, and that yet managed Ferox, wheeling him between the swirling knives on the chariot hubs, spurring him into a momentary space away from a brandished club, and twisting to plunge his lance at a tartan-covered chest. The world had turned blue—the blue of woad stripes and circles on the savage faces, and it had turned to the red of blood.

At one time he felt a streak of fire run through his thigh and then forgot it. A wild Parisii lunged at Ferox's bridle, Quintus leaned over and bashed his face in with the sharp boss of his shield. The Parisii fell across the corpses of British horses, isolating Quintus behind a momentary bulwark; the fighting had surged forward and beyond him, as the Roman legions advanced with disciplined and murderous precision.

Quintus found that he was panting and forcibly quieted his breath while he soothed the trembling Ferox. Then he stiffened, paralyzed at a sight not far from him but across a barricade of overturned chariots and thrashing horses.

He saw General Petillius on foot, the white stallion dead beside him, fighting desperately with Navin, the Trinovante chief, who was still mounted. Navin's mouth was lifted in a snarl beneath the stripes of woad. His spear had knocked away the general's lance. Petillius was parrying the continual spear thrusts with his shield and short sword, but the Briton was backing him steadily into a corner formed by overturned chariots. Navin's spear darted down again and again; Quintus with horror saw that Petillius was tiring. He lifted his own lance and aimed it at Navin's constantly whirling back, praying that it could carry that far, and not hit Petillius.

But while he still aimed and hunted for a chance to throw, a horseman streaked up to the fighting pair. Quintus saw the lightning gleam of a Roman lance plunging into Navin. He saw the spurt of blood from Navin's breast, then saw the chief in a reflex action hurl his spear straight at the Roman who was knocked sideways by the impact and slid slowly off his horse and fell to the ground.

Quintus spurred Ferox, galloped to a better spot, then jumped the barrier and reached the three he had been watching. Petillius was standing, staring at the two men on the ground. The general was still dazed from the blows he had received, from the shock of nearly fatal combat. He looked up at Quintus without surprise. "The chief of the Trinovantes is dead," he said, "and it seems this lad has saved my life."

"Lucius!" cried Quintus, gaping at the crumpled figure lying beside the dead chief.

"Ay—Lucius Claudius—so he came to fight after all," the general said in a wondering voice. "But he's still breathing!" Petillius gave himself a shake and became his usual brisk self. He glanced down the plain where the

167

fighting now was—a plain strewn high with mangled corpses of men and animals. British corpses. "Here," he said to Quintus, "help me carry him under that tree."

Navin's spear had cut deep through Lucius' armpit into the lung. Quintus and Petillius stopped the bleeding by binding the wound tight with Lucius' undertunic, after laying him carefully down. He breathed in wheezing gasps as they left him, but his heart was beating well.

"Your horse is dead, sir," said Quintus. "Here's mine."

The general nodded and mounted Ferox. "Follow as quickly as you can," he cried and galloped along the side of the carnage.

When Quintus arrived on foot at the scene of battle, it was nearly over. The Britons' confidence had at last turned to terror. They had tried to flee, though the Queen herself hoarsely begged them to fight on. But blind panic had seized them, and they had surged back in mad confusion, only to be stopped by their own cumbersome wagons, which now blocked the retreat. The wagons were full of women who had come to watch the sport.

The legions' work from then on had been easy, and they had carried it out with merciless thoroughness.

Thousands of Britons had been slaughtered by twilight of that day when the groans and shrieks of the dying lapsed to a silence broken only by long-drawn-out wailings—the Celtic keening for the dead.

For Boadicea lay there too amongst her people, on the ground. Her shield was beneath her head, her spear beside her, the golden hair outspread. The terrible face of fury was calm now and white, and still. When she had seen the last of her people fall, she had not waited for the Roman capture, which she knew would come. There had been a tiny vial of poison hidden in her bosom, and she had swallowed the contents.

She had died on the British trackway at the north end of the battlefield with no one near her but her daughters and four old Icenian noblemen, her relatives. It was the dirge of the two princesses that wailed through the evening of the Roman victory.

The Romans did not disturb them. This forbearance was General Petillius' doing. Suetonius would not have been so merciful. Even in the midst of his great triumph, he had been infuriated that Boadicea had eluded capture. He wished to seize the princesses, at least, and drag the corpse of the rebel Queen throughout the land as an example.

Petillius had had the courage to combat his governor, pointing out that such a course would make a martyr of Boadicea and keep the British flame of hatred so hot, that never could the Romans hope to rule here peacefully.

"Show them that Romans can be merciful, Excellency," he pleaded. Suetonius consented grudgingly to let them mourn the Queen until he decided what to do with the princesses. But before he had decided, they had gone. The six had taken their Queen with them and rolled away in a wagon along a secret path through the forest to bury her with their own rites.

While the dreadful keening of the princesses could still be heard down the plain, Quintus and General Petillius had gone to Lucius, taking stretcher-bearers with them.

Lucius lay beneath the tree where they had put him. There was bloody froth on his mouth, but he looked up at them with a faint smile, and said, "We won?"

"We won," said Petillius. "The most glorious triumph against the worst odds Rome has ever had. Thanks be to the gods. I believe we've not lost over four hundred men, while all the British forces are wiped out—and Boadicea dead."

"Good," gasped Lucius painfully. He turned toward Quintus. "I surprised you, didn't I? You never thought to see *me* die a hero's death!" His weak voice still had an edge of bitter mockery.

Petillius made a sign to the bearers, who carefully moved Lucius to the stretcher. "I believe you will *not* die, Lucius Claudius," said the general gently. "You'll live to find that your brave act on the battlefield today has wiped out all that's gone before. It is forgotten."

Lucius sighed and shut his eyes. The stretcher swayed as the bearers picked their way amongst the scattered corpses. Petillius and Quintus walked on either side. Suddenly Lucius spoke again in the dream voice of half consciousness. "And yet I did not fight today either. I waited on the hillside watching, until the moment that I saw the general in danger—then only I forgot my fear."

"I know," said Petillius. "*All* that came before your slaying of the Trinovante chief is forgotten."

"I'm a patrician. I'm of the blood of our divine Emperor Claudius," the voice went on unheeding. "I wasn't

169

made to be a common soldier in a barbarian land, I've been miserable—full of hate and fear—hate and fear——"

"Hush!" said Petillius sternly, and the rambling voice stopped, though the labored breathing continued.

Quintus' eyes stung, he swallowed hard against the dread that Lucius might die. He didn't try to understand the complex misery that Lucius had suffered—from self-indulgence, from cowardice, and arrogance combined—the rotten streak which had been redeemed by one selfless gallant action. He felt only pity and the old affection, purged now of contempt.

They put Lucius down on a bed of leaves at the back of the ravine, amongst the other wounded, and the Fourteenth's skillful surgeon examined his injury by firelight and gave the young man a powerful medicine to drink. "I think he may pull through, sir," said the surgeon to Petillius. "Too soon to tell—— Hello," the surgeon added, looking at Quintus, "you seem to have quite a bit of gore yourself, Centurion. Is it yours or some Briton's?"

Quintus looked down in astonishment and saw that his left thigh and upper leg were a shiny mass of clotted blood. "I hadn't noticed," he said ruefully, though now he remembered the streak of fire he had felt in his thigh.

"You *will*," said the surgeon grimly, while he washed the leg in warm water. "Stiff as a log this'll be tomorrow! You'll have something to remember the battle by for quite a bit." He drew together the edges of a great jagged spear gash. "Lie down there beside your friend while I bandage this."

So Quintus lay down on the leaves beside the sleeping Lucius, and found that he was very glad to do so. But he was happy. An exultation shared by all the exhausted troops, too deep for loud rejoicing, almost too strong for realization; and yet some, like Quintus, suspected that this was a moment the world would not forget. Roman rule was once again established in Britain.

The next three weeks were a haze to Quintus, whose wound festered as almost all wounds did. He developed a high fever and was only dimly aware when he was taken back to base camp on the other side of the Thames and put in the tent hospital there. Various impressions penetrated the jumble of battle dreams, home dreams, and love dreams that chased each other through his confused brain.

He knew that Dio and Fabian had both escaped injury beyond a few cuts and bruises, and that they came to see him. He knew that of his own company only one auxiliary had been killed, that the over-all fatalities had been miraculously few and almost entirely suffered by the infantry's shock troops.

He knew that Lucius, who lay in a different hospital tent, still lived, though he was not out of danger.

At last there came a day when Quintus awoke without fever, felt an interest in breakfast, and managed to sit up shakily to consume it. While he was eating, Dio trotted into the tent bearing a plate on which reposed a bunch of fragrant purple grapes. "Aha! So we're much better, I see!" said Dio, squatting down by Quintus' pallet, and shoving the grapes under his nose. "Look what I've brought you!"

"Jupiter Maximus!" whispered Quintus, sniffing. "I haven't seen anything like those since I left Rome. How in the world. . . ?"

"A ship, loaded with provisions for us, arrived yesterday from Gaul. It's tied up at London, which, by the way, we've already started to rebuild!"

"A cargo of *grapes?*" exclaimed Quintus, with the first real smile he had produced since the battle.

"Well—no. There were a few bunches destined for His Excellency. I happened to be around when they were unpacked—and so——" Dio shrugged expressively, pulled off a grape, and popped it in his mouth. "I doubt whether the governor's much interested in grapes right now anyway."

"Oh?" Quintus leaned back on the straw pillow. "Not trouble?"

Dio looked around quickly before replying. Quintus, as an officer, had been given a corner of the tent, slightly isolated, and the patient nearest him was asleep. "The trouble is of Suetonius' own making," said Dio seriously and very low. "We've got a new procurator, Julius Classicianus, sent direct from Rome. A really good fellow, not like that fat scoundrel of a Catus who started the whole Icenian mess. I've been back and forth a lot with messages to Classicianus, so I know what he's like."

"But what's the trouble, then?" asked Quintus. "Unless

Suetonius doesn't like sharing the rule of Britain again with a civilian."

"Exactly. Suetonius is a superb general and man of war, and he's puffed up over his extraordinary victory. Can't blame him. BUT, the trouble is he won't stop fighting. He wants to go on slaughtering Britons and making examples and crushing what's left of a people who are thoroughly beaten already. He's even beginning to anger our allies, like the Regni. Classicianus wants all this stopped."

"I believe General Petillius feels that way too," said Quintus after a thoughtful moment. "That Rome has always managed to make friends with conquered nations— once they're subdued. Look at the Gauls, the Spaniards, the Germans—and all the rest of them, they're as loyally Roman now as we are."

"As a matter of fact—*I'm* mostly Greek," said Dio with his little chuckle. "Which clinches the argument. That's enough deep talk for a dashing young centurion who's been balmy as a butterfly for weeks. You scared me one day when you took me for an Icenian and tried to throttle me, but you terrified Fabian another time when you called him 'Regan' and tried to *kiss* him!"

"Great gods——" said Quintus reddening. "Did I?"

"You did, my lad. . . . Well, I better be going. Got to report in a few minutes. Hope I get sent to London again. It's unbelievable how quickly it's being cleaned up. Of course, we got all those troops in from Germany."

"Troops?"

"To be sure, you don't know. Replacements for the Ninth. Your legion's being built up fast. They landed last week. Suetonius announced he was glad they didn't get here for the battle, more glory the way it was." Dio grinned affectionately and turned to go, but Quintus stopped him.

"Wait a minute, Dio—I've been wondering—in my lucid moments—what about the Second? Did it ever come at all?"

Dio sobered and leaned over Quintus' pallet. "Three days after the battle, Suetonius sent the general of the Fourteenth and a vexillation of a thousand men to Gloucester. They found the situation much as we left it; Valerianus still mad, Postumus still shut up by himself in an agony of pigheaded dumbness. But this time . . ." Dio paused with a shrug, letting his hands fall open. "This time the prefect, Postumus, was *forced* to face the truth. When they finally got it through that ox-brain of his how he had dishonored his legion, made it a laughing stock, and shamefully disobeyed his governor and his Emperor . . . well . . . he ran himself through with his sword."

There was a silence, while both young men thought of the strange experiences in Gloucester's fortress. Then Dio added, "They've got a new general now. Promoted one of the tribunes. . . . So long Quintus, I've got to run."

After Dio had gone, Quintus ate his grapes and stared up at the tent roof. His thigh wound ached, and he was weak, but his mind was quite clear and capable of thinking through certain personal problems.

His thoughts started with Postumus' suicide and traveled back to the Arch-Druid's house at Stonehenge. Now that every detail of that lost day was vivid to him, he remembered the surprise he had felt that Conn Lear had let him proceed to Gloucester, and suddenly he saw the old man's sad stern face as he had said, "And you—young Roman soldier—will go to summon the Second Legion as it is your destiny to do, *but*——" And there had been the peculiar smile in his eyes, as he added, "No matter, you'll find out for yourself. . . ."

And Quintus guessed now what he had meant. The Arch-Druid had foreseen that Quintus' mission would be a failure. As everyone knew, there were some people who could tell the future. The augurs and the sibyls could, and the prophets. And Conn Lear had said another thing. "There will be blood and yet more blood, anguish for my people—and in the end——" *Disaster for them*—those were surely the words Conn Lear had not spoken, and the reason for his dreadful sadness. He had foreseen that Rome would conquer, had seen the coming of twilight to the Celts.

In his ears now Quintus heard again the agonized wailing of the princesses by their mother's body on the battlefield. He had scarcely noticed it then, had felt nothing but exultation that the fierce terrifying Queen was dead. But now there was no more cause for hatred and much cause for anxious uncertainty—because of Regan. She had said "Your people and mine . . . killing each other . . . it's no use, Quintus . . . there can never be a future for us . . ." But she had given him the brooch.

I must get back to her, Quintus thought, I must find out. . . . But how? He was a centurion responsible for a company. As soon as he was on his feet, he knew what his orders would be; either work detail in London or return to their own garrison at Lincoln. The life of a Roman soldier did not allow for romantic excursions.

Nor were these things the only barriers to his love for Regan. Roman soldiers were forbidden to marry Britons. He had managed to forget that fact in the vague rosy dreams he had had in the past. Impractical fantasies they were, he saw now with the clarity of convalescence and of the new maturity the violent experiences of the last months had given him.

It was a grave and quiet Quintus that Petillius found when he entered the tent that afternoon. "Surgeon says you're out of the woods now," said the general, smiling and accepting a camp chair from a bowing orderly, to sit down by Quintus. "That leg had us worried for a while. But you're a tough young sprout. You'll soon be riding Ferox as recklessly as ever. A very good horse that."

"Yes, sir," said Quintus with a faint smile.

Petillius looked at him keenly. "I've been sent a good many replacements and more're coming. When you're able, you'll have your own proper century in the Ninth instead of those auxiliaries. We'll pull out for Lincoln pretty soon, and after that we're probably going to be stationed at York to keep order in the north."

"Yes, sir," said Quintus. "Thank you for telling me. . . . How's Lucius today, sir? Do you know?"

The general nodded. "I've been to see him. He's not been doing well. The lung's almost healed, the surgeon thinks, but he's been very difficult—wouldn't speak or eat unless forced. But he's better now, since I saw him." The twinkle appeared in Petillius' eyes. "*Much* better. Quintus, I'm invaliding Lucius Claudius out of the army and sending him back to Rome. You should have seen his face when I told him!"

"That's wonderful for Lucius, sir!" Quintus cried.

"Yes. He was always a misfit, and I owe him that much, poor fellow. He wants to see you, Quintus. Have yourself carried into his tent."

"I will, sir." And Quintus thought that Petillius would certainly leave now, but he did not. He scratched his chin a minute, while gazing down thoughtfully at Quintus.

"His Excellency," the general said at last, "is having trouble believing that the rebellion is over, except of course for scattered demonstrations which *I* feel should be dealt with firmly but without bloodshed. . . . In fact most of the remaining north-east Britons are starving, since they were so sure of getting our provisions they didn't bother to sow any crops. The new procurator, Classicianus, is trying to help them out, which infuriates Suetonius. . . . I'm speaking very frankly to you, Quintus. You'll see why in a moment."

Petillius frowned as though remembering an unpleasant incident. Then went on, "Classicianus has unlimited civilian administrative powers from Nero and has managed to curb the governor so far, but now Suetonius has started the Druid persecution again. If he can't fight Britons in general, he wants to at least exterminate Druidism—ah, I thought that would interest you," said Petillius, smiling, as Quintus raised himself on his elbow and began to breathe faster.

"Classicianus, being a typical Roman senator with tolerant religious views, isn't at all interested in wiping out Druids, unless they're definitely hostile to us. However, he's compromised with Suetonius to the extent of permitting an investigation—a peaceful mission to that mysterious land of the western plain to confer with the Arch-Druid and ask his co-operation. The governor and procurator finally agreed on me as leader of this expedition, chiefly because I seemed to have special knowledge of Stonehenge and the Arch-Druid."

The general paused and gave a dry chuckle. "I did not mention that my knowledge came mostly from an impetuous young centurion, who had got himself romantically involved with the Druids and, moreover, has managed to forget the most important day of his whole experience with them!"

"Not any more, sir!" Quintus cried. "It's *all* come back!"

"Fine," said Petillius, rising. "Then you'll be useful, I hope. I'm taking a full cohort, by Suetonius' orders, and we'll leave tomorrow."

"Tomorrow . . ." Quintus whispered, glancing at his leg. "Then you're not taking me, sir . . ." The disappointment was so black that he could not hide it and he bit his lips.

"Tomorrow, because I'm urgently needed in Lincoln

175

and can't waste much time down here, and yes, I *am* taking you. You'll travel by litter until you're able to ride. And those are your orders."

"Oh, thank you, sir," said Quintus, his face transfigured.

"Not thanks, Quintus," said the general sternly. "It's neither from favoritism nor a sentimental desire to please you that you're included in this expedition. You're going because you can help Rome. Any romantic hopes you may be nourishing are entirely irrelevant. More than that— they are *forbidden*. You understand that?"

"Yes, sir. I understand." Quintus meant it with all his heart. His loyalty to his general, his legion, and to Rome had become the most important thing in life to him—and yet he could not prevent himself from thinking that at least he would almost certainly *see* Regan again.

In a little while Quintus had himself carried into the tent where Lucius lay, and deposited beside that young man, who greeted him warmly.

"By Mercury, Quintus, I'm glad to see you. Heard you had a bad time with that leg. . . . Quintus, did the general tell you. . .?"

Lucius, though he was pale, hollow-eyed, and had lost much weight, gave forth an eagerness Quintus had never seen in him.

"Did the general tell me he was sending you home?" Quintus asked, smiling. "Yes, he did. It's what you want, isn't it?"

"What I *want*," repeated Lucius, his eyes shining. "How could anybody help but want it!"

"Well, I don't," said Quintus temperately, "which is lucky, since I'm in for plenty more years' service here. But, as a matter of fact, I'm getting fond of the country. It has a lot of beauty when you get used to it."

Lucius snorted almost in the old way. "You're welcome to it, AND to the army. I'm through with that forever. Petillius said he'd write a letter to my father that would make it all right." He paused, and Quintus, who had been about to offer congratulations, did not speak, for Lucius reddened and looked away, and moistened his lips in obvious embarrassment. He murmured after a moment, "I hope you'll forget all—all the things I—I mean what happened here—Quintus, I'm awfully fond of you—I admire you. I always have."

Quintus reddened in his turn. He gripped Lucius' thin arm in a quick clasp. "Don't be a fool," he said gruffly. "We've both done a lot of floundering since we got here. I'll miss you." He cleared his throat and said, "Lucius, there's something I want you to do for me when you get to Rome. Will you?"

"Of course."

"Deliver a letter to my mother, Julia Tullia. I'll get it ready tonight, because I'm going west with Petillius tomorrow. And also I've got a lot of army pay saved up. I want you to take a purse."

Lucius nodded. "I'll be glad to, and keep an eye on them too. You know my father—is not without influence," he added with a trace of the old arrogance.

"I know," said Quintus, chuckling. "Someday I may write to ask you to use that influence to get Mother and Livia sent here to join me."

"Great Jupiter! You wouldn't do that to them!"

"Someday—perhaps," said Quintus softly. "If there's peace. I think they'd like it. But no use talking of that now. And mind you, don't tell them about my wound, or anything to worry them."

"I won't," said Lucius. "I'll just tell them you've become a puff-headed centurion and gone completely native as well!"

They grinned at each other, and Quintus signaled the orderlies to carry him back to his own tent. When he got there, he lay for a while and wondered that his mother would think if he mentioned Regan in the letter, and knew that he could make her understand, but what was the use? He sighed heavily. Nor could he report the slightest success in the quest. Well, but Julia had never expected success anyway. She was a sensible woman. Quintus sighed again and set about composing a thoroughly cheerful letter that could in no way disturb his family.

CHAPTER XI

EAGER AS HE WAS to get back to Stonehenge, Quintus was glad that the hundred-mile journey took them over five days, because he felt foolish in his horse-drawn litter and was extremely anxious not to appear before Regan in such a subdued, undashing way. He had looked ridiculous enough last time she had seen him as a fake Silure, anyway. So he gritted his teeth over the first sharp pains in his thigh, ignored his spinning head, and daily mounted Ferox for brief periods. And his strength came back fast.

Their marching time was below standard for several reasons. As far as Calleva, the Atrebate capital, they were accompanied by several cohorts of the Fourteenth who were bound for their own garrison at Wroxeter. And they all paused overnight at Calleva while Petillius and the general of the Fourteenth inspected the former Roman camp there and drew up plans for its rehabilitation.

Calleva itself was a city of mourning; doors were shut and barred, the streets were empty; but now and then at a window a woman's face would look out and gaze at the legions with a listless despair. In some of the isolated farms, where the news of defeat had taken longer to penetrate, they were still keening for their dead. Once an old woman with matted gray hair rushed out of a hut and spat directly at General Petillius, while she waved her skinny arms and screamed curses. The general rode on apparently unnoticing.

But another time on the outskirts of Calleva they passed two well-dressed little girls with neat blond pigtails and bright tartan tunics fastened by rich brooches. The children were huddled under a tree, sobbing. They clung to each other frantically as the legions marched by, too frightened and bewildered to run away.

This time Petillius reined in his horse and spoke to the Regni interpreter who rode behind him. "Ask the children why they are crying."

Quintus heard the children's answer, when the interpreter had finally soothed their fear enough so they could speak. "Because we're so hungry, and our father was killed, and we can't find our mother."

Petillius smiled sadly down at the little girls and said to the interpreter, "Take them back into Calleva, put them with some kind trustworthy woman who can search for their mother. Tell them that the Romans are sending food to their town, and they need not go hungry any more, but give them some now." He gestured to his orderly, who took a packet of marching rations from the general's own supply and handed it to the awe-struck children.

See, children, Quintus thought, all Romans aren't cruel monsters, as no doubt you've believed. And he hoped there would come a time when the beaten people might look on the Romans with something besides hatred, or the apathy of despair.

But as they left the land of the Atrebates and approached the great sacred plain, the feeling of the country changed. Here the war had brought no desolation or famine. The little farms looked prosperous; the natives watched the Romans pass with startled curiosity and drew together murmuring and wondering, for this country was apart from all previous Roman military travel, and the trackway they followed would have been hard to find without their Regni guide.

As it was, on the last day's march when they had reached the edge of the great plain, they got lost. The Regni could not find a way amongst the myriads of tumuli and barrows that dotted the plain. These grass-covered mounds—the burial places of the ancient people of long ago—made a landscape so weird and yet monotonous that the Romans marched in circles amongst them. All that day there was no sun to help them get their bearings, nothing but a fine foggy drizzle through which they could not see more than a hundred yards.

When night had fallen, they gave it up and struck camp. Soon afterward the general sent for Quintus.

Quintus, who had seen little of the busy general since they left the Thames, limped hastily to Petillius' tent and presented himself.

The general greeted him with his quick smile, said, "Sit down—I'm glad to see you're getting around so well. . . . Now, have you *any* idea where we are?"

Quintus shook his head. "I'm afraid not, sir. I came into the plain before from the south, you know, and left it to the west, also I had a guide."

"I thought I did too," said Petillius dryly. "That Regni said he knew this country like the back of his hand, but he obviously doesn't. What's more, I think he's frightened. He keeps saying the spirits of the dead are haunting him, and that the Druids have raised this mist so we can't find Stonehenge."

Quintus had a sneaking sympathy for the Regni. There was a strange atmosphere in the spot where they were. The dark silent mounds of the dead seemed to press around them, as though they were watching.

"It's ridiculous," said Petillius impatiently, "that six hundred men should be lost like this. We must hope for clearing weather."

"I know we have to cross a big river—the Avon," said Quintus hesitatingly. "It would be west of us—if we knew where west was—I'm sorry I'm not more useful, sir."

"I'll send scouts out at dawn to see if they can locate that river somehow," said Petillius. Then he answered Quintus' rueful apology with his usual crisp justice. "You can't help our being lost. I didn't expect you to be a guide. I've brought you along because the Arch-Druid knows you. WHEN we finally get to him, I hope he'll be more willing to negotiate because you're with us."

"I don't really know if the Arch-Druid likes me or not, sir," said Quintus frankly. "There was a moment when he certainly didn't." He thought of Conn Lear's fury when Quintus had mentioned Gaius Tullius.

"Well—but his granddaughter likes you, I gather," said Petillius with the sly twinkle, "and it's amazing what women can accomplish when they want to."

Quintus stiffened. His tone was cold as he said sharply, "I'll not take advantage of Regan, sir, or any feeling she may have for me, since there can be nothing—no future —between us."

The general raised his eyebrows, surveying the stern

handsome young face, the resolute set to the mouth. "Indeed . . ." he said without any expression at all. "So. . . . Good night, Centurion, that'll be all at present."

Quintus went back to his tent, wondering uncomfortably if he had annoyed the general, and was startled at his own anger at the suggestion that Regan's love might be made a tool of. Calmer thoughts later showed him that the general's remark had been reasonable enough, viewed from the Roman side. But it was almost impossible for Quintus to use reason when it came to Regan, and one part of him actually began to hope that they never would get to Stonehenge.

It looked for a time next morning as though that hope were on the way to being granted. The drizzling mist continued. Petillius' scouts, who had orders not to go out of shouting distance lest they too get lost, came back from various sorties to report that they saw no sign of a river, or indeed of anything but more mounds and rolling downs.

The general had just given orders to march anyway, in a direction the nervous Regni had guessed at, when the last scout returned with a captive. Quintus saw the commotion in front of the general's tent and heard loud gobbling noises, so he rode over on Ferox to see what was happening.

The captive was Bran—the Arch-Druid's ape man. He was standing in front of the general, thumping his chest and pointing over his shoulder into the distance.

"He was watching us from a mound over there, sir," the scout was explaining to Petillius. "I can't make out what he is, sir."

Quintus rode forward and saluting said, "I know who he is, General Petillius. It's the tongueless servant of the Arch-Druid that I told you about."

As he spoke, Bran turned, and, upon seeing Quintus, broke into a wide grin; ducking out from under his captor's grip, he ran to Quintus.

"I see he knows you, all right," said Petillius. "Can you make out what he's trying to express?"

Quintus, relieved to find that his general's tone and expression were exactly as usual toward him, answered that he would try.

He questioned Bran slowly in Celtic, and the familiarity he had learned earlier with the stocky little man's sign language helped him to understand.

"I think, sir," said Quintus at last, "that he's been sent out by Conn Lear to look us over." As he spoke the Arch-Druid's name, Bran nodded violently and flapped his hands like wings beside his head, to represent the high priest's ceremonial crown.

Petillius nodded. "That seems likely, though how would Conn Lear know we were on the way?"

"Grapevine, sir," said Quintus. "Some secret runner from the farms we passed. We've probably been watched all the time. I think Bran wants to guide us to Conn Lear —at least he wants to take us somewhere."

Again Bran thumped his chest and pointed repeatedly.

"So it would seem." Petillius studied the beetle-browed cave-man face, the long brawny arms, the garment of mangy otter skins. "But can we trust him? He might lead us into a bog—any kind of trap."

"Bran would never've let himself be captured like that, sir, if he weren't friendly. As for where he's taking us, I'm sure——"

Quintus stopped. He was nearly sure of Bran, but there was a way to make certain, a way that cost Quintus a moment of sharp struggle. His sense of duty and loyalty won, of course, reinforced as they were by shame because he had snapped at his general last night.

But Quintus could not prevent himself turning brick-red, as under the startled eyes of Petillius, the scout, and several other officers, he fumbled inside his breastplate and pulled out Regan's brooch—the brooch no Roman had ever seen except Dio and Fabian.

A snicker from one of the other officers was sharply suppressed by the general as Quintus, holding the brooch under Bran's eyes, said solemnly, "Do you swear by this Druid sign of the ruby snake that you are leading us in peace to Conn Lear?"

Bran stared at the brooch in obvious awe. He nodded slowly. Then he leaned over and placed his forehead on the brooch in token of submission.

"Bran has sworn by this Druid emblem, sir," said Quintus. "We can trust him."

"Good," said Petillius. "Then we'll march at once."

Bran led them in quite a different direction from that the Regni would have chosen, and in less than an hour they came to the river. Soon after they had forded it, Quintus' heart began to beat fast. The mist lifted, a watery sun came out, and he recognized many features that he remembered; rows of grass-covered earth rings, a particular long barrow shaped like a crouching lion. And then they saw ahead the long avenue of upright stones that led to the great temple.

When Quintus had seen the avenue before, it had been thronged with Britons going to the festival of Lugh. Today it was deserted as the Roman cohort marched along it.

When they entered the avenue behind Bran, Petillius had motioned Quintus to ride up near him, but the general did not speak until they topped a rise of ground and saw ahead of them Stonehenge, huge and mysterious, its great up-ended stones looming dark against the green down and forest grove behind.

"That's most impressive," murmured the general, in surprise and half to himself, as he stared. "I'd no idea."

They rode on slowly, and even the tough legionaries in the cohort behind them let out murmurs of wonder as each in turn came to their first sight of Stonehenge.

Quintus, who had been on the watch, saw how they were to be met. "There's Conn Lear, sir," he said, pointing.

The Arch-Druid stood on a mound against the "Heel," or Holy stone that guarded the entrance to the temple. They saw the gray beard, the long white robe, the winged crown, and the golden sickle of office in his hand. Around him, densely packed, were a thousand Druids of all the orders; the Bards in green, the Ovates in blue, the priesthood in white. They were unarmed, except that, ranged on either side of Conn Lear, were twelve Druids-of-Justice with their golden spears. The spears were raised and lowered once, as the Romans approached, while from all the Druids there came a high weird chanting. Again the twelve golden spears were raised, and this time remained poised, aiming in the direction of the Romans.

"Is this a *friendly* reception, Quintus?" said Petillius with a dry laugh, staring at the spears. "It looks as though if we get nearer there may be one general the less in Britain—possibly no great loss. But it might be wise to alert the cohort." He turned to give the command, "Javelins up."

Quintus called sharply to Bran ahead. "What are you leading us to? You swore there was no danger!"

Bran gesticulated frantically and pointed.

183

"He wants us to go forward ahead of the cohort, I think," said Quintus. "And see, Conn Lear is motioning."

"Very well," said Petillius after a moment. He spoke to a centurion behind him. "If they cast those spears at Quintus Tullius and me, you'll know what command to give the cohort!"

The centurion saluted grimly and went back to the men. The general and Quintus continued to advance in tense silence, watching the golden spears in the Druids-of-Justice's hands. The Druids' strange formless humming pulsated through the air. It was like the rush of water, yet there was menace in it too, like the buzz of angry bees, an eerie sound, and frightening. Quintus felt the palms of his hands go moist on the bridle and sighed with relief when the sound suddenly stopped at a signal from Conn Lear.

The Arch-Druid descended majestically from beside the Holy stone and took three steps toward the general and Quintus, who were now two hundred yards ahead of their cohort.

"What brings you here—Romans?" called the Arch-Druid in Latin, his stern resonant voice echoing amongst the great stones.

"Peace! Conn Lear. Peace for your people and mine!" Petillius called back.

"Why then do you bring soldiers with you?"

"It was the command of Governor Suetonius that we bring a cohort. But would the centurion, Quintus Tullius, and I have dared advance alone in the face of your spears if we did not come in peace?"

"The Romans dare many things," said Conn Lear coldly. "Advance further!"

The general and Quintus obeyed. The Arch-Druid also moved forward a few steps. "Now dismount!" he commanded.

They obeyed this too, and Quintus, while he tried to hide the stiffness of his leg, knew that Petillius must be much impressed by the Arch-Druid or he never would have acceded to this request.

Conn Lear walked yet three more steps until he stood before the general. "Now," he said, "we are equal. You have come to me, and I have come to meet you. It is so that it must be, if you wish peace in Britain."

184

"That is true, Arch-Druid," said Petillius gravely. "We shall understand each other."

Conn Lear turned and signaled to his guard. The Druids-of-Justice slowly lowered their spears.

"Leave your cohort there to camp on the plain," said the Arch-Druid to Petillius. "You have no need of it. Then come with me and we will talk together."

"Shall the centurion, Quintus Tullius, stay with the cohort?" asked Petillius.

The Arch-Druid looked at Quintus directly for the first time—a veiled considering look, neither hostile nor friendly. "The centurion may come with us," he said. "There is a foolish girl in my house who will be glad to see him."

Quintus' heart jumped. It took all his will power to keep his face impassive as he walked behind the general and the Arch-Druid on the road to the sacred grove. The Druid company followed at a distance. Quintus stared hard at the outside of the Arch-Druid's strange house, and the enormous tree that grew up through its center. The oak's leaves and gnarled branches cast a canopy of shade, not only over the roof but all the palisaded enclosure around the house.

Conn Lear's door and windows stood open. It was light inside when they entered the circular room with the painted hangings on the walls.

As Quintus stepped in, he heard a sound, half gasp, half cry, and he whispered, "Regan." The girl ran forward around the tree trunk, with her hands outstretched. Quintus bounded toward her but the Arch-Druid quickly barred the way between them, as he had when they had parted here before.

"No, daughter of my daughter, you shall not speak to the Roman centurion, until I have decided many things," said Conn Lear. "Sit down where you were, and you"—he pointed at Quintus—"over there."

The girl gave Quintus a quick, involuntary look. Biting her lips, she raised her chin proudly and obeyed her grandfather. Then she returned to a stool near the small fire, picked up the distaff she had dropped, and began to twirl yarn around it slowly.

Quintus, from the bench indicated by the Arch-Druid, could just see her. She wore a new violet and yellow tartan, her lovely hair rippled with chestnut lights down to her waist. Around her neck there was a crescent of beaten gold, beautifully carved, that lent a sparkle to her charming down-bent face.

She did not look at him again and he gazed at her until he knew just how the tendrils sprang from her white forehead, the way a mole accented the corner of her full red mouth, and the way her long lashes shadowed her cheeks.

He paid no heed to the Arch-Druid and Petillius, who were conversing at the other side of the room, until he was jolted from his absorption in Regan by the Arch-Druid's suddenly raised voice.

"Ay, General—it surprises you that I am willing to make peace with our conquerors? It was not always so. Once I hated the Romans as fiercely as ever Boadicea did. I hated as did the Arch-Druids before me, back through the years to the invasion of your Julius Caesar. But I am old now, and of what use is it to hate that which *is*—and will be!"

"Who can tell what WILL be—Conn Lear?" said Petillius in a grave, thoughtful tone.

"*I* can," said the Arch-Druid. "Because Lugh has granted me the vision. I have made the sacrifice of the bull. I have lit the sacred fire at midnight in the great stone temple out there. And I have seen."

"What have you seen, Conn Lear?" said the general softly.

The old man rose, turned his head toward the east window, and gazed toward Stonehenge. Then he raised the hand which still clasped the golden sickle and spoke in the chanting voice of power. "Blood I have seen, and defeat. I have seen the coming of darkness to the Celts in Britain —to my people. I have seen the Roman legions marching into every corner of this land. But more than that. . . ." He paused. "Ay, more than that, I've seen that the blood of Briton and Roman will someday mingle here, and they shall become one race and for hundreds of years this shall endure."

"You are wise, Conn Lear," said Petillius very low, "I believe that you have seen the true sight of what will come."

"The gods will mingle too," went on the resonant voice, unheeding. "Our own gods, our Celtic gods that you Romans will adopt and call by Latin names, just as you would dilute and Romanize our Druid lore in time—if we permitted it."

186

"Permit?" cried Petillius sharply. "Now you speak as though you would resist!"

The Arch-Druid lowered his head and looked at the Roman, a sad smile came to his lips. "We shall not resist. For if we did, it would be slaughter for us, as it was for Druids on the isle of Anglesey. I know your Governor Suetonius' nature. No—you must give us but a little time, a month will do—then we shall leave this land to its own destiny."

"Where will the Druids go, Conn Lear?" Petillius leaned forward earnestly.

"To the Islands of the West across the Irish Sea. There no Roman will pursue us."

So the Druids were planning to leave Britain, thought Quintus in sudden panic—and what of Regan? He saw that she too had heard; her mouth was tight. Suddenly she threw her shoulders back and got up. "Grandfather," she said, walking toward him. Her voice trembled. "I am frightened of your anger, but I must speak."

"Speak then," said the Arch-Druid, sitting down and looking at her steadily.

"You know what is in my heart, Conn Lear," said Regan, "and I know the condition you have made. Put it now to the test, I implore you. Tell Quintus Tullius."

"You are impatient, child—you interrupt me," said Conn Lear sternly, but his eyes were not unkind. "Yet because I love you, daughter of my daughter, it shall be as you wish. Come here, Centurion!"

Quintus rose and walked to stand before the Arch-Druid, wondering much and worried because he saw that something portentous was coming.

"The Druids will go to the Islands of the West without me," said the Arch-Druid, "for I am old and sick and very soon will die. When I die I would be laid here in this room beside the tree, and burned—my spirit to mingle with the spirit of this oak in fire, as in the ancient rites of long ago. I would that nothing here should be disturbed until the ashes of my body, and the oak, and my house shall all sink down and mingle with the quiet earth beneath . . . *undisturbed*," he repeated solemnly, "by any mortal hands forever."

What has this to do with me? Quintus thought, profoundly uneasy for the piercing gaze seemed to be searching his soul. Petillius too looked puzzled, as he sat a little withdrawn, watching. Regan's hands were tight-gripped, her breath came rapidly. Her eyes moved from her grandfather to Quintus.

"When you first came to Britain, what was it that you wished to find, Quintus Tullius?" asked the Arch-Druid quietly.

"The body of my ancestor Gaius," murmured Quintus after a moment.

The Arch-Druid rose and pointed with the golden sickle.

"The body of your ancestor lies here amongst the roots beneath this tree."

Quintus gasped. He stared at the great trunk in the center of the room. Petillius made a sharp motion, but Regan held still—waiting.

"That Roman, Gaius Tullius, profaned our holiest things. It was for this that the Arch-Druid of that time built the stronghold of our religion here, to counteract the evil. Now that you know, Centurion, what will you do?"

Quintus breathed deeply, and looked into Conn Lear's eyes. "I don't quite understand, Arch-Druid, but I've changed since I came to this land. I will not profane your holy things as Gaius did, unknowing, nor disturb that which you wish left untouched."

The old man's face quivered, the biting coldness vanished from his gaze, but he said inflexibly, "There is Druid gold buried with your ancestor, Centurion—much gold. You wanted that, did you not?"

"Yes," said Quintus slowly. "I wanted that, but there are things now that I want far more."

He looked at Regan and saw joy shining in her eyes.

"You have chosen well," said Conn Lear. "And I will tell you this. If the spirit of your ancestor has been unquiet, it will be so no longer. For in the fire that will consume us both, all differences shall be resolved—the Roman invader and the Celtic high priest shall both pass together into the paradise where there is always peace."

The old man stopped and bowed his head. He walked to his chair and sat down wearily. There was a throbbing silence in the room of the living tree. Tears rolled down Regan's cheeks, she knelt by her grandfather and kissed his hand.

Petillius stirred at last and spoke; in the roughness of

his voice, Quintus recognized the strong emotion that he felt in himself.

"It shall be done, Conn Lear, all as you wish it. Quintus has spoken and I have spoken."

The Arch-Druid nodded slowly. "You are good men. You are of the stuff that shall build up the new Britain." He sighed, then his mouth lifted in a faint smile. He put his hand on the girl's bowed head. "Ay—Regan," he said tenderly, "you may speak to your Roman now. Take him outside, for the general and I have still many things to talk of."

Quintus caught his breath, as the girl rose from her knees and came toward him, but he turned to look at Petillius.

The general answered his look with a softness Quintus had never seen, and he smiled as he said, "Yes, go with her, Quintus. And speak to her as you wish, for the Arch-Druid is right. From such as you and Regan will come the new race in Britain. You must have patience till the law is changed, but I'll see that it won't be long before permission will be granted."

"Thank you, my General," said Quintus very low. He took Regan's hand and they went out into the grove of trees, both silent, feeling only the clasp of their hands together, so deep in wondering happiness that they could not speak.

They stopped together, as of one accord, beneath an ash tree in the grove, and looked into each other's eyes.

"Regan," Quintus whispered, "did you understand what the general meant?"

"Not quite," she whispered back. "Oh, Quintus, I've prayed for this—I didn't know how much I—I—until you were gone, ah—but you're wounded—what has happened to your leg . . . ?"

He put his hands on her shoulders and held her thus, looking down into her candid beautiful eyes. "I was wounded by a spear thrown by one of your own countrymen, and I killed many of them, Regan, in the battle that wiped out half of Britain. The battle in which Queen Boadicea died. You must know and face this."

Her lids drooped for an instant, then lifted. Her pupils were dark and steady as she gazed up at him. "I know. I have mourned bitterly for my people who are dead, for the Iceni and my foster mother who once was good to

189

me. But it is past. Soon the snows will fall, then spring will come, and grass will grow again—even on the battle-field."

"Yes, my Regan," he said on a long breath. "So now I will tell you what the general meant. There's still a law, a barrier between us for a little while, but when the grass has grown again upon that battlefield, then—I can ask you to become a Roman soldier's wife. And will you, Regan?"

She did not answer in words. She slowly raised her arms and put them about his neck. He caught her to him, and they stood clasped together beneath the tree. The slanting sun filtered through the leaves and glinted on the girl's bright flowing hair and it glinted on the breastplate of the young Roman centurion, who had found in this land not the thing he had once searched for, but instead a new home, and love, and his destiny.

A NOVEL OF POWER, INTENSITY AND BURNING TRUTH

Anya

SUSAN FROMBERG SCHAEFFER

The story of the magnificent life-odyssey of Anya Savikin —from an idyllic European childhood, to the terror of the death-camps, to survival and escape to America, to middle age . . .

"ANYA is a myth, an epic, the creation of darkness and of laughter stopped forever in the open throat. Out of blown-away dust Susan Fromberg Schaeffer has created a world. It is a vision, set down by a fearless, patient poet . . . A writer of remarkable power." WASHINGTON POST

SELECTED BY THE BOOK-OF-THE-MONTH CLUB

 25262 $1.95

ANY 1-76

AVON ⬢ THE BEST IN BESTSELLING ENTERTAINMENT!